Dark Designs

His lips brushed the exposed skin of her stomach, causing butterflies where he made contact.

'I said it was strictly business.'

'And so it is. Strictly my business to get you off.'

'Futile promises.' She tried to sit up. Damn him for interfering. She was probably spiting herself, but she wasn't going to retract her promise, just because she was horny, *yaoi*-kiss drunk and had a beautiful man drawing his tongue across her clit.

'Oh, oh!' Her body sighed, as the soft lashes continued. 'Not fair.'

'That's right,' he said, and began sucking instead.

Remy feebly pushed at his head, his shoulders. 'We're not doing this.' Her voice was rising, as her resistance weakened.

'Oh, but we are.' He climbed on to the bed on top of her. 'Let me make this easy for you.' He grasped her wrists, pinning her to the narrow bed.

The feel of his cock bruising her thigh was too much. Why did he have to take control, and be so bloody composed about it?

'I don't want you: I want Silk.'

'No.' He breathed the denial into her mouth. 'You want me to have Silk.'

By the same author:

A Gentleman's Wager
Passion of Isis

Dark Designs
Madelynne Ellis

BLACK LACE

Black Lace books contain sexual fantasies.
In real life, always practise safe sex.

First published in 2006 by
Black Lace
Thames Wharf Studios
Rainville Road
London W6 9HA

The right of Madelynne Ellis to be identified as the Author of
the Work has been asserted by her in accordance with the Copyright,
Designs and Patents Act 1988.

Typeset by SetSystems Ltd, Saffron Walden, Essex
Printed and bound by Mackays of Chatham PLC

ISBN 0 352 34075 4
ISBN 978 0 352 34075 7

To TJC.

Ai shiteiru.

1

He wasn't sure what had first drawn his attention, the girl, or the word *yaoi* being bandied about the tiny provincial comic shop. She was visually stunning; there was no question of that. From the red dip-dyed ends of her black hair to the toes of her buckled boots, she was simply too stylish to dismiss with a casual glance. But the word itself had its own powerful attraction.

'*Yaoi*,' he whispered, rolling the syllables over his tongue. It had a unique taste – bitter dark chocolate surrounding a sweet liqueur centre. A taste he associated entirely with seduction and the sort of man-on-man action he could expect from one of the *manga* being discussed. In his Japanese homeland, the gay-themed books featuring huge-eyed androgynous-looking men were considered an entirely female province. After all, what could possibly be the appeal of heartbreakingly beautiful men engaged in complex, romantic and exceptionally tortuous relationships to an ostensibly heterosexual man?

He grinned, and absent-mindedly picked up a comic from the rack. Why did everything in the world have to be viewed so starkly? Wasn't there room for a few shades of grey? He liked the uncertainty of monochrome, the way in which one shade bled into another. He liked the uncertainty he felt right now about this woman. It buzzed at the back of his brain, an exotic tickle like a premonition. She was important somehow. His admiration and the attraction he felt were more than just high points on an otherwise dreary Saturday.

He moved closer to her, paused a few feet from the counter and pretended to scan his randomly selected title. To his dismay, it turned out to be a superhero pin-up special. He flicked through the images of scantily clad women in the western comic, but there was nothing to compare with the woman at the counter, whose eyes, now he was close enough to see them, were wide and luminous. She turned her back to him, so he stared at her bum instead. It was heart-shaped and pert in her cropped black jeans, framed by the hem of her black, ostentatiously braided military jacket and a belt of silver links, hung like a charm bracelet with occult pendants and *objets d'art*. He wondered whether they jingled when she walked, and how they'd sound against her hips as she writhed otherwise naked on a bed of black silk strewn with rose petals. Would the gentle tinkle mimic her sighs as she came? He could see her. The *yaoi* novel open on the pillow, her hand between her thighs as she imagined herself sandwiched between the two male leads of the book.

'They're perfect,' she said, holding the graphic novels up to the light. There was a man on the front of the foremost one, with large, striking, green eyes and a veritable sea of blond hair.

'That's a relief,' said the shop owner, 'after the effort it took to get them. Colour fan translations, rarer than *Swamp Thing 37*. First appearance of John Constantine,' he explained, when she failed to make the appropriate 'ah' noise. 'Mind, they cost more too.'

He watched her peer at the price tags. 'Bit more than I'd expected.'

The man behind the counter shrugged. 'I did say I couldn't guarantee the prices.'

She nodded, causing the red tips of her hair to bounce, then fall in a sharp line against her cheek.

So they were special imports. There weren't going to be any duplicates he could buy, which meant there was only one way he could guarantee a closer look, since striking up a conversation was never a given.

He watched them go into a shop carrier. Four in total, pristine in their plastic envelopes. The proprietor took her card and slotted it into the machine, then waited while she punched in her number. The bag was just lying on the counter; its handles pointed conveniently outward, just waiting to be picked up.

It would guarantee her attention.

It would be easy, the work of seconds.

It might even be fun.

The premonitory thrill he'd felt earlier spread to his fingertips, and tugged his lips into a smile. It had been a while since he'd been such a bad boy. He dropped the pin-up book, and took a step forward.

2

Where was he? God help him when she found him. And she *would* find him.

Remy Davies peered down the alleyway at the back of the tiny comic shop, then sprinted past the bins towards the thrum of the evening traffic. No idiot stole her bag and got away with it. She could hardly credit his audacity. He'd simply lifted it straight off the counter while she was returning her bankcard to her wallet. Of course, it meant she'd had a good look at him: angular, Oriental, about five foot ten, with incredibly dark eyes and glacial blue hair. She wasn't likely to forget that bit. It made him look as if he'd walked straight out of one of the graphic novels she'd just paid for. Reason enough to be interested in pursuing him even without the extraordinary circumstances. However, exotically gorgeous or not, she was still going to wring his neck when she caught him.

The high street was a dreary grey. Remy slowed to a fast walk and joined the other shoppers. It had been one of the wettest Aprils on record, and the pavement was dotted with oily puddles and soggy pastry crumbs. Even the spring collections in the shop windows seemed to have had all their vibrancy washed out of them by the constant rain. Not that she was much for pinks and pastels, anyway. She'd much rather see a dramatic blood red or midnight blue. Something striking and stylish that engaged the senses. Something like the fantasy image on the back of the biker jacket ahead – a curvy flame-haired temptress, provocatively dressed in bottle green with thorns growing up her arms.

It was him.

It took a moment for her brain to register the pale silver-blue hair grazing the leather collar. Well, nobody had ever said that thieves couldn't be stylish too. Better yet, he still had her bag.

Relief and adrenaline surged through Remy's chest, spurring her on between the huddles of umbrella-wielding die-hards. It was gratifying to know that her precious comics weren't floating in a puddle – the victims of failed opportunism by some X-dweeb who thought he was completing his collection. Still, the sooner she had them back in her hands, the happier she'd be.

It had taken six weeks for her four carefully packaged *manga* translations to arrive from Japan. She'd only glimpsed them through the protective plastic covers before he'd swiped them, but the vividly rendered cover drawings promised so much. One particularly exquisite image of a blond-haired, green-eyed sex god had especially caught her attention. Right now, she should have been on her way home to an Irish coffee and an hour of indulgence, not chasing a thief in the rain.

He reached the main road ahead of her, stepped out behind a bus, and cut across the traffic. Remy more sensibly waited for the lights to change, trying to keep one eye on him and another on the traffic. To her dismay, he disappeared through the park gates just as she left the crossing.

'Hell, not the park!'

Chasing him through the centre of town where there were plenty of witnesses was one thing, but a lonely confrontation in the shrubbery? Who knew what sort of weirdo he was? He'd already shown a lack of morals and a willingness to take risks.

Remy paused at the gates. She wasn't afraid of taking chances either, but was it worth the risk for forty quid's worth of books? Not that money was the real issue here. Those comics were her bit of escapism as she tried to get her life back on track, and the fictional men between their pages, her muses.

She needed the inspiration. Her fledgling fashion-design business was barely off the drawing board yet. She had one paying client on which everything was riding; her start-up capital had gone on materials and sequins; and, if things didn't come right soon, it'd be back to the factory-based pattern-cutting job she'd quit in January. The memory of her former life in Leeds was all the incentive it took. It would be the work of minutes to nip along the path and see if he was out in the open. It wasn't as if she were pursuing him into the undergrowth.

There was nobody in sight along the main park thoroughfare or by the swings, the normal collection of families and layabouts apparently chased away by the rain. Remy pushed her damp hair back off her face and breathed out hard. It was over. He was gone – and so were her books.

Just then, the drizzle turned into a downpour. She turned around and began retracing her steps towards the gate. Within seconds her hair was plastered to her head and her prized replica Black Brunswicker's jacket was losing the battle to keep her dry. She needed shelter and fast, or she was going to make a drowned rat look stylish.

The gents' loo was just ahead, off to the left behind a sprawling rhododendron. Shelter. Presumably, it'd be as deserted as the rest of the park, but even if it wasn't she was still going in.

Remy shoved the graffiti-riddled door and stepped inside. Her nose immediately wrinkled at the ingrained reek of men and caustic cleaning fluids. It was dry and almost warm, though, and she could sit on the counter by the sinks and curse the prick who'd stolen her comics.

Who, as luck would have it, had taken refuge too.

The girl on his jacket seemed to wink at her – a trick

of the blue light, which flickered overhead and hummed like an electric flytrap. He was standing with his back to her at one of the urinals. Remy's image rippled across the warped mirror as she marched up behind him and clamped a hand on his leather-clad shoulder.

'I want my stuff back.'

She'd expected him to jump, to protest, and perhaps mutter a denial. Instead, he made a single sharp exhalation, which, like a yogic breathing exercise, drained all the tension from his body.

'Give me a moment. I'm nearly done here.'

'Now.' She paused as she caught a glimpse of colour over his shoulder. Horrified, she shoved him sideways. He had one of her precious comics precariously balanced on top of the white ceramic urinal. It was open at the centre spread: a three-frame image showing the pretty blond she'd noticed earlier impaled on the cock of a second man with long, dark, straight hair.

As her eyes feasted on the image, it also dawned on her that he wasn't just having a piss.

'You're wanking over my comic,' she screeched, lashing out at him. 'You fucking wanker!'

'I'm not hurting it.' He crossed his arms in front of his face to ward her off.

'You're disgusting.'

'You're the one who buys this stuff. I don't suppose you get it just to admire the artistry. And it certainly isn't for the story.'

Yama nashi, imi nashi, ochi nashi, thought Remy, recalling the phrase from which the *yaoi* genre derived its name. No climax, no meaning, no resolution. Although some jokers insisted it was actually a euphemism for '*Yamette! Oshiri, itai!*' 'Stop it! My arse! Ow!' Exactly how this bastard would be feeling, if he didn't hand her comic back. She reached out to take it, but he stepped back in front of her, his palm spread over the explicit image.

7

'Get out of my way.' She tore at his arm, although she doubted he felt it through the thick leather.

He clasped her upper arms in response and swung her about. Remy's insides lurched as they might on the Waltzer at a fairground. Sticky, nervous heat seeped from between her thighs. A second heart seemed to have taken up residence in her stomach. The sudden movement ended, their eyes level, mouths only inches apart. He had her pinned between himself and the row of cubicles behind. 'You're awfully familiar with those hands.' He stroked the line of her jaw where the red ends of her wet hair shaped her face.

Remy couldn't breathe. Close up, his eyes were like dark rum, seductive and laced with the forbidden. He looked right into her as if he could see all the things that made her tick and knew how best to use the knowledge. His mouth set in a tightly pursed line, making her feel guilty and apologetic, even though he was the thief. The words of an apology sat on her tongue, making her throat thick. Hesitantly, she looked down. His fly was still undone, and his erect cock poked from the elastic of his designer shorts to brush the hem of his tightly fitted T-shirt. It lay between them like a bargain waiting to be struck.

Remy anxiously raised her gaze. The corners of his mouth turned up into a sly smile. 'Want to do something about it?' he asked.

'You what?' The exclamation broke through the thickness in her throat.

'You heard.'

'You're crazy if you think I'm going to let you come anywhere near me with that.'

He was a thief. A crazy, good-for-nothing thief, who had no right to demand anything of her. But, even as she thought it, her gaze slipped down to his crotch again. Above the elastic of his shorts, there was a tantalising glimpse of toned stomach and a fine smattering of short dark hairs – a hint at his real hair colour.

'In here.' He pushed her into the nearest cubicle and followed her in. Remy backed up against the toilet, while he kicked the door shut behind them and slid the bolt. The sharp snap it made seemed to announce the crossing of a boundary.

'Let me out!'

He put his back to the door and folded his arms. She stretched forward to slide back the bolt, but instead her hand closed over his open palm. His fingers immediately laced with hers.

Remy jerked backwards as if she'd just touched a hotplate. He moved with her. 'Too pushy,' she growled, trying to twist free. Instead of escaping, she found herself wrapped up in his embrace facing the cistern with his hard cock branding her arse through the seat of her cropped jeans.

'Something tells me you like pushy.' His breath was warm as it whispered against her ear. His lips alighted near the pulse point in her throat, gently brushing the exposed skin. Remy's heart was thundering now. She felt as skittish as a racehorse. Instinct told her to lash out, to bring her elbow back hard into his ribs or his stomach, but something about the gentle brush of his lips was enthralling. It seemed to light nerves elsewhere in her body that had no right to be connected. She felt his lips part and the trace of his tongue. Then he was sucking and the sensation was too exquisite, too incredibly sweet to pull away from. A strange eddy of fear and excitement fizzled inside her chest. It tingled through her nipples and shot electric arrows down towards her cunt. She didn't want to pull away, but she didn't want to be overcome so easily either.

One of his arms slipped around her bared midriff. A single digit toyed with the piercing through her navel –

a stem of blood-red stones. 'Enough.' She twisted out of his grip, grasped both his wrists and pinned him against the door. 'Let's see how you like it.'

'Like to be in charge, do you?' He jerked his wrists as if to check her hold. 'Regular Amazon, aren't you? What's the plan? The door's behind me.'

Remy looked into his almond-shaped eyes, and saw her image reflected in his pupils. She wasn't exactly sure what to do with him. Her focus had been the retrieval of her property. She certainly hadn't anticipated ending up locked in a toilet cubicle cottaging with a guy, his attitude, and an impressive erection, which was currently bruising her thigh. It appeared to have grown since her first glimpse of it. She wondered how much more it would thicken with her palm curled around it, her lips nuzzling the flare around the head. Dangerous thoughts, she chastened herself, only to find her breath coming faster and her hips moving unconsciously against his loins.

'Still want to escape?'

There was warmth in the brown depths of his eyes as well as humour when he spoke, which hinted at the same sensuality he'd already displayed with his kiss. There was also a tight stubborn turn to his mouth that plumped his lower lip, and made her long to taste him.

'I don't lip-kiss,' he said, as she closed in on him.

'Yeah, well I do.'

She pressed up against him; in her boots, he was only a fraction taller. For someone who didn't kiss he didn't resist. She suspected he'd just said it to sound cool, because his lips whispered over the surface of hers, rekindling the earlier sparks. They tingled in her throat, and along her jaw. His erection nuzzled against her stomach. Heaven, she thought, as their mouths finally locked in an exotic sparring dance.

Remy slowly released her hold on one of his wrists,

and slipped a hand inside his jacket. Beneath the cold leather and tight-fitting T-shirt his body was firm. Not gym-muscled, but lean and wiry. She stroked her palm down across his skin, following the sparse dark hairs towards his cock, which jerked eagerly as if begging for contact.

Smooth and hard, his cock head fitted neatly into the palm of her hand. She rubbed the shiny helm, drawing pre-come down over the shaft for lubrication. His free hand closed over her bottom – squeezed.

Remy took a step back, breaking off the lengthy kiss. They were both breathing hard. There was a rosy sheen high up on his cheekbones. It would be easy to throw caution to the wind and let him slide deep, fill her molten core and ease the longing and madness she felt, but that wasn't her way.

'Punishing me?' he asked.

'Wondering what the hell I'm doing, actually.'

'Living the fantasy. Isn't that obvious?' He twisted her around and pulled her close again so that his cock pressed against her bottom. 'Let me show you how it's done.' He popped the top two buttons of her fly and wriggled his fingers into the front of her pants.

Remy groaned. She was wet, embarrassingly so, slick and eager for his touch. One digit brushed her clit; another slid lower into her cleft. This was ridiculous. She could hear the rain drumming on the corrugated roof. She tried to focus on its music, to keep herself from succumbing to the magic of his fingertips, but the rhythmic patter seemed to match the slip and slide of his hand, lulling her into complicity while heightening the depth of her response.

He was a common thief, a criminal, regardless of his pretty-boy looks. Why was she letting him get away with this?

He unfastened the last button of her jeans, and they

slid off her hips, only to cling to her legs. Undeterred, he pulled them lower and slid his cock between her bared thighs.

The heat in his shaft rushed straight to Remy's cheeks, colouring them an animated rose pink. His tongue traced the curve of her ear. 'Think of the blond,' he whispered. She couldn't help it. She did.

There had been both uncertainty and ecstasy in his eyes as he'd looked up from the centre spread. He was exquisite, clearly tortured by the nearness of his *Seme*, his Dom. Still, there was a stubborn defiance about the way he'd crooked his chin upwards as the male hands gripped his bottom, and the hard hot cock of his lover dipped inside him. She could almost hear him as he came, sighing in time with each buck of his master's hips and exhaling with a startled 'Aagh!' as his own penis jerked.

The sound was also her own. She stretched out her arms, bracing herself against the cubicle walls. He was slippery and hard between her closed thighs, his pacing bordering on frantic, an urgency that translated into the less than subtle rub of his fingers over her clit. He was almost there, and he was going to take her with him. She felt so close now. Each brush, each caress felt like a nettle sting. The prickly heat it caused made her long for him to slip upwards rather than forward, so that he'd sink in deep. She wanted him to take her hard, pump into her and drive away the crazy itch. She wanted more – more than just a quickie, more than just a hand job.

Quite suddenly the bubble burst, jerking her backward into his arms, panting and cursing as he continued to pet her until the fire in her clit started to fade. It was only when she felt the nip of his teeth that she realised she was drifting and that he was supporting her weight.

Remy peeled herself away from his grasp. Her cheeks were burning, and probably clashing with her hair. He'd come between her thighs, leaving an opalescent puddle on the tiled floor. She was sticky with sweat and their combined moisture. She leant against the cistern, trying to find a sense of balance. Who was this guy? What was she doing here?

The cubicle walls were etched with names. Cartoons, both gaudy and crude, jeered down at her. Someone had replaced the toilet chain with a leather belt, and even that hadn't escaped the graffiti.

'What's your name?' he asked, from behind her.

'Remy.' She hitched her pants and trousers and turned to face him. 'Yours?'

'Takeshi.' He pointed upwards with a pen, to the head of a list he was adding her name to in purple marker. Remy stared at the column of names feeling slightly sickened. 'All the rest are men.'

'It's a gents' loo.' He shot the bolt.

'So, what, you're part-time gay?'

'I'm opportunistic. Men are just easier to pick up, easier to fuck and don't give you a twenty-question follow-up.'

'I've only asked two.'

She followed him out of the cubicle. Uncertain what else to do, she reclaimed her book from the top of the urinal. It seemed to have survived unscathed, unlike her neck. She stared at her flushed image in the mirror.

'You marked me.'

He nodded, retrieved her stolen carrier bag from beneath the end basin and handed it to her. 'It'd be cheaper to get these off the Net, you know.'

'Maybe if you can read Japanese, which I don't. Besides, I don't have time to wade through all the crap to get to the good stuff.' She couldn't prevent a touch of animosity from creeping into her voice, but he merely smiled at her outburst. His good humour only made her feel more irritable.

'Busy schedule?'

'Yes, actually. I'm starting my own business.'

'Whoa!'

Remy's grip on the carrier bag tightened. She was tempted to hit him with it, except that it would likely do more damage to her books than his smug expression. 'All right, Mr Cool, what do you do that's so impressive? Just doss about?'

'I trade on eBay. And before you knock it, how much did you earn last week?'

Remy shrugged. Nothing. She wouldn't get her first paycheque until Chelsea's wedding dress was finished. Her first commission was also her first piece of *haute couture*. Everything was riding on it. The wedding was going to be a big affair. Her friend was planning a midnight ceremony, and had invited something approaching two hundred guests, all of whom were potential clients for her Gothic- and fetish-wear-inspired designs. She'd had some business cards printed, but still needed photos for her catalogue, and she couldn't afford to pay even a mediocre model. Chances were it'd have to be her and a few mates.

'Well?' Takeshi prompted.

'How much did you make?' she countered. 'And if it's so much, why did you need to nick my bag?'

He stiffened almost imperceptibly, then combed his fingers through his spiky silver-blue hair. 'Maybe I was trying to attract your attention.'

'Bullshit!'

'It worked, didn't it?'

'You could have just introduced yourself.'

Takeshi zipped his jacket. There was a metal *kumadori* mask pinned to the lapel. He fondly brushed a finger across the grimacing visage of the *kabuki* theatre character. 'I thought about it, but this seemed so much more dramatic. I know you goths like your theatrics, so I figured what the hell.'

Remy slapped her palm on to the counter by the sinks. 'One, I'm not a goth. I just hang out with them. Two, a high-street chase and a gent's loo aren't my idea of theatre. And three –' she hitched the collar of her braided jacket '– you had no way of knowing that I'd chase you. You'd have been stuffed if I'd called the police.'

'I figured it was worth the risk. I had a good feeling about you.'

'Did you, now?'

'Yes, and it was right.'

'I suppose you'll be claiming you're psychic next.'

He shook his head, a smile forming on his lips. 'No, just intuitive.' He drew his marker pen from his pocket again and plucked off the lid.

'Another list to add to?' she asked scathingly. She was too old to be acting as lookout for someone scrawling his name on a toilet door. There was no longer any point to her being here. She had her stuff. It was time to get out before she did anything else stupid.

Takeshi's smile widened into a grin that crinkled the skin around his eyes and showed his teeth. 'Actually, I thought you might be needing this.' He stepped forward and, before she even thought of stopping him, he lifted her short jacket and top and scrawled his phone number across her midriff.

'Excuse me.' She pulled her clothing down. 'As if I'm going to call you.'

'You'll call.' There was a certainty in his voice that was unnerving.

'I won't.'

'You will, and before the week's out. Who else are you going to indulge your *yaoi* fantasies with?'

Remy pushed her shoulders up and her chin high. It was true. He could have been a *yaoi* model. But he was far too confident, far too full of himself, and she didn't like the way he made assumptions about her, even if his guesses were accurate. 'I don't need to indulge them,' she snapped. 'Not with you, anyway.'

He laughed in response, his voice sharp and high. 'So

why did you?' He was still laughing as he left the building.

Remy sprinted to the door after him, but he'd already vanished into the undergrowth of the rain-drenched park.

3

After forty minutes of dodging between shop doorways and bus shelters, Remy finally reached home and curled up in her favourite leather armchair, the one classy item of furniture among the flat-pack pine in her attic flat. She felt chilled to the bone, even with a blanket pulled around her shoulders. She lifted her mug and let the swirling steam heat her face as she breathed in the fresh coffee aroma. Immediately, her senses perked. She swallowed a mouthful of the soothing black liquid and felt it seem to wash through her bloodstream, leaving her with a warm afterglow. But it didn't chase away her shakes. The cold wasn't responsible for those.

They were Takeshi's doing, the blue-haired *oni* who'd given her way too much to think about. She'd been trying to edit him out of her thoughts ever since she'd left the park.

She glanced warily over to where her new *manga* translations lay on the coffee table. One glance at the blond was all it took to release the memory of Takeshi, cock in hand, living out some fantasy at her expense. Eventually, she hoped that association would fade, letting her enjoy the story between the pages, but right now – right now he was still pushing buttons in her subconscious she wasn't sure she wanted pushing.

She still didn't understand how she'd ended up cottaging. She wasn't a thrill seeker, and, while the romantic *yaoi* imagery of gay sex certainly fired her senses, the sticky sordid reality was less than inviting. Actually, it seemed rather sad. And yet she'd let him take her as he might have taken a man. She could picture him in the exact same position working some guy's cock instead of her clit, their skin damp with sweat and raindrops, slightly luminescent under the blue lighting. She could see his eyes, his beautiful, almond-shaped, near-black eyes, and hear the breathy whisper of his voice, coaxing his partner towards orgasm in combination with his wrist action.

How many times had he played out that scenario? She hadn't read all the names on his list, but there'd been at least seven, and now her.

Remy stood abruptly and pressed her palm to the windowpane. The sky had turned black, and thick rivulets of rainwater were streaming down the outside of the glass, now clouded with condensation. Some had seeped under the sash to form a puddle on the windowsill.

She wasn't a man, but he'd fucked her as if she were. Remy lifted her top and stared at the inky shadow across her stomach. His phone number. Why had he given it to her? Not for casual sex, she was sure. No, phone numbers implied intimacy, and intimacy equalled relationships and emotional turmoil. She'd been there in the past, got engaged, got serious, got out, and now she preferred her passions to play out on paper. But he seemed to have taken the spice out of that. After waiting six weeks for her novels, she no longer wanted to turn the pages.

Remy traced the digits of his number on to the windowpane. Maybe she'd feel different after a shower, when she'd washed the ink and the other evidence of their encounter away. She crossed to the door and flicked on the main light. Shame, though, because he was gorgeous, and she sensed that, beneath their outward façades, they might actually have a few things in common.

An hour later, Remy was squeezing cat food out of the packet when the doorbell rang. 'Chelsea,' she hissed. She'd forgotten their appointment. Her friend had started turning up every Saturday evening after she shut up shop downstairs, to check how her wedding dress was coming along. The gown was currently spread over Remy's double bed, still fifty black seed pearls short of being finished.

Remy scooped Shadow off the workbench and plonked the cat on the floor next to his bowl. 'Focus,' she told herself. Chelsea was an old friend, but she was also a paying client.

The bride-to-be looked exhausted. She wasn't wearing makeup, and there were grey smudges beneath her eyes. 'Coffee? It's fresh,' Remy offered, guiding her into the tiny kitchen.

Chelsea slipped on to a stool by the breakfast bar, so that her PVC raincoat hung behind her like a pair of folded wings. It was where the shop name had come from – Batwings – specialising in anything alternative, from clothing to tarot cards and incense sticks. She sighed into her clasped hands. 'No. I'm jittery enough as it is. My dress is finished, isn't it?'

Remy regarded her curiously. She'd been fretting over the wedding for months but the dejection in her voice sounded rather more serious this time. 'It's fine. I've still a few beads to sew on, but it'll only take a few minutes.' She lifted a couple of mugs from the rack, which was blackened to look like a withered tree. 'You sure I can't tempt you? You look like you need it.'

'Go on, then, but I'm picking my mum up from the station in ten minutes.'

Remy poured and pushed one of the mugs along the bench. 'Sounds as though you need the help. You look frazzled.'

'Help! Fat chance.' Chelsea grimaced into her cup. 'Interfere, more like, as if it isn't enough of a disaster already.'

'Don't be daft. You've been planning for ages. It's going to be perfect.'

Chelsea pinched the bridge of her nose. When she looked up, her blue eyes were shiny with the tears she was just managing to hold back. 'Help me, Remy. I've just seen the bridesmaids' dresses. They're terrible. They're going to look like three overstuffed pincushions, and that's on women who don't amount to a size twelve combined.'

'I'm sure they're not that bad.'

'They are.'

Chelsea pressed her brow to the counter. 'I'll pay you, whatever you want. You've said all along that you wanted to make more of the outfits.' She turned her cheek to the worktop and peered up hopefully, her tears almost ready to fall.

'That was months ago. Your wedding is next weekend.' Remy padded over to the sink and back. How did you break it to your only paying customer that you couldn't help? It wasn't that she didn't want to. Several months back she'd been desperate to outfit them all, but Chelsea had gone with another friend's recommendation, and commissioned her to make only the bridal gown.

'You don't have to make them from scratch. You've got stock. You must have something suitable. Paper bags will be better than what I've got.'

'There's nothing I've got three of.'

'Well, something you have two of, then.' The tempo of her voice wavered between desperate and frantic. 'You can easily run up another one by Thursday.'

'I suppose.' If she went for something simple, there was no reason why she couldn't put something together in an afternoon.

'Come on, Remy. Or it'll be your fault that the bridesmaids are dressed by Bhs.'

'Not fair!' Remy snarled, but she couldn't help feeling sorry for her. 'Damn it, all right.'

'I knew I could rely on you.' Chelsea combed her

fingers through her white-blonde hair, causing it to cascade over her shoulders. 'You're a star.' The shadows in her expression vanished, so that her normal golden succubus glow returned.

Remy shook her head. What had she agreed to? Hopefully, the chance to blow people's preconceptions away, and not just a total nightmare. Chelsea's wedding was going to be huge. If she was dressing half the wedding party instead of just the bride, it'd make a fantastic showcase for her designs. She could see them now, standing in the shadow of the church, the moonlight playing across the stained glass, rose-petal confetti floating in the air, and her designs resplendent across a centre spread. Chelsea had already agreed to her using photos of the event for promotional purposes. It'd make a terrific advert. All she had to do was pull it off.

'Why Thursday?' she asked, backtracking to an earlier point. 'The wedding isn't until Sunday.'

'Yes, but we're all going over on Thursday night, so we can perfect everything. I did tell you, and it's written on your invitation.'

Remy frowned. She wasn't actually sure she'd opened her invitation. It hadn't seemed all that important when Chelsea had handed it to her in person and told her what it was. It was still sitting on the mantelpiece in the lounge along with the gas bill and the tax forms for the Inland Revenue. 'When am I supposed to shoot my catalogue in all this? It's getting urgent.'

'Do it at the castle. I need you there, Remy. You're going to have to fit the dresses anyway, and brush Shaun into shape.'

'Whoa, back up a moment.' Remy raised her hand. 'You never said anything about dressing Shaun.'

'But you've got loads of menswear. You've shown me more coat designs than dresses. And, well, he's missed half his appointments with the tailor, and it's the same place that's screwed up the bridesmaids' dresses. I don't trust them. I don't want him turning up looking like Robert Smith.'

An image of the groom in a scruffy suit with garish lipstick smudged across his face briefly struck Remy as amusing, but she could see why Chelsea wouldn't want him to walk down the aisle like that. Still, it meant adding to her already substantial workload. 'So it's just Shaun?'

'And the best man.'

'Oh, God!' Remy took several exasperated gulps of hot coffee, then slammed the mug down on the counter so that it sloshed over the surface. 'Let me get this straight. You want me to come up with three matching brides-maids' dresses, no meringues –'

'Not too sexy.'

'And tailored outfits for the groom and best man by Thursday.' Remy gazed forlornly at the black puddle. She stretched across, tore off a kitchen towel and dropped it over the spill. She was going to have to work every available minute to get all this done, and it would still be touch and go. 'Do you even have measurements for these people?'

Chelsea immediately produced a folded wad of paper from her coat pocket. 'Full sets, for all of them.' She smoothed the papers, and pushed them towards Remy.

'Chelsea!'

'Just take them, will you. You don't have to create anything new. Use whatever you have that'll work. They'll be Dark Designs exclusives, anyway. Nobody else has commissioned anything from you yet.'

Remy dug her fingertips into her scalp. Suddenly, she felt mentally weary. Too much had happened in too little time. It was only two hours ago that she'd been shagging a stranger in a toilet.

Chelsea pulled up the collar of her shiny coat. 'You needn't let me know what you decide on. You can just show me on Thursday. I trust you. I know you'll find things that work. Oh, and don't forget the invoice when you come. Now I've gotta go. Mum'll be getting off the train about now.'

'But what about my catalogue?' She followed Chelsea to the door.

'I've told you: shoot it at the castle.'

'And my models?'

'Use the guests.'

Remy frowned. Chelsea raised her hands in surrender. 'OK, bring your own models along. There's two spare beds, if they don't mind sharing. Jem and Toni decided they'd prefer to stay in luxury at the Dower House.'

'The photographer? My cat?'

'Bring Shadow along – he'll fit right in. And I figured that you'd be using Alix. She's already coming along to photograph the wedding, so where's the problem?'

'Actually, I hadn't decided on Alix yet.'

'No, it's fine. I already spoke to her. And don't worry about – you know. She's grown up loads recently. I'll see you Thursday.'

'Sure.' Remy watched her trot down the stairs as far as the first landing. Trust Chelsea to interfere and organise things behind her back. If it weren't that her friend was also her generous landlady – she was living virtually rent-free – she'd have seriously considered hexing her for involving Alix. Remy made a choking motion with her hands. She very much doubted Alix had changed since Christmas, when things had come to a rather emotional head, because, contrary to Chelsea's opinion, one didn't generally grow out of being a lesbian – although people did outgrow crushes. Besides, Alix had never been what you'd have described as immature, so God knew what the 'grown up' remark referred to.

She slapped her hand against the banister and sighed. She'd better work on finding those models. Models! Huh, that was a joke. All her friends were going to be at the wedding, anyway, and most of them were up their own arses already, without inflating their egos any further. Besides, she really wanted people who were visually striking, who'd be able to carry off her designs without making them look like every other weekend goth or PVC-clad wannabe bondage queen. Sadly, the only person she'd met in that category recently was the egocentric idiot she'd screwed earlier, and she wasn't about to call him.

Back inside her flat, Remy headed for the spare room. It was still without a lampshade, and she'd improvised a curtain from a swathe of purple voile. She pulled the plastic sheets from her clothes racks and began rifling through the bagged garments. She hadn't put that much stock together yet. OK, so some of the designs came in three or four different colours, but Chelsea wanted something to match her black and purple velvet and taffeta dress. She also wanted the bridesmaids to match each other, so that made things more difficult. On top of that, there was how they'd look alongside the groom and best man. She had to get this right, since it could make or break her business. There'd be several influential relatives among the guests, and a fair few upper-class freaks. Shaun, the lucky groom, might look as if he'd been dragged backwards though Kensington Market, but his father was landed gentry, and a former member of the pioneering goth band Toys in the Attic.

After a few minutes of rummaging, she managed to whittle the selection down to three potential brides-maids' outfits: a plain, black, boned corset with a long netted skirt; a mediaeval-style dress in black and purple velvet; and a Jane Austen-inspired number.

Chelsea had made it clear that there were to be no meringues, even black ones, and no sassy outlines apart from her own. So, after a few minutes of deliberation, she went for the last option. It was predominantly black with a touch of purple to match Chelsea's dress. It had a

Regency outline and lace powder-puff sleeves, and a velvet choker and lace evening gloves to match – tasteful, stylish and easy to run up on the sewing machine. With the measurements Chelsea had provided, she could adjust the pattern accordingly. She moved the sample dress to a rack on the opposite side of the room. Now for the men.

Remy rubbed her brow. What a nightmare! All that was missing was the mother of the bride. She was never going to get it all done.

The sound of the telephone ringing dragged her out of her moment of despair. She sprinted back to the kitchen to pick it up.

'Remy,' said a familiar voice. 'Chelsea. My mum's outfit, it's pink. Fuchsia-bloody-pink.'

What had she been saying? 'I'll add it to my list.'

'Thanks.'

Remy hung up. She stared at the phone, then purposely dropped it in the kitchen bin. 'Enough!'

Back in the workroom, she scanned the list of measurements for the two men. Chelsea was right: she did have an abundance of menswear, possibly because she enjoyed dreaming about men in smart clothing, and she'd been using images from her *yaoi manga* as inspiration. She'd have to dress them from her ready-to-wear range, and make any adjustments necessary on location, since there simply wasn't time to tailor things properly. She opted for white ruffle-neck shirts, black brocade trousers and coats, with burgundy-coloured, patterned silk waistcoats. She could imagine Shaun in the outfit, and that would have to do. The best man wasn't one of the usual crowd, but hopefully he wouldn't look too out of place.

Once she'd hung the outfits alongside the single bridesmaid's dress, she returned to the women's wear to find something appropriate for Chelsea's mum. Except that she had no measurements, and couldn't recall their ever having met. She tried to think back to graduation day four years earlier, but the memory was far too hazy, probably as a result of the amount of champagne she'd drunk. She was going to have to take a guess, or else sort out the outfit on location from the stock she was taking for the catalogue shoot.

From the kitchen, she heard a sudden clatter. 'Now what!'

Shadow had toppled the bin, which was vibrating with the ringing of the phone. Remy righted the silver cylinder and retrieved the handset, dusting off the remains of Super Noodles and sardines before she put it to her ear.

'Hello.'

'Hi, Remy. Remember me? It's Alix. We used to hang out together.'

Oh, hell! Remy made a goldfish expression at the receiver, while she recovered her wits. 'Hi. Yeah, I've been meaning to call.'

'Sure you have,' Alix drawled, and Remy could picture her, hand on hip, her flaming red hair cascading down her back. 'Someone mentioned that you need a photographer. Thought we'd better speak and sort it out. You don't have to hide just because I got plastered and came on a bit strong.'

'It wasn't that.'

'Yes, it was. I was there when Gary Stevens did the same to you that time after the Christmas ball. You reacted in exactly the same way.'

'Maybe,' Remy sighed. 'Chelsea was still jumping the gun, though. There's no way that I can afford your fees.'

'So, I'll give you a discount.'

'I can't let you do that.'

'We're mates. We're supposed to help each other. I've sold a few prints recently, so I'm flush.' The line went silent a moment as she awaited Remy's acceptance. 'OK, so pose for me as payment. I'll do a few black-and-white stills and we'll call it quits. It's a darn sight better deal than you're going to get from anyone else. And you know I'm good.'

Remy covered the receiver and bit her knuckle. When she wasn't selling out and doing family portraits and wedding albums, Alix was a connoisseur of the female form. Her particular speciality was a nicely shaped bum. She'd been bugging Remy to pose since their university days. The problem was, Remy suspected it would be the forerunner to another major come-on, and, after the previous messy episode, she didn't fancy risking a repeat. However, her 'friend' was talented when it came to photography. She had a way of catching light that really expressed the essence of what made a person unique. It would probably be a useful tool for selling clothes, provided the models were interesting enough.

'I'll think about it,' she virtually whispered.

'Great!' Alix gave a whoop. 'I'll pack plenty of film. See you Thursday, lover girl.' She hung up.

'Shit!' Could the day actually get any more complicated? Between Takeshi and the wedding outfits – and now nude photos – the day sucked. She just hoped the rule of threes was going to hold, because she honestly didn't think she could take any more.

It was late when Remy finally quit working that night. She'd adjusted the patterns for the bridesmaids' dresses and cut the main sections out from material left over from Chelsea's dress. The additional pieces would have to wait until she could get some organza on Monday.

She evicted Shadow and slumped into her armchair. Her brain felt kinked, as if someone had driven a very large stake through her skull. She was tired but – hell! – if she didn't unwind she'd be adjusting dress patterns in her sleep. Which reminded her, Chelsea's dress was still lying across her bed.

Unthinking, she reached forward and picked up a graphic novel from the coffee table. Carefully, she peeled back the magic tape and slid it out of the plastic cover. Immediately the knots of tension in her brow started to ease. The first page contained no dialogue. It was a collection of four boxes, predominantly blue and gold in colour, depicting a park in autumn. Two men entered the frame: an unearthly assassin and the son of a *yakuza* boss. The stage was set. Remy ran her tongue across her canines, already anticipating the interactions to come, the clashes, the tragedies as a twisting tale of forbidden love emerged.

A roll of thunder boomed outside the window, tugging her gaze upwards from the page just in time to see a fork of lightning brighten the dead sky and highlight the windowpane's slightly tainted condensation. Takeshi's phone number. The thought of him triggered a curious chain reaction. It was as if she could suddenly feel the storm's charge dancing in the air, as the myriad tiny particles replicated his earlier coaxing caress.

Remy traced her fingers down her neck, trying to wipe away the sensation but managing only to heighten it. A staccato beat pulsed between her thighs. He'd claimed that she would phone, which was reason enough not to, but was she only spiting herself by resisting temptation? Despite leaving her with certain reservations, he had given her an undeniable kick.

She clenched her thighs together, which only caused the beat to quicken. That part of her remembered only the joy he'd given her, not his attitude or her misgivings. It wanted to feel the pitter-patter of his fingers again, to enjoy the infuriating bliss sparked by his thumb slipping in and out of her hot core. She stared blankly at the book open on her lap; her interest in it had evaporated. He'd insinuated himself into her most intimate fantasies.

Remy closed the book and slapped it back on to the coffee table. She was going to have to meet him again just to prove to herself that he was ordinary, and to erase the scorch mark he'd left across her psyche. But what to say when she called? If she didn't have something in mind, he'd think it was all about sex.

Shadow pushed his way on to her lap. Remy absently petted his head. The only other thing prominent in her mind now was her design business. It was a split-second decision. She'd phone and ask him to model. There were certain designs, the more casual end of things, that he'd off-set to perfection. She'd been hoping for unusual models. Maybe she could even persuade him to pose for free.

Remy snatched up a pen and paper. It took the better part of fifteen minutes, but she managed to reconstruct his number from the greasy finger marks on the glass.

He met her in the park the following afternoon and took her back to his place: a basement flat you reached via a rickety iron stair, on a street of Victorian town houses facing the park.

'Sorry about the mess,' he said, as they pushed their way past boxes of packaging materials and collectable trade goods to reach the sofa. 'Do you want a drink?'

Remy nodded, and watched him head through a door to what looked like an under-stairs cupboard. A moment later she heard a tap running and then the chug of a coffee machine.

'Black, no sugar,' she called.

'Naturally.'

Remy took off her braided jacket and laid it over the back of the sofa. It seemed the appropriate thing to do, since they were behaving like old friends, exchanging pleasantries and companionable silences. She'd mentioned her purpose in meeting him when she'd called, not wanting to give him the wrong impression, and so far he seemed to have accepted it. Leastways, he hadn't tried anything on.

There was a corkboard by the computer, which held a collection of snapshots of motorbikes and what looked like the Japanese teenagers' equivalent of the Hell's Angels. A younger version of Takeshi stared out from the centre of one picture, full of easy charm and wearing something that resembled a punk version of a motor mechanic's uniform.

'Are these in Japan?' she asked, when he came up behind her.

'Yes.'

'What are they, some kind of biker gang?'

'*Bosozoku*,' he replied stiffly, without bothering to elaborate, and something in his expression suggested that the subject was closed. A detail to file away for future reference, she thought, turning her attention to the stacks of boxes instead. Beneath the layers of packaging were collections of My Little Ponies, Star Wars figurines and silver jewellery. 'Nice.' She lifted an ornately carved ankh.

'The toys sell better.' Takeshi handed her a pint-sized mug. 'A friend of mine makes that stuff. I sell it for her online.'

Remy thoughtfully traced her thumb over the top loop of the ankh. The finely cut ridges and flourishes were pleasingly tactile. 'Do you think this friend would let me use some of this stuff in my catalogue? It'd go really well with some of my designs.'

'Maybe, if you made her something in exchange.'

That seemed fair, provided that what she wanted wasn't too costly in terms of materials. Remy replaced the ankh in the box of bubble wrap, and briefly traced the curve of a dragon's-tooth pendant.

'She's into corsets,' Takeshi elaborated. He leant past her and flicked his computer monitor on.

'So am I.'

'Yeah, but you don't need one. Marianne's a big girl on top. A corset's about the only thing that'll keep them in check. You could probably drown in them.' He straddled the swivel chair and offered her a perch on the cluttered sofa.

Remy sat down between a box of agate spheres and a Lego Dalek. She watched him clear his mail folder and check his eBay listings. She'd expected him to be far more brash on this second meeting, more pushy bad boy and less genuinely odd, although it was also pleasantly surprising to find her expectations were false. Mind you, his flat wasn't really what she'd expected, either. It was cluttered with boxes, but not untidy in a traditional sense and certainly not littered with dirty socks. He owned far more books than she'd expected, and some genuinely arty objects, such as the series of makeup impressions from *kabuki* theatre stars that were hung above the bed, and the freakish collection of specimen jars on the mantel.

'What's that?' she asked, staring at the lifelike mannequin sitting on a stool looking out of the window. It had been carefully dressed and arranged, with its head tilted upwards to peer up at the blue sky outside.

'Tifa.' He left his seat and crossed to where she sat. 'She's a *real doll*.' He stroked his fingers through her long brown hair and planted a kiss on her plastic cheek.

Remy gaped at him. 'That's warped.'

Takeshi shrugged, smoothed the doll's miniskirt, then returned to the swivel chair. 'No more warped than your *manga* collection.'

'Yeah, but I don't have sex with them.' She got to her feet.

'No, you probably have a vibrator for that.'

'So?'

'Typical! If women use sex toys they're empowered, but if men use them they're sad. Totally hypocritical.'

Remy felt herself blush and sat down again. She guessed he had a point. It was still a bit weird, though.

'They make male dolls, as well,' he said, and gave her a sly grin.

'As if I'd want one? *Yaoi* isn't about taking part.'

'You mean you don't want to be sandwiched between them?'

'No. It's about the relationships.'

Takeshi rolled his dark eyes incredulously. 'The Japanese girly obsession, I understand. It's a safe fantasy, isn't it? A vicarious thrill they get to giggle over without actually having to do the deed. It's the ultimate secret club. But you – you I don't understand.' His gaze flickered over her face. 'You're not the type to fear sex or a bit of power play. In fact, I know you don't. So, what gets you off so much about two guys, if it's not the possibility of being sandwiched between them?'

'Maybe I just like looking at beautiful men, and watching how their relationships play out.' Remy rubbed her nose, feeling vexed by his probing. She hadn't come here to be grilled. 'Anyway, what about you?'

Takeshi turned to the massive computer screen and started flicking between search screens. 'I thought I stated my interest yesterday.'

True. Masturbating over them was a clear statement of his position. At least he wasn't pretending there was some other, higher, cause behind his behaviour.

'Why settle for dull reality when you can live the fantasy?' He flicked along a line of navigator tabs. 'You should have a website.'

'You mean for my business? Yes, I know. It's on my plan, but I need a catalogue first. A website for a clothes emporium isn't going to get much traffic without any pictures.' That brought them back nicely to the point of her visit. Whatever else he was, he was visually stun-

ning, and, with Alix's wonderful photography, his attitude would leap right off the page.

'Ah, here it is,' he said, and urged her closer to the
screen. He'd opened a Japanese language site, and
started a movie clip running. 'The *anime* companies are
just catching on to the trend.' Remy strained forward, as
two impossibly pretty men argued, and then fucked: the
green-eyed, dark-haired male forcing the slighter blond
down on the bed, bottom up. They watched the three-
minute clip in silence until the end.

'Again?' Takeshi said, when it finished. His breath
tickled against her ear.

Remy shook her head. Her heart was racing and she
was sticky between the thighs. A repeat would likely
have her sprawled on his bed. She guessed that yesterday's encounter in the toilets hadn't entirely wrecked
her appreciation of the *yaoi* art form. That, or maybe his
presence injected potential.

'Can we get to the point of this visit?' she said, before
he could distract her with any more. She sat back on the
sofa to reclaim some personal space. She wanted this to
be a formal, nonsexual arrangement, which meant getting him to quit before he realised exactly just how
much the vignette had turned her on.

Takeshi drew his hands through his hair, adding to
the spiky effect. 'Yeah. You wanted me to model.' He
stood, thrust his hips forward, struck a pose, then
twirled on the spot, and struck another. What do you
want – sexy, sultry, rebel, misfit?'

Remy shook her head at his poses. 'Do you think you
can do it without mucking about?'

He grinned, displaying his teeth. 'Maybe. What's in it
for me?' He perched on the arm of the sofa beside her.

'A four-day holiday in a Jacobean fortified house.'

'Hmm.'

'And an outfit, as long as it's within reason.'

'How about I get to see you in the outfit of my choice?'

Remy scowled. 'Alix already has me posing naked. I'm not selling my soul over this.'

'Forget the outfit, I'll sit in on the photo shoot.'

His expression of delight made her regret the admission, although she suspected he wouldn't be the only male of her acquaintance who'd be jockeying for a ringside seat when she stripped. She could only hope that Alix would veto the audience as a distraction and pack them all off to the showers to cool down. Which, judging by the lecherous gleam in his eyes, was where he ought to be headed now.

'Who's this Alix guy, anyway?'

'Girl,' Remy corrected. 'She's the photographer for my catalogue, and the wedding we're shooting it at.'

Takeshi's rubbed his hands together in glee. '*Yuri*, how exciting. Like *yaoi*, only featuring women.' He brushed a stray hair off her cheek.

Remy batted his hand away. 'I know what it is, and don't get your hopes up. Nothing's going to happen.'

'That's a poor deal you're offering, Remy, if I don't get to dress you, undress you or fuck you silly.'

It was the first time he'd actually said her name. A thickness gathered in her throat at the realisation. She liked the way he said it. 'Remy,' he said again, and pleasure echoed in her chest. 'Are you listening?'

'What?'

'I just messaged Marianne.' He was back at the computer again. 'She says she's got some other stuff you can use as well: earrings, bangles, hair thingies, the works.'

'Sounds great. What does she want in return?'

He began typing, his fingers skimming lightly over the sensitive keys. 'OK, a mention in the catalogue, a web link and the chance to pose. I told her I was.'

'Is that reasonable?'

Takeshi shrugged. 'She's not bad-looking, just busty.

Some guys go for that sort of thing.' Remy glanced across at his well-endowed doll. He was clearly one of them.

'OK. Tell her to come along on Thursday. I'll leave you the details to pass on. She'd better be all right, or I'm going to hold you personally responsible.'

'As you wish.' He laughed.

Remy bowed her head. Why had she just agreed to use a model she'd never seen? She was shooting a fashion catalogue to launch her business, not a school project. If this actually worked, it'd be a bloody miracle.

4

Thursday evening came around too quickly. Remy's sense of excitement built as she sped north out of town in a black cab loaded with trunks. The last few days had been mental: cutting, sewing, adding all the essential trims and details that made an outfit. She was finished. Exhausted, but finished. She just hoped that all the measurements had been correct, that everything fitted, and nothing clashed. Chelsea's crowd were unpredictable. She just hoped no one had green hair.

The fields slowly rolled by, and the lights of the city vanished into the middle distance before blinking out all together. Soon only the cats' eyes lit the road over the wuthering hilltops. A billowing mist was coming down, stretching across the windy road like ghostly fingers. Remy sat in the back enjoying the tranquillity, only occasionally disturbed by the driver's radio messages, and Shadow's meowing. She hadn't spoken to Chelsea since Saturday, when she'd landed the job of outfitting the entire wedding party. Takeshi had phoned once, to check the dress code, and the bride's name, to avoid embarrassing anyone. He was being far too endearing, which just made her suspicious.

The driver took a sharp left into a lane. The road dipped and ran between two rocky outcroppings canopied by trees, and overhung by a rickety-looking bridge. They made another sharp upward turn, past a wall of brambles, and then there it was, lit up like a paper lantern. Castle D'Amon: five storeys high, golden light spilling from its windows and arrow slits, inspiring reverence and wonder.

Remy got out of the cab and stared up at the ancient stone edifice as the taxi driver unloaded her suitcases on to the gravel drive. She'd arrived. She wished she was coming home. Oh, to live in a place like this! Her fashion business would *really* have to take off it she was going to aim this high. Its summit seemed to scrape the stars.

She paid the driver, and watched him go until his taillights were swallowed by the dip. Then, leaving her possessions in a heap beside a very flash-looking motor-bike, she hoisted the cat box and followed a trail of foot-high lanterns to the door. It was a huge oak affair with iron pins and no knocker, so she braved her fist against the wood. She was unsuccessfully trying to peer through an adjacent spear hole when she finally got a response.

'Remy! Thank God! We were wondering what had happened to you. Your models arrived an hour ago.'

'Well, I had tons of stuff to pack, didn't I?' She glanced around Chelsea into the castle interior. The door appeared to open on to a landing partway down a broad spiral stair. 'It's all sitting on the drive. I'll need some help getting it all in.'

'Hang on.' Chelsea jogged up the bottom four steps of the spiral, orange light dancing through her golden hair. 'Get your bums down here. We need some help,' she yelled, then turned back to Remy. 'You're on the top floor in the cap house. Shaun figured you'd feel at home up there.'

Remy let Shadow out. He immediately darted past Chelsea, off in search of mice to terrorise. At least he was happy. Remy retraced her steps and grabbed her personal case and overnight bag.

Takeshi was coming out of the castle when Remy got back. In the moonlight, his pale-blue hair was shot with silver, and his eyes glittered like twin black sapphires. 'Hi,' she whispered. Her mouth curved upwards into an open greeting. He'd clearly put some effort into sprucing himself up for the occasion, or else she'd managed to convince herself that he was far more ordinary than he was.

'Hi. Much stuff?' He leant in to kiss her, and their lips briefly touched sparking memories of hurried intimacy.

'Loads.'

He stepped aside to let her pass, then headed towards the luggage pile.

Face it, she thought, you like looking at him. It's why you're using him as a model. She'd liked doing something else with him as well, but she was adamant they wouldn't be doing any more of it this weekend, despite the awakening she felt in response to his kiss. Theirs was going to be a business relationship, largely because she hadn't got over being taken like a guy. OK, so she had other issues with claustrophobic relationships, but nothing she couldn't handle.

She entered the castle. It was lit with wall lamps designed to look like wooden torches. To the right, the stairs descended five or six steps towards what looked like the dungeons. Left, they turned in a sharp spiral upwards, with only a thick rope as a rail. Remy adjusted the position of her overnight bag on her shoulder, swapped her suitcase to her right hand and grasped the rope. She began counting – numerous glassed-in arrow slits, three doors and three floors later, the main spiral ended on a landing and a tiny stair continued up. 'That'll be me,' she reasoned. She dumped the suitcase. It was too narrow for her to carry both it and her overnight bag in one go. She'd have to come back.

The staircase was a tight squeeze, extremely worn and creepy. Through the wall she could hear high-pitched shrieks – like a Space Invaders game. Bats, she realised – how Gothic! The short staircase led straight into a diamond-shaped room with two small stained-glass windows. There was a candle flickering by the bedside and no overhead light. Remy shivered. It was also a bit chilly. She crossed the board floor and closed the single set of shutters, then dropped on to the narrow bed to catch her breath after the climb.

There was an old-fashioned closet against one wall, a chest of drawers under the window, and a faded green armchair she'd walked past without noticing. The drawers would do for her casuals but the closet was hopelessly inadequate. Actually, she doubted she'd get all her cases up the tight stairs. She sat up again, just as the suitcase she'd abandoned came through the low arch of the stairwell. Chelsea followed it in, and dropped a vanity case beside it before clambering over both to collapse in the armchair. It creaked ominously.

'Takeshi's taken the rest to the Old Kitchen. You can use it as a workroom.' She puffed a breath upward, ruffling her silky blonde hair. 'I'm not going to ask where you found him.'

'Good.'

Her friend rose again, looking slightly disappointed. 'Look, I've said it before, but thanks for doing this. I thought I had everything sorted, but it's all gone pear-shaped over the last week. I'd be stuffed if you hadn't agreed to sort out all the outfits.'

'Fingers crossed I have. Do you want to see them?'

'Later. Get settled in first. We'll be in the lounge. Two floors down at the end of the corridor.'

'Right. Um, Chelsea, about this.' She pointed to the top of the gloomy stairwell. 'Isn't there a door?'

'Just the drape.' Chelsea drew a faded velvet curtain, which was about ten inches too short, across the gap. 'Sorry.'

Remy shrugged. It would do.

Once Chelsea had gone, she unzipped her ankle boots and collapsed back on to the pillows. The bed had an old-fashioned, dark, wooden frame, which made her think of 1930s boarding schools. It was made up with blankets and a purple tasselled bedspread. A single person's bed, of course, that just sparked an image of Takeshi above her, smiling as he stroked into her with deep, slow thrusts, as if the narrowness of the bed demanded extra care.

No! She sat abruptly. Why couldn't she shake him out of her head?

She emptied her suitcase into the chest of drawers, and got out her alarm clock. Was he in the lounge? she wondered. Eyes straining from the lack of decent light, she ventured downstairs to find out.

The heat in the lounge flooded her cheeks with blood. There was a long sofa and two squishy armchairs, all in rich green, positioned around a roaring fire. Shuttered windows on two walls, numerous sideboards and book-cases, and three occupants: Chelsea, a plump girl dressed in black and an older, blonde woman.

'We were beginning to think you'd turned in.' Chelsea stood. 'Mum, this is Remy, the dress designer.'

'Hi.' She assumed since they hadn't been introduced that she was supposed to know the other girl. Remy took a surreptitious second glance at her. There was nothing familiar about her; she was just another alternative in a band T-shirt. Then she saw the trays of jewellery and realised with a start that this was her other model. When Takeshi had described her as busty, she'd thought he'd meant just that, not that she was plump all over. 'Marianne,' she said, recalling her name. The woman nodded. OK, it wasn't what she'd expected but she wasn't so bad, she had a nice pout, and her curves would definitely look good in a corset.

Meanwhile, Chelsea's mum waved a champagne flute at her. 'It's Dolores.' She forced a glass into Remy's hand. Remy stared at her. She was dressed in a soft-pink cashmere suit. Her mouth fell open. This was Chelsea's mother! Maybe it had been the fuchsia-pink outfit that had made her imagine Hyacinth Bucket, complete with an atrocious accent and flowery hat, but Dolores Pen-shaw-Paige was anything but. Twenty years Chelsea's senior and probably twenty pounds lighter, Dolores was bottle-tanned, angular and wearing far too much gold.

She dabbed at her glossy lips, as if fearful that Remy's stare was a result of her drooling. 'We were looking over some of Marianne's pieces. She's rather gifted. I was suggesting to Chelsea that we pick out some pendants to give to the bridesmaids as gifts. Perhaps something they could wear with their dresses.'

'I've brought velvet chokers for them.' Remy transferred her gaze to the jewellery trays.

'But some silver as well, dear. Don't you think?' Dolores lifted two different pendants: a pentagram with a goat motif and an inverted crucifix.

'No, Mother!' Chelsea seized them. 'You'll look, won't you, Remy?'

Remy picked out some oversized ankhs, all similar but subtly different, and easily connected to the velvet chokers.

It was as she was bending over doing this that a hand closed over one of her up-thrust cheeks. Shocked, she stood only to find herself hard up against another body. 'Takeshi?'

'I see your arse is as lovely as ever,' said a female voice.

'Alix!' Remy peered over her shoulder, and saw the top of a head of flaming red locks. 'I see you still can't keep your hands to yourself. Haven't you heard you can get arrested for groping people?'

'I'm not groping anyone. I'm just being friendly. So, when do I get to see you in these outfits you've designed?'

Remy shook her head. 'I'm not modelling. I need to make sure everything is just right.'

Alix gave a great bellowing laugh that seemed too loud for her petite size. 'Don't be a dope, babe. You look ace in your stuff. It'd be criminal not to photograph you. Besides, I'm looking forward to seeing you *nekkid*, too.'

'You're finally going to pose?' asked Chelsea.

Remy nodded. 'Apparently. Where is Takeshi?' she asked, suddenly uncomfortable in a room full of women.

'Is that the cutie with the blue hair?' asked Dolores, between sips of champagne foam. 'He's gone to take a bath in the dungeon. He said you were welcome to join him.'

'It's not a dungeon: it's the old jail cell, Mother,' Chelsea said. 'From when they used to hold the assizes here. Anyway, it's been converted into a bathroom.'

'What about Shaun? And who else is there?'

'Stag night.' Chelsea sucked her bottom lip. 'God knows what they're up to. Hopefully, Silk will manage to bring him back here once the clubs close. The brides-maids are coming tomorrow.'

'Silk?'

'The best man,' Dolores said, with a definite purr in her voice. 'Why have cotton –'

Remy exchanged a look with Alix, the closest they'd come to a real connection in some time, and a big reminder of how close they'd once been. 'Care to clue us in?'

'Blond, six-foot, gorgeous,' Dolores said, before her daughter got the chance. 'A real pretty boy. You'd think he'd walked out of one of those Japanese kiddies' pro-grammes – *Beyblade* or whatever it's called.'

'Oh,' said Remy, feeling an excited tingle in her cunt at the mention of *anime* and pretty boy in the same sentence. Silk sounded just her sort. Mind you, the result of her last such encounter was currently soaking downstairs, and was probably plotting some mischief. Maybe it'd be wise not to let her imagination wander too far. Sounded as if he might be good catalogue material, though.

'Anyway, I plan to be in bed long before they get in,' Chelsea was saying. 'I think I'll take a hot drink up now. A bride needs her beauty sleep.'

'I thought the idea was to look like a corpse,' sniped Dolores.

Chelsea scowled.

'Well, you are getting married at midnight in a graveyard.'

'Actually, I'm getting married at midnight in a church. It happens to be Shaun's family's chapel, and it's just down the lane. They own this place as well. Shaun's hoping they'll offer us it as a wedding gift.'

'Nice prezzie!' Alix said, from the depths of a curious-looking cupboard she was investigating.

Remy nodded. 'Beats my apartment. Although you fitted it out very nicely.'

Dolores was scowling at her daughter. Clearly, they could expect some squabbling over the next few days. Remy got the distinct impression that Dolores had turned up only to hobnob with Chelsea's future in-laws, and maybe piss off her daughter a bit.

'What are everyone else's plans?' Remy asked, figuring it was about time she looked into what had become of her cases. 'I'd better go unpack, or everything's going to be creased to buggery.'

'Stay for another drink,' Dolores coaxed.

Remy waved her off. She'd barely touched the first glass, which she slipped on to the bookcase by the door, among the collection of spotting guides, coats-of-arms collections and ghost stories.

'Alix?'

Alix emerged from the person-sized cupboard. 'This is a cool place to play sardines. Where'd my kit go, Chels?' She ignored Dolores's offer of champagne.

'It's in the Old Kitchen with Remy's stuff.'

'Why didn't you bring it?' Remy asked. She edged towards the door.

'I brought my bike.'

'What, that flashy thing is yours?'

43

'The black and silver Honda Fireblade? Nope. I still have my old Ducati Monster.'

'It's Takeshi's.' Marianne caught up with them in the doorway. 'I had space in the mini but he wouldn't have it. He just gave me his suitcases. Did you want to take this stuff down?' She offered Remy a stack of jewellery trays.

'Yeah, thanks for the loan.' Remy accepted the trays.

They paused by the door to the first-floor kitchen. 'I'll leave the kettle on simmer,' Chelsea promised. 'Night.'

Remy and Alix continued down, following the spiral past the oak door and the spear hole. Then along a dingy corridor that smelled suspiciously of a mix of Old Spice and air freshener.

The Old Kitchen was exactly as its name implied. Alix's aluminium cases were arranged in a neat stack beside a worn table, while Remy's stuff had been dumped on an oversized rug without any thought to order by Takeshi.

The rug, a lurid floral affair, clearly wasn't an original feature. In fact, the only original feature was the enormous fireplace, large enough to accommodate four people standing shoulder to shoulder.

Alix walked over to it and stuck her head up the massive chimney. 'Long way up. Bit sooty, too. Mind you, they've got the fire going upstairs.'

Remy laid Marianne's jewellery collection on the table, and lifted a case from the top of her pile, causing several smaller items to tumble.

'Need some help?'

Remy stared at the jumble in dismay. 'I thought you had your own stuff to check.'

Alix swept her gaze over her neat silver cases. 'Yup. All present and correct.'

Remy thrust one end of a portable clothes rail at her. 'Help put this up.'

Five minutes later they flipped the catches of the first

trunk. Chelsea's dress came out, followed by the brides-maids' outfits, and the men's. 'Not too rumpled, either.' Remy gave each item a shake before smoothing the protective plastic coverings and hanging them. They filled a second rail with samples for the catalogue.

'We'll go out in the morning and scout some loca-tions.' Alix ran her fingers over a panne-velvet, Rosetti-inspired dress. 'The interior's mostly a bit dull. Not so sure about your models, either. You'll set this stuff off far better than Marianne.'

Remy shrugged. 'She'll look good in the corsets, and a deal's a deal. Maybe we can persuade Chelsea. I don't know what the bridesmaids are like apart from their measurements. They're Shaun's relations, I think.'

'I bet Dolores will be up for it.' Alix narrowed her eyes and grinned wickedly. 'Especially if you manage to recruit the best man. I'm guessing he's the only reason she's here.'

'Yeah.' Remy trailed her hand along the rack of clothes. 'And I thought my mum was bad. Her worst crime is dressing like a vicar's wife.'

'Well, she is one.'

Remy rolled her eyes. Her horribly straight parents were probably tucked up safe in bed with their evening cocoa by now, just like her elder siblings and their made-in-Stepford spouses.

'So, who's this guy you've brought along?' Alix asked, hands on hips, and her expression suddenly serious.

'Takeshi. You'll like him. He's got a cute arse and can talk bikes.'

'If you say so.' Alix shrugged, much to Remy's relief. Perhaps her friend really had outgrown her crush.

'Last suitcase.' Alix flicked the catches. 'Is this yours?'

Seeing her broad grin, Remy hurried over. 'No, it's bloody well not.' She stared at the carefully positioned doll and its oversized boobs. 'Shit! I can't believe he brought that.'

'Hi, there. I thought I heard voices.'

Remy turned sharply. Takeshi was in the doorway, wrapped in a navy bath sheet. His chest was bare, and he still had foam clinging to his shoulders. Remy stared at his penny-shaped nipples feeling decidedly hot around the collar.

'I see you found Tifa.'

'She's *yours*?' Alix spluttered.

'Yes, indeed. She's a great listener. Come on, darling.' He clasped the doll around the waist as if they were about to dance a tango. 'You and me have a hot date tonight. Unless you're going to cut in?' He looked at Remy, who shook her head. 'Night, ladies.'

'Night.' They both said, and then burst into giggles.

'Is he really gonna take a doll to bed?'

Remy grimaced. 'Don't go there. What he does with her doesn't bear thinking about. I mean, I hope he cleans her.'

Alix slapped her thigh and a tear rolled down her cheek. 'And you chose him over me. Dear God!'

Remy chased her out of the door.

The hours grew long. One coffee with Alix became three and a nightcap. Eventually, Remy staggered up the stairs to bed at around 3 a.m. It'd been months since they'd properly spoken, but Takeshi's doll had blown away all the ghosts of Christmas, and lightened the mood. Admittedly, they'd skirted the topic of relationships and Remy had adamantly denied being involved with Takeshi.

She slept lightly. The half-hearted curtain across the archway nagged at her subconscious. She kept expecting Takeshi to sneak up and pin her down. She woke, confused, to a very dark room. There were noises on the stairs that weren't anything to do with the Space-Invader bats.

Remy wrapped herself up in an oversized jumper and

some purple-and-black-striped over-knee socks, and padded down the narrow stairs on to the top landing. The commotion was coming from further down. Remy grasped the rope and continued down the main spiral. Further down, there were shadows on the wall where the lamp splashed light over the steps – an amorphous lump that writhed and shuddered. It split in half, revealing a tall figure with very long hair, and a hunchback.

Remy hung back a moment, then followed, intrigued by the silhouettes. The door to the second-floor corridor was off the latch, and the light was on. She stepped into its amber glow, treading carefully across the dark, stained boards so as not to make a sound. The first door stood open, revealing freshly made twin beds, but no occupants, the second a bathroom.

Remy squinted into the gloom. Whoever it was hadn't bothered to turn on the lights. The two figures were huddled by the toilet. Shaun, Chelsea's fiancé, was bent over the bowl, and standing by him was the most startlingly beautiful man she'd ever seen.

Silk, she realised, staring, – blond, angular and demonically gorgeous. Dolores hadn't been exaggerating. He could have passed for one of the *Daoine Sidhe*, the legendary fairy nobility. You could get drunk just looking at him. Right now, just his oceans of long hair had her transfixed.

Remy loved long hair, on anyone but herself. She admired the tenacity of anyone prepared to carry around all that extra weight and keep it tangle-free, but mostly she loved men with long hair. She loved how it tickled as it tumbled over her breasts, or brushed against her thighs when a guy went down on her. Silk's was so long that, although the bottom foot was plaited, it still brushed the backs of his knees.

She watched him reach out and gently scoop back Shaun's black hair and hold it in an ebony ponytail, while he retched. So he was a gentleman too, she thought, especially since he was risking getting a truly gorgeous frock coat splattered.

The coat was rich coffee-bean black, obviously made to measure. The fabric shimmered slightly with each movement, hinting at a subtle pile to the fabric. This man definitely knew how to dress. She wanted to run her hands along the seams of the coat, admire the artistry and skill that had gone into its creation – although the flaring heat between her thighs told her the biggest kick would come from feeling his hard body, and his even harder cock.

'Exquisite,' she whispered, only for him to turn his head at that very moment and look straight at her.

Or maybe that was into her. He had the piercing green eyes of the *Sidhe*, too.

Remy froze. He could also have been the *uke* from her book – the submissive blond Takeshi had wanked over. Except here he was made flesh and clearly dominant. Nothing in his expression, in the foxfire green of his eyes, said he would be anyone's toy.

'Think I can make it to bed now,' mumbled Shaun, his voice husky. He pushed himself to his feet and pulled the chain.

'Er, night,' mouthed Remy to Silk, before Shaun turned around and recognised her. She didn't want him to know she'd been here.

Silk inclined his head a fraction. The very corners of his lips curled upward, but he let most of his response come from his eyes.

Remy swallowed hard. It was like getting a come-on from a panther – aggressively, knicker-wettingly sexual. She turned on her heels and scampered back up the stairs to her room. Next to him, Takeshi was like a lovable puppy dog.

Back in the safety of the cap house, Remy snuggled under the covers, with her hand between her thighs. She didn't think she'd ever seen another man so poised, so breathtakingly beautiful, so sexually predatory, at least not outside the pages of one of her beloved *yaoi* stories. He'd obviously been sent to torture her.

Well, one thing she knew: she *had* to have him as a model. And she couldn't wait to see Takeshi's reaction to him. Her bisexual blue-haired *bosozoku* was going to have kittens when he saw him. Mind you, so was she if she ever got to see them kiss.

5

Remy woke late the following morning, despite her best intentions to get up and explore the grounds while the dew was fresh on the grass. She sat up and looked around. The sun was pouring through the stained-glass window in her turret, painting the tiny space in coloured light. The bedside travel clock said it was half-ten.

Remy showered, dressed and headed down to the kitchen in search of food and company. The yummy smell of bacon and sizzling eggs greeted her as she took a seat in the dining area at the huge oak table between Alix and Takeshi. The pair were warily eyeing each other up.

Remy glanced around the broad dining space and took in the squat iron stove, the tall wooden divide that hid the kitchen, and, curiously, the large pocket in the castle wall to her right. A commemorative plaque proclaimed it as an old cannon emplacement, once accessible by a wooden platform, but now out of reach.

Alix pushed a cup of stewed tea in her direction, then waggled the cereal box. Remy shook her head. 'I'll save myself for Chelsea's full English, thanks. It smells delish.'

Across the table, Dolores rolled her eyes in disgust. She was picking at a bowl of strawberries with a tea-spoon, doing her best imitation of royalty at a rock concert. She must have been up since eight perfecting her outfit and applying lip liner. Remy glanced down at her own outfit: she hadn't exactly dressed down herself, although she had opted for comfort, and her makeup had been a five-minute job. Takeshi and Alix were both wearing jeans. She guessed Silk had been uppermost in her mind when she'd opted for a lacy crop top. Dolores had obviously been thinking along similar lines. Her expression suddenly brightened. Silk had arrived.

Remy watched him prowl around the end of the table. He'd dressed simply in black boot-cut trousers and a high zip-necked T-shirt. The black cotton pulled tight across his abdomen as he moved revealing the musculature beneath – six clearly defined ridges, of the variety you normally saw only on posters or marble statues. He'd tied back more of his hair this morning, so that it framed his face, then hung in a thick braid from the level of his shoulder blades.

Remy traced her finger around her lips. If possible, he was more enchanting by day than he'd been by lamplight, when a brief glimpse of him and a moment's eye contact had resulted in her masturbating herself to sleep, thinking of him and Takeshi fucking.

He sat down near the head of the table, away from both her and Dolores, who was anxiously fluffing her hair.

Seeing the older woman preening made Remy aware of her own body language. What signs was she giving off? She immediately pushed her hands under the table. Just because she fancied him, it didn't mean she had to broadcast it to him and the rest of the table. Luckily, they seemed preoccupied with their own thoughts.

Tearing her gaze away from his blond perfection, Remy focused on Takeshi instead. He seemed equally entranced by Silk's appearance. 'Your eyes are bulging,' she whispered.

'They're not the only thing.' He took her hand and guided it towards his crotch. 'Is he for real, or am I hallucinating?'

'Real, or it's mass hysteria.' She pulled her hand away from his trapped cock and patted his thigh. She felt strangely affectionate towards him this morning. Perhaps because with a new predator on the scene she no longer felt so threatened. Still, that was no reason to be lulled into intimacy.

'Look at those talons. I bet they feel good raking against your back,' Takeshi mused.

Remy dug her fingertips into his thigh. Silk's nails were manicured, sharpened to points and painted with clear lacquer so that they gleamed. His fingers were long and slender, just perfect for finding her G-spot if they ever got intimate. Well, if he cut his nails first. Then she noticed that one nail on his left hand was filed right down. How strange!

She wondered what he did for a living. Nothing manual with those hands: they were too soft and smooth, unlike her own, which were a little rough from days of frantic sewing. Computer analyst, maybe, or some sort of consultancy role. Definitely, something that allowed him to swan around with an unconventional image, and probably in an environment largely free of women. She defied any heterosexual woman to concentrate on work when they had this guy in front of them. She was going to have to manage that somehow. She glanced along the table at Alix, who was spreading marmalade on a piece of toast. At least she could be relied on to keep her head.

'Good night?' Chelsea's voice crossed the tall wooden divide from the kitchenette.

Silk turned towards the wood panelling. 'Dreadful. Your fiancé spent the whole evening stone-cold sober and boringly faithful. I suggested a brothel, but he wouldn't have it.'

'Yeah, right,' replied Chelsea, but she sounded pleased with the report.

Silk returned his attention to the table, poured himself a cup of milky English breakfast tea, and then glanced bemusedly around the table at all the gaping expressions. 'Morning.' He winked slyly at Remy.

She suddenly felt hot and breathless. She had to say something, quickly, to cover her confusion. 'I need some models,' she blurted, hoping he'd volunteer. He smiled, but the only actual affirmatives she got were vague mumbles from Dolores and Marianne, who plonked herself into the seat next to Silk, after sliding a huge tray of bacon, sausages and black pudding on to the table.

Chelsea brought over eggs, mushrooms, tomatoes and a stack of warm plates, and they all began to eat.

Remy watched Silk help himself to a bit of everything, and followed suit. Takeshi, she noticed, was poking dubiously at the black pudding with his fork.

'It's congealed blood and fat,' she said.

'Seems appropriate for a bunch of vampires.' He took a nibble. 'Not even too gross.'

'When are the Gorgons arriving?' asked Silk, immediately attracting everyone's attention again.

Chelsea brushed her honey-gold hair over her shoulders. 'Not till later. They're seeing the dentist this morning to have their fangs fitted.'

'Gorgons?' Remy said, around a mouthful of fried bread. She forced herself to chew and swallow.

'Fangs!' Takeshi blurted.

'My bridesmaids. Their dad, Steve, and Shaun's dad were in Toys in the Attic together.'

'But why Gorgons?'

Chelsea shrugged, and looked at Silk, who stirred his tea thoughtfully. 'Do you know the legend of the Gorgons?'

'Medusa was one, right? Snaky hair, turns people to stone.'

'Exactly.' He took a sip of tea. 'They've perfected a hard stare that cracks mirrors at twenty paces. When they were nine-year-olds they took that stare to a Hallowe'en party along with fangs and demons' wings, and called themselves Medusa, Stheno and Euryale. They terrified the adults and scarred the other kids for life.'

'Nine-year-olds, period, terrify me,' said Alix. She licked a smear of marmalade from her fingertip.

'Who did you go as?' Chelsea asked, ignoring her.

'Dorian Gray.'

How cool are you? Remy thought.

'Didn't the Gorgons have beards?' Marianne asked, raising smiles all round.

'Well, beards or not, I need to see them as soon as they arrive.' Remy speared a grilled tomato, and frowned at the resulting mess. 'I need to see everyone else, too, except Chelsea, for a final fitting.'

'I might come down and check mine again with the bridesmaids.'

Wonderful! Remy glanced skyward. She didn't have time to play dress-up with Chelsea, but the path of least resistance seemed like the best option. And it would be useful to see them all together. 'I'll concentrate on the men this morning, then, until the bridesmaids arrive.'

'You'll have to wait till Shaun crawls back up the evolutionary ladder. Even without a hangover he's never up before midday.' Chelsea glared pointedly at Silk, who tilted his head and blinked twice in a 'Who, me?' sort of way.

Dolores immediately broke into a more exaggerated smile. The strawberry juice had wrecked her carefully applied lipstick. 'That's just fine with me, honey,' she purred in Silk's direction, clearly the start of an epic flirt. 'Although I still don't see what's wrong with the outfit I brought.'

'Remy's made something for you, Mother. You'll fit in better with the other guests this way. Like we discussed.'

Dolores flexed her swanlike neck, and peered down her nose at her daughter. 'Like *you* discussed. What makes you think I'd want to fit in anyway?'

'Mother!' Chelsea brought her fist down hard against the table. 'Just get with the programme for once. It's my wedding.'

Everything went silent, as all five other guests stopped chewing to watch.

'Well, really.' Dolores jerked her chair backward with a screech. 'There's no need to throw a tantrum. It makes you sound just like your father.'

Chelsea went an unearthly white. 'Don't you dare mention Dad.'

Dolores leant over the table towards her daughter. 'Don't tell me what to do.'

Remy forced herself on to her feet. It was too early in the day for squabbling. 'I'll see everyone downstairs in the Old Kitchen. Shall we go down?' She caught Dolores's eye and nodded meaningfully in the direction of the rickety kitchen door.

The cool air on the stairs was a relief after the tension of the kitchen. Remy could hear Dolores clattering after her in her stiletto heels. Hopefully, Silk would follow once he'd finished eating. She thought longingly of her own half-eaten breakfast. Oh, well, her hips would thank her.

The Old Kitchen was predictably gloomy. Remy flicked on the lights, and began rifling through her samples rack. Dolores was a little flat-chested and frankly a bit boyish to carry off most of her designs, so she opted for something to emphasise the few curves she did have.

'Try these on.' She handed Dolores a black velvet bodice with a boned floral-print panel in black and white, and a narrow ankle-length skirt with a split to the knee on one side.

'Am I just suppose to strip on the carpet? Don't you have a screen?'

Remy scowled with her back to Dolores, but she dragged the clothes racks out and used them to section off a changing area in one corner. She found a stool for Dolores's neatly pressed clothes.

The fit on the skirt wasn't perfect, but it was passable. Dolores clutched the bodice to her front as Remy laced the back, threading the silky ribbons through the many eyelets.

'She thinks her father's a saint,' Dolores said stiffly. Remy could see her jutting chin in the mirror. 'Actually he's a selfish tosser. I notice there's been no mention of why he's not here. Too busy screwing baby-dolls in the Bahamas to come to his daughter's wedding. And all I get for turning up is criticism.'

'You're all done.' Remy patted her on the shoulder. She knew Chelsea's father had sent her a substantial cheque to cover the wedding expenses, but Chelsea had never mentioned why he couldn't make it. Really, it wasn't her concern. Families always had issues. She knew. Her own had plenty.

Dolores shuffled a couple of steps closer to the mirror, adjusted her breasts, and jiggled. 'Woo! It's better than a Wonderbra. I like it.'

'You need something to set it off. Where's Marianne's jewellery?' Remy spread the trays over the old table. 'You need something to rest just there, at the top of your cleavage. A nice, wide, heavy pendant.'

'Like one of her dragons or something.'

'Or a bat, maybe.'

'Hmm.' Dolores gave her a pernicious stare. 'I hope you don't mean anything by that.'

'You need gloves, too.' Remy started sorting through her box of accessories, ignoring Dolores's remark. She'd meant what she'd meant. 'Try these. They're fingerless, so you can still show off your nails.' Dolores wiggled her perfectly manicured nails, which were painted a shimmery pink. 'Well, I wouldn't want to hide them.'

'No, but you might want to change the colour.'

'Is red acceptable, or does it have to be black? Honestly, all this effort, and with so much black about, we'll be lucky if we can find each other in the dark.'

Dolores hung around for another thirty minutes after Remy had finished accessorising her outfit. She pretended to be interested in the bridal gown and then in

Remy's fashion business, but it was blatantly obvious that she was waiting for Silk.

Remy was waiting, too. The anticipation had her insides fluttering like a net full of butterflies. She couldn't wait to start smoothing fabric over his skin, tracing his lean contours and moulding her designs to his shape.

But time dragged on, Dolores gave up and left, and Remy's excitement turned to impatience, and finally to annoyance. Where in hell had he got to? She had better things to do than hang around.

Remy checked her watch again: almost two. It was no good: she simply had to get on with things. She lifted Shaun's outfit off the rack, and decided to knock him out of bed. At least she knew where he'd be and how to wake him. His errant best man would have to wait.

Two floors up, Remy knocked on Shaun's door, waited, and then knocked again. When there was still no response, she let herself in.

The thick brocade curtains were drawn tight across the long windows. There were two beds, the nearer of which had been neatly made. Remy laid his outfit over the covers, and headed for the blackest part of the room.

'Rise-and-shine time.' She wafted the scent of black filter coffee towards the bed. Shaun groaned and rolled over, tugging the bedspread up over his chin. 'What time is it?'

'After two.'

'Ergh! Just five more minutes, Mum.'

'Up.' Remy put the mug next to the alarm clock. 'I need to fit you.'

'Remy?' Shaun pushed himself into a sitting position and groggily clasped the mug. 'Thanks. This wasn't necessary, you know. We had outfits sorted.'

'I guess Chelsea just wanted to make sure you were matched up.'

'Wanted her way, more like,' he mumbled into the steaming mug. 'Our stuff was fine from the other place. It was just the bridesmaids' dresses they mucked up.'

'Are you gonna get up?'

'All right, already.' He thrust back the covers and climbed out, revealing a stark white body and a pair of skimpy black slips. He tripped over a suitcase and landed on the other bed, narrowly missing his outfit.

'Oh, no,' said Remy, when he plucked at the plastic cover. 'Wash first. You stink of sick and you need to take the makeup off. How much did you put on last night?'

'We went clubbing. How much would you put on if you were going out with him?' He glanced towards the head of the bed he was sitting on.

Remy shrugged. She hadn't thought about the Silk effect from a heterosexual male perspective. She guessed he could make you feel pretty inadequate. That didn't excuse Shaun's pan-stick white, though. 'Bathroom. I don't want grey smears on anything.'

Shaun dutifully headed next door. Remy heard him running the taps and scrubbing his teeth. She crossed to the light switch, then changed her mind and drew the curtains. Bright white light flooded into the room. Remy flung up the sash, letting the chill spring air spill in and blow away the acrid reek. There were several large conifers bordering the lawn on this side of the castle, all swaying merrily in the breeze. The pungent scent of pine needles reached her. She'd find Alix after this, and head outside to find some good backdrops for photographs. The interior was airy but gloomy, and, while the fire-places were impressive, everything else was tastefully nondescript.

She was still staring out of the window when Silk came in. He sat down on the edge of his bed by Shaun's clothes.

'I thought you could use some air in here.' Remy pointed at the open window. 'It smells a bit sicky.'

Silk's warm smile and green gaze showed that she had his full attention, but he didn't say a word. Her earlier impatience melted away and she felt compelled to keep talking.

'I need to dress you.' She pressed on. He'd look fantastic in her coachman's coat, a long, fitted, wool coat with capes and a high collar. Hell, he'd look fantastic in anything, and equally in nothing. 'Have you got – I mean, can you spare a few minutes after I see Shaun?'

Silk lowered his gaze, then flicked it back up. 'I suppose,' he said. 'Shall I meet you in the Old Kitchen?'

'Stay and offer an opinion on Shaun's outfit. Yours is similar. I'd like to know what you think.' Stay and convince me you're real, she thought. He was too perfect, like Takeshi's doll. She wanted to know that he had some flaws, some feelings that she could appeal to.

'Shit!' The yell came from the bathroom. A moment later Shaun returned, his eyes bloodshot and watering, and his pasty face blotchy. There was still a greyish smear around his eyes. 'I left my bloody lenses in all night, and they're glued to my eyeballs.'

Both Remy and Silk peered across at him. Sure enough, he still had yellow cat's eyes.

'Leave them for a bit,' said Silk. 'They'll come loose again, once you've been up a while. It's just because they dry out while you're sleeping.'

Shaun rubbed at them.

'Don't rub. If they're stuck you could take your cornea off.'

Shaun stopped, and bit his lips in irritation. 'Thanks for that cheery thought.' He turned to Remy. 'Will I do?'

'You still have a fake bite mark on your neck.'

'Who said it's fake?'

Remy raised both eyebrows. She hoped he was joking. She noticed that Silk was smirking. Shaun picked at the dry wound, and a trickle of blood resulted. 'Oops,' he said, and went back to the bathroom.

'Tell you what,' Remy called after him. 'I'll bring your outfit down. Take a shower and I'll see you afterwards. I'll sort Silk out now.'

He followed her down to her workroom, persistently two steps behind. Remy couldn't decide whether he was avoiding conversation or checking out her bum. She went to the rail, hung Shaun's clothes and found Silk's outfit: heavily woven brocade trousers and a crisp white shirt with a ruff front.

'This is yours. The coat is slightly different from Shaun's. His is cut like a morning coat, while this has a straight front.'

Silk ran his long fingers over the brocade. 'You made these?' He made the simple question sound like a compliment.

She nodded.

He undid his zip.

Va-va-voom! thought Remy.

He pulled his top off in one fluid motion, then kicked off his shoes and stepped out of his trousers. Instead of the translucent white she'd expected, his skin was creamy. The hinted-at six-pack delivered on its promise, too, lending him an aspect of power that completely wiped away any hint of androgyny implied by his long hair.

Remy handed him the trousers, but held open the shirt to pull on to him herself. The soft cotton whispered against his biceps as she slid it up his arms. He seemed bemused by the intimacy. Deliberately avoiding his gaze and pouting in what she hoped was a serious manner, she smoothed the front from his collarbone to waistband. She didn't know what it felt like to him; he breathed in sharply as she traced his stomach, but it sent a shiver of delight from her brain to her cunt. She fastened the hidden button at the neck next, and arranged the froth of fabric. 'Now the waistcoat.' He was watching her intently, the scrutiny raising pinpricks of heat across her cheeks.

The burgundy fabric gathered the loose shirt to his chest, giving him a more defined shape, and emphasising the breadth of his shoulders. Remy swallowed, and held out the coat for him to try on. He looked too scrumptious for words. She wanted to see him in every item of men's clothing she'd brought, right down to the cobweb-effect pyjamas. Actually, what she wanted to see him in right now was her coachman's coat. 'Try this.' She snatched it off the rail. She loved this coat. It was her favourite. More precious, more exquisite to her than even Chelsea's wedding dress, which she'd poured so much effort into. She'd constructed fantasies around this coat, usually involving a pretty winter garden, a quaint chocolate-box cottage hung with icicles, and the man who owned the coat making angels in the snow beside her. Right now, it smelled of freshly laundered wool. By Monday, she hoped it would smell of him.

Silk let her tweak and smooth the coat without comment. She was being especially fussy over it. It had to be just right. It was a fraction too long, not drastically, but it had to be perfect. Remy grabbed the seam ripper, tore away the stitching, and then began repinning.

'How long have you known Shaun?' she asked, trying conversation in order to seem less neurotic.

'Since high school.'

'Surprised he's getting married?'

'No. He's a romantic, and it's the romantic thing to do, isn't it?'

'Ouch!' Remy sucked the red pinprick on her finger. 'I don't know, I chickened out.'

'At the altar?'

Remy swallowed hard, wishing she'd kept quiet. How to look stupid: tell a guy about how you jilted someone a fortnight before your own wedding. 'He was my parents' choice.' Silk's silence seemed to invite her to continue. 'We didn't suit. He married my elder sister in the end. They have three kids, a huge mortgage and a pair of Irish wolfhounds.'

She carried on pinning for a few minutes, feeling irrational and irritable after her outburst. The thought of Duncan always awakened old resentments. He was nice, just boring, and she'd been only nineteen. The pressures had been enormous. She could still remember all the lectures. He's got a good job, fine prospects. He's from such a respectable family. He'll help you settle down. You need to sort yourself out, forget the pipe dreams, get involved in the church more.

What she'd actually done was got blind drunk, snogged the lay preacher at her father's church and run off to Leeds and fashion college. Her parents had nearly disowned her, but it was still the best decision she'd ever made.

'Penny for them?' Silk was looking down at her with one eyebrow raised and his bottom lip plumped. He seemed to care, but she'd done with confessions for today.

She shrugged. 'Ancient history. What about you? Any plans for a white wedding?'

'Too exclusive. I don't make promises only to break them.' He held her gaze as if challenging her to have a problem with that.

'So you're easy, but not cheap,' she said around pins in her mouth.

Silk lowered his eyelids. 'How do you know I'm not both?'

She bowed her head. The wicked gleam in his eyes was too devilish to hold. If she kept looking at him, she might embarrass herself by kissing him just to find out how easy he was. 'You're all done.' She sat back on her haunches. 'Finished.'

'Mirror?'

She pointed to the one she'd stolen from the bathroom earlier.

'Very nice.' He rotated so that the coat skirt swirled. 'Gloves. And my pocket watch.' He disentangled the chain from his own trousers and attached it to his wedding outfit.

Remy licked her lips. The effect was perfect. His looks and her clothes – they were a deadly combination. With him as her model, she'd sell oodles in no time at all.

He extended a hand towards her. She accepted, and he pulled her up quickly. Her heart rate quickened as she stumbled forward, almost head-butting him in the groin. His grip tightened just before they collided, bringing her upright instead. Remy stared into his bright-green eyes.

'Will you model for me, please?'

'What's in it for me?'

'What do you want?'

He gave a faint smile. 'All sorts of things.'

Like a kiss, she thought, tilting her head. She wondered how soft his lips would be. Whether his skin was as smooth as it looked. How he'd look naked beside Takeshi, their limbs entwined, a black satin sheet gliding over them as they moved together. Who'd be the bottom? Who'd be the top? There was a giddy, bubbly sensation in her chest. He touched a finger to the ends of her hair, lowered his eyelashes and dipped his head towards her.

'Wow,' said Shaun, from the doorway. 'Man, you look fantastic.'

'I think we'll do,' Silk replied, turning his head.

Remy jerked away from Silk, as Shaun rushed forward, pulling his tie-dye T-shirt from his leather jeans. He held out a hand out for his shirt.

'Here, let me,' said Remy when he started fumbling with the neck ruffles.

'This is great. This is so great.' He turned towards Silk, grinning maniacally. But Silk was gone.

* * *

Silk paused halfway up the stairs and peered back over his shoulder. His body was tingling with an electric thrill from her hands running over his body. Beneath his shirt, his nipples were erect, and his body was aching for her – well, for someone. He smiled to himself, shook his head, and continued up to the kitchen, his long braid sailing behind him.

'Remy Davies,' he mouthed to himself. He'd known she was interested, from her reaction last night. Still, he was used to covetous stares, and he wasn't going to pretend to be modest about it. The plump one and Chelsea's tanned, svelte mother were already eyeing him up, and he had no preference for soft or hard bodies. He just liked women. And, of course, there were the Gorgons to think about.

He reached the kitchen, dumped his own clothes on the end of the workbench and peered around. He needed something to ease the tension in his groin. Jerking off would do it, but there was nothing stylish about reliev-ing yourself in the bathroom. Besides, it wasn't what he wanted. He didn't want to eradicate the slow erotic burn she'd caused. He just wanted to temper it.

Silk stuck his head into the pantry. It was full of crockery. Backtracking, he moved to the fridge and found a 400g bar of Dairy Milk. He wolfed down three chunks. The taste tingled on his tongue. Mmm, better. He broke off another three chunks and returned the rest to the fridge.

At the dresser, he poured himself a shot of Scotch, and swallowed it in a single gulp. Better now, much better.

The door to the back stairs opened. The plump pouty one appeared. He tried to recall her name as he watched her walk the length of the room, broad hips swaying. She was full of soft curves in all the obvious places: thighs, stomach, breasts, and a few less fashionable ones. Her bottom lip was fleshy, too, and painted blood red.

She went to the fridge, took out the chocolate, and irritably flicked the ripped foil wrapper.

'Sorry, I pinched some,' he confessed.

Her annoyance vanished. 'That's OK. Have some more.' She handed him another chunk.

Silk took it, using the exchange to narrow the gap between them. Sex, chocolate, sex, chocolate. There was no contest, really. Chocolate was always a substitute. If he could have had sex five times a day, every day, he'd never have needed to eat chocolate again. As it was, he'd never felt completely satisfied by any woman he'd ever had. Still, that was no reason to knock chocolate as foreplay. The next piece she offered, he took with his teeth.

She seemed so startled he had to struggle not to grin. Instead, he masked his mirth by licking a smear of chocolate from her thumb. He curled his fingers around her wrist, extended the tease to her inner wrist, her forearm, and then her elbow, feeling like a dreadful parody of Gomez Addams. But the gesture worked like magic.

Her eyelids fluttered, and her mouth opened in a soft 'ah'.

His kiss reached her shoulder, where the edge of her top clung to the lily-white skin, defying gravity. It slipped as he touched it, exposing a cleavage that no push-up bra would ever achieve. Oh, to feel those curves envelop his cock. The soft sensual slide would be amazing. He dusted their surface with his lips, imagining the vision of her nipples – huge, brown and sensitive.

He brushed his body against her, connecting them from thigh to chest as he rose to meet her gaze again. 'I'm Silk.' He kissed one corner of her mouth, then the other. 'Pleased to meet you. I don't think we've been formally introduced.'

'Marianne,' she squeaked.

Do you want to fuck, Marianne? He didn't say it. He

let his eyes convey the question instead. It never failed. However, her next move took him by surprise. Her lips sealed over his and her hands shot straight to his groin. Clearly, she wasn't planning on being passively seduced.

She backed him into the tiny pantry, her hand inside his fly, coaxing life into his shaft. Silk felt the wall against his back. Talk about cornered! There was barely room to stand, barely room to breathe, as she leant into him, kissing him as if he might suddenly disappear.

She was good with her fingers, though. A stream of fire was flooding through his cock, making a pleasant buzz in his loins. He wanted something more encompassing, though. He wanted to slip inside, feel her clamp her soft thighs around his hips and dance to his rhythm. His hand went to his pocket.

Bugger! He'd left his condoms in his other trousers.

Marianne rubbed her thumb over his sensitive eye, making him forget everything. Back and forth, her circling made his muscles clench. It was too sweet, dangerously addictive. She'd make him come too soon.

Gently, he urged her down, breaking their lengthy kiss and her skilful tease. She knelt, nuzzled up to the hair at his root, and then licked along the underside of his shaft from base to tip.

Silk gave in to the sweet pleasure. He stroked her hair, gripped the shelf to his left and let his head fall back against the angled window ledge. The tip of his cock throbbed with need, while the silky wet caress of her tongue whispered across its tightly drawn surface. But the relief of each brush was bittersweet, heightening his need for release.

He wanted to be doing this with Remy. Wanted to be still in the dingy kitchen, watching her dip-dyed hair swing against her cheekbones as she fellated him, while surrounded by the tiny slivers of silver that were her spilt pins.

The girl he was with was good, but she was too

willing. He wanted more of a challenge, he supposed, more resistance. When Remy looked at him, it wasn't just simple attraction that made her eyes go wide. There was something more, as if she were inserting him into a complex fantasy life that rendered physicality obsolete. Touch was a bonus. She didn't need it to gain pleasure.

Marianne cupped his balls. They already felt high and loaded. She was doing fantastic things with her tongue as she sucked. He looked down at her. There was a pretty smattering of freckles across her nose, which she'd tried to cover with makeup. He was almost there. The blood-red lipstick prints she'd left on his erection were what triggered the final ascent.

Sensing his arrival, she dug her nails into his buttocks, helping extend the moment of liquid bliss before orgasm. The nerves in the tip of his cock were singing. He couldn't maintain it, couldn't delay it, either. The ecstasy built to volcanic proportions. He let go.

There was no fantastic explosion. Definitely, no feeling of bullet-time vertigo as his senses helixed out of control, just a physical jolt and the momentary pleasure of release. It took the edge off his lust, but failed as a total catharsis. Silk let his muscles go slack. He was going to need to fuck again, and soon. There was too much eroticism in the air for him to ignore it and get on with his duties as best man.

Marianne clung to him. He stroked her head absently, soothingly. Now that his brain wasn't so fried with erotic thoughts, he realised that he'd made a big mistake. The possessive grip on his thigh said it all. It was just a quickie, he raged internally. Nothing more.

Silk drew her up into his arms and pressed a kiss to her clever mouth. He had a favour to repay her and then they were quits.

6

After she'd finished with Shaun, Remy went to find Takeshi and Alix. They took some of the more casual articles out along the gravel causeway that led to the Dower House. There was a set of old stone steps partway along, where a line of heavy shrubs divided the garden widthways. Remy looked at the heavy, grey sky and grimaced.

'Don't worry, we're OK for a while,' said Alix, positioning Takeshi on the steps, where a solitary shaft of golden light rippled over the worn granite.

After straightening Takeshi's collar, Remy had little to do except hold the remaining clothes, so she sat back on the crumbling base of an upturned urn and watched the show. Alix knew her stuff, and, after a brief moment of awkwardness, Takeshi settled into a rhythm. He was a natural, flirting with the camera in subtle yet provocative ways. It was wonderful just to watch him pose, to see him curl his lip in a surly smile or glower menacingly. Once or twice, his air of wounded machismo seemed more than just an act. Either he'd watched a lot of Marlon Brando films, or he was for real. She wondered again about his past and the snapshots of Japan. In any case, he would make a fine and exotic contrast to Silk's refined androgyny, assuming Silk ever agreed to help.

The minutes ticked by, the clouds growing steadily darker. Remy pulled the last outfit, a mesh T-shirt featuring a Chinese dragon screen print, over Takeshi's chest. The fabric was clingy, and accentuated the hollows and curves of his wiry frame. His nipples, steepled by the wind, showed clearly through the pattern. Remy stared at them distractedly. She liked male nipples. Liked to suck on them, loved the feel of them against her tongue. She wondered if Takeshi would enjoy that. Some men got off on it, while others always hurried her towards their groins. She wondered if he thought about Silk exploring that area with his tongue.

'Your fingers are cold,' Takeshi growled, as she moved upwards to smooth the neckline. He grasped her hands, and held them around his neck.

His brown eyes were warm and open.

'What do you say we share some friction to warm up after this?'

'We agreed this was strictly business.'

'I don't remember that.' He ran his index finger up and down along the inner edge of her thumb. The area was unexpectedly sensitive. Remy tried to pull away, before the sweet shivers became too seductive. Already she could feel echoes of his caress hurtling towards her groin. Takeshi held her tight, and tilted his head forward so that their brows met. Their mouths were just millimetres apart. His warm breath whispered against her lips, light as a feather, and more intriguing than a kiss. I know what makes you tick, his eyes said, coaxing her towards lip and hip contact.

'I'm sure this is all very exciting for you.' Alix snapped her tripod closed. 'But you need something more original than a blue-haired moron, I mean model, and a castle backdrop if you want to stand out. Anyone can dress their boyfriend up and take snapshots around some stately home.'

Remy turned her head away from Takeshi's tease, although she didn't need to see Alix's face to know she was scowling. She may have made light of Takeshi and his doll last night, but currently there was no disguising the jealousy in her voice.

'Cosplay,' Takeshi announced. He turned a circle. 'You

should include a section like that in your catalogue, make a statement with it.'

Remy looked blankly at him. 'That costume play thing where fans dress up as their favourite *anime* characters? How's that supposed to help?'

Takeshi shook his head. 'Use your imagination. It's not about being exact. It's about attitude, and fantasy. Think about Silk. Have you ever met anyone who looked more like Sephiroth from *Final Fantasy VII*? It'd be a wasted opportunity not to use that to make a statement.'

Remy's brow further wrinkled. 'I don't see how dressing up as video-game characters is going to help me sell clothes.' Yet Takeshi was right on one score: Silk could've walked straight out of the popular game.

'No. It'll be fantastic. I can loan you Tifa. You could be –'

'Has anyone ever mentioned that you're a total geek?' Alix said, cutting him off.

'So sue me.

'Does Shaun have black hair?'

'Yeah,' Remy said, 'but I'm really not convinced about this.' It sounded like one of those name-your-ideal-film-cast-for-your-favourite-book articles. Good fun to talk about down the pub, but hopelessly unrealistic. And nerdy.

'Actually, he might have something, Remy.' Alix favoured him with a grudging nod. 'It might work as a spread over a couple of pages. A catalogue's supposed to do more than just show people what you've got. It needs to sell an image, and that means style and fantasy. Anyone looking at the images should be thinking, I want to be this person or be with them. Of course, we could use any theme, not just cosplay.'

Remy turned her back on them and walked up the steps. 'Look, I get what you're saying. Maybe we could even make it work, but Silk hasn't even agreed to model yet.'

'So *make* him agree,' said Alix.

Remy glanced back. 'And how exactly am I supposed to do that?'

'Give him a blowjob.'

'Great idea,' Takeshi snapped. 'And, since you thought of it, why don't *you* do it?'

'You've got to be kidding. I'd rather suck on an exhaust pipe.' Alix zipped her jacket up to the neck.

Remy narrowed her eyes at Takeshi. 'You sound a bit jealous, pal. Did you want that job for yourself, or are you telling me what to do?'

'I'm telling you what you need. I've heard you come, remember.' He wet his lips as he stared at her. 'As for Silk, I've got a few ideas about what I'd like to do with him, but he's not into men.'

'What?' Remy came back down the steps. There was no way someone as poetically beautiful as Silk was just heterosexual.

'Remember my list?'

She nodded.

'Well, I know a straight guy when I see one, and that guy's so straight you could ram a broom handle up his arse and he wouldn't notice. The pretty-boy thing is just a way of getting him laid. Girls love androgynous men. They're less threatening.' He leant towards her, baring his teeth.

'But – but –' Remy stammered. Paper images of Silk and Takeshi together burned to ash in her imagination.

'You make him sound like a real conniving bastard,' said Alix.

Takeshi nodded. 'I'll guarantee he'll have slept with eighty per cent of the castle by the end of the weekend.'

'And you'll have slept with none,' sniped Remy.

'I'll have slept with two. You and him.'

'You just said he was straight.'

'Who said I played by the rules?'

He took the tripod from Alix, leaving her with the camera to carry, and tramped off towards the castle.

Remy snatched up her bagged clothes and followed, feeling vexed. She wasn't sure what had annoyed her most: his cool assurance that he'd have shagged her by Monday night, his jealousy or the way he'd destroyed her hopes of a little live-action *yaoi* from him and Silk. Arrogant sod! Ha! She couldn't wait to see his reaction when she snared Silk before he even made it to first base.

There was another car on the drive when they got back: a black hearse complete with starched lacy curtains and black satin ribbons. There was bedlam in the hallway, too. A collection of suitcases was blocking the stairs, and somebody's sexy smalls were strewn over the bottom eight steps. After stowing the clothes and Alix's camera back in the workroom, they began to pick their way around the obstacles.

'Lucretia, you old bat, you've left a trail of knickers down the hall,' screeched a high-pitched voice.

'They're not mine, they're Sev's.'

A figure appeared just above them on the spiral steps from the kitchen. She stopped short and gave them a wide grin, which showed off her dentally enhanced canines. 'Hi! I'm Eloise. One of the bridesmaids. You must be Remy.' She extended a bony hand. 'We're up for modelling. Chelsea's just been filling us in.' She glanced at the other two. 'Alix and Takeshi,' said Remy by way of introduction. 'Alix is the photographer; Takeshi's one of the models.'

'Nice hair,' said Eloise, giving him an entirely predatory grin. 'Very *Visual Kei*.'

'You know that stuff?'

'Yeah. Gackt and HYDE. I'm into the imagery more than the music, mind. And, of course, *Moon Child* was très cool.'

Remy and Alix stared at the pair as though they were speaking a foreign language.

'They're singers and it's a film,' he translated.

'You could've picked them up for me.' A second figure came out of the kitchen and down the stairs towards them, scooping up underwear as she approached.

'My sister, Severina,' said Eloise. 'Another part of the triune. Sev, this is Remy, Takeshi and Alix.'

'Um, hi.' She peered up at them, holding a pair of scarlet pants. Although she was otherwise identical to Eloise, Sev's hair was pulled back in a thick black pony-tail, her teeth were her own, and her dress code was Wednesday Addams.

'You're twins,' said Remy, imagining endless mirror-image-type possibilities for the catalogue.

'Test-tube triplets,' they both replied.

'Lucretia's with Chelsea,' explained Sev. 'Shall we go up?'

Takeshi lingered at the back of the group, and continued up the stairs when the others headed into the kitchen. Too much oestrogen.

Away from the twittering girlish voices and the clack of stiletto heels, the upper floors of the castle were filled with welcome quiet. He breathed a sigh of relief, and lingered by a glassed-over arrow slit.

Cosplay and X-Japan – the images of a past life, not memories he expected to be evoked by a nineteen-year-old with fake fangs. The sights and sounds slid easily into focus, flooding his senses. Painted youths on street corners, ghosts in high heels and short skirts posed against a black sky shot with neon. The smell of rain and gasoline, the thrum of the engine beneath him, blending with thumping music as he soared through a rainbow of wet tarmac. There were sirens screeching in the distance, but he was wild and free. Free as only a teenager who'd sneaked out of the house to scavenge for bike parts and run with the pack could ever be.

Takeshi put his hand to the glassy slit, wishing he

could push through it into the open space beyond. He was already half frozen from modelling, or he'd have pulled on his leathers and taken the bike out along the lush country lanes, just to feel the wind rushing by and to know that nothing had really changed.

But everything had changed. He was no longer in Japan. He was no longer a *bosozoku*. No longer a bad boy running errands for the *yakuza*. Bike rides were just to get from A to B, and all his thrills were tied up in sex. Remy's designs were good, even if they weren't exactly his taste, but he wasn't here to be a clotheshorse. It had felt crazily good when they'd fucked in the graffiti-riddled cubicle in the park – far better than he'd ever expected. He'd come here to have her again, not to watch her go all doe-eyed over some *blondie*. Then again, he couldn't deny his attraction to the other man. Silk was a bitter chocolate, a sensual feast. He licked his lips. One he intended to taste. He'd meant what he'd said to Remy: he would have them both. But he'd have to keep his cool, not lose it as he had outside.

Silk embodied Remy's *yaoi* fantasies, and he knew his own image played heavily on that. He smirked. This was just like one of the dating sims that were so popular in Japan. Seduce, cajole, trick and treat your way to the perfect clinch. It was dangerous; there were risks involved. She might just decide to quit game playing and exclude him, but not to play the game would guarantee failure, anyway. He knew his limits, and, in a straight contest with Silk, he was destined to lose.

He left the stairs on the second floor and passed his shared bedroom. The sounds of Marianne clattering about inside were enough to drive him onwards down the hall towards the lounge. Hopefully, he'd find a roaring blaze and no company.

Silk was in the armchair to the right of the fire, and another man wearing black lipstick was sprawled along the length of the sofa. Shaun, evidently. It seemed the only peace to be had was on the stairs. Maybe that was why the English thought of castles as claustrophobic. Everyone seemed to huddle together in pockets of warmth.

Shaun turned his head towards the door. 'Come and join us.' He swung his legs off the sofa, creating an obvious space in which to sit. Not wanting to appear rude to his host, Takeshi joined him. At least the blaze was strong. He stretched his legs out, letting the heat wash up his calves. He hoped the next shoot would take place indoors.

'So how do you know Remy?' Shaun crossed his legs and sat holding his toes.

Takeshi stared at his black socks. He didn't know if Remy had said anything about how they'd met and he didn't want to piss her off by contradicting her. 'We met in a comic shop. We like the same books,' he said, opting for an abridged version of events.

'What, all that sappy *manga* homo crap? I've seen her collection. No offence, mate, but only the Japanese could come up with that stuff.'

'Go on! A bit more and you'll be up to your neck.' Silk put aside his magazine. 'The Japanese aren't the only ones who write slash. Westerners have been at it for years.'

Shaun shrugged. 'Not my scene.'

Takeshi turned his head in Silk's direction, surprised at his depth of knowledge. Perhaps he was being unfair. Silk hadn't given him any reason to believe he was homophobic or narrow-minded.

'Interesting place for a wedding,' Takeshi said, deliberately changing the topic. 'Didn't your family object to a midnight bat fest?'

'You're joking, right? They think all this is incredibly tame. Mind you, they might spice it up a bit. Dad'll probably turn up in his kilt and Mum as the Lady of Shalott.'

'Loopy and loaded,' said Silk 'His gran's a bag lady as well as an art critic. It's amazing he turned out so sane.'

'Ah, so you finally admit that marriage is sane?'

Silk rested his hand on the chair arm. 'In your case, yes.'

'Are you saying nobody else'll have me?'

'I'm saying Chelsea wants you.'

Shaun rested his elbows on his knees, and leant forward eagerly with his chin in his hands. 'When are *you* fixing a date, then? Everyone wants you.'

Silk ran his thumb across his lips in order to hide his smirk. 'And everyone can have me. Just as soon as I get around to it.'

'Pass me a pin so I can deflate your head.'

'I'm not the one who reckoned they could neck a bottle of absinthe in one go.'

Shaun chucked a cushion 'Did it, though, didn't I?'

Silk snatched the velvet square out of its flight path, and tucked it behind his head. 'A half-bottle, yeah. And then puked it straight up again.' He turned his cheek towards Takeshi, his liquid green eyes wide and luminous with intent, almost the colour of absinthe themselves. 'So, are you and Remy together, or not?'

Takeshi, startled by the shift in conversation, paused a little longer than a straight answer required. The question sounded innocuous enough but he knew it was loaded, and he had his own game plan. 'Why? Do you want to get in on the action?' he said, making it clear he understood the subtext. ''Cause I'm sure she's up for a threesome.'

Silk ran his tongue over his teeth in response and eyed Takeshi thoughtfully. Clearly, the idea of sharing with another man was giving him pause for thought. Takeshi was sure Silk had had two women at once, so it wasn't just the notion of group sex making his fingers tighten over the chair arm.

Takeshi couldn't resist pushing it a little further. He

was enjoying watching the sleek white panther squirm. 'Scared I'll make you look bad?' he said, making it sound like a challenge.

Shaun snorted in amusement. Takeshi guessed that he didn't see many people challenging his friend's alpha-male status.

Silk's lips pursed almost imperceptibly. His irises seemed to respond to his moods, and were now the venomous green of a Hollywood ghost. Push me more, they said, and I might bite.

Takeshi pushed. 'Unless you're afraid I might touch you.'

Silk rearranged the cushions so that he was sitting straighter. 'Why would I be afraid of that?'

'Why wouldn't you be? You've never had a man make you come before.'

Shaun shoved the heel of his hand in his mouth, but failed to stifle the guffaw.

Silk glared at him. 'That's a big assumption.'

'It's not an assumption.' Takeshi leant towards him, holding his gaze. 'It's a fact.' He stood. 'I'll be around if you feel like joining the dark side.'

The Gorgons liked to talk, Remy had discovered. During the afternoon fitting they'd chatted constantly about music, bra sizes, literature and lipstick. Constant noise, but at least she could now tell them apart. Severina was the most distinctive: she didn't have fangs, and she was definitely only a weekender, as she worked for a solicitors' firm. Eloise was the friendly but weird librarian. And Lucretia, or Lulu, as her sisters called her, was just bats. From what Remy could gather, she was involved in some sort of wacky performance-art collective called Murder of Crows.

Everything they did seemed to line up on a sliding scale. Books ran from Laurell K Hamilton through Anne Rice to Poppy Z Brite; lipstick from Brazen Bean-sidhe to

Black Widow. They'd insisted on changes to their outfits so that they were more individual, too. Nothing drastic, just extra lace and more sequins. They'd managed to talk Lulu out of a fringe of crow feathers.

Remy put aside the dress she'd just finished taking in, and stretched to ease the tension out of her neck. Someone was heading her way along the corridor. She hoped they were bringing her something hot – either a cup of coffee, or a sexy man. It had grown finger-chillingly cold since the sun had gone down. She needed something to warm her up.

'Dreaming of me?' Alix strode towards her, sadly empty-handed.

'Nope. I'm working.'

'Well, stop working. There are more important things to concentrate on. We're playing hide and seek, kisses as forfeits, and we have about fifty seconds to hide.'

'Count me out.'

'Silk's on.'

'Count me in! But how's that supposed to make me hide?'

'The winner gets a spanking.'

'Kinky.' Remy shoved a coat hanger through the neckline of the dress and hooked it over the rail, then looked around frantically for a hiding place. Alix had climbed up the chimney, and was comfortably braced with her feet against one wall and her back to the other. 'Why are you hiding?'

'That's the game. I'll explain the minor by-laws later.'

Remy opened her largest trunk, thought of Takeshi's doll and almost changed her mind. Then she got inside and pulled the lid down, leaving it open a crack. There were more footsteps hurrying this way.

Expecting Silk, she was disappointed when it was only Marianne.

Remy frowned. With the whole castle full of nooks

and crannies to hide in, why come to her workroom? Marianne looked purposefully about, and, apparently seeing nobody, she scrambled over the trunk in which Remy was hiding, into the space behind the clothes rail that was serving as a changing room. Moments later, Silk slid into the room like a shadow drifting across the moon.

He paused at the threshold, then began to move around the perimeter. Remy watched him from her box. There was a graceful swagger to his creeping movement, which, coupled with his black outfit, made him look like a cat burglar. He was getting closer, peeking between the bagged outfits. Remy was tempted to wait until he was close enough to touch, and then leap from the trunk like a jack-in-the-box. She wondered if he'd maintain his poise while startled. The blond in her *manga* novel would. Even when his *Seme* was sliding his cock into him for the first time, he'd still exude liquid grace. Her concentration blurred. It was so easy to imagine Silk in the same position, bottom raised, his cheek pressed to the mattress, with his skin aglow, coated with a delicate sheen of perspiration.

Suddenly, being caught seemed like a good thing. Her throat thickened at the thought of his lips meeting hers, and the taste of him on her tongue. OK, so it'd just be a kiss, but it would increase the odds of Takeshi's getting the winner, and then she'd get to watch a real show. Remy licked her lips. She wondered how she could ensure Takeshi was the last one to be found. The thought of Silk even touching him was making her uncomfortably wet. The possibility that she might get to watch him discipline the pretty-boy biker might actually induce a spontaneous orgasm.

She slid her lips over the back of her own hand, imagining Silk's mouth locking with Takeshi's as they embraced following the chastisement. Their heads tilted, eyes closed so that their eyelashes dusted their cheeks. She tasted the kiss as if it were real and she was inside their skin, feeling each spark, each melding of breath.

The fantasy was compelling. It trembled through her limbs, wakening a hungry ache between her thighs. Then her brow furrowed. If Silk was as straight as Takeshi had claimed, how come he'd agreed to give kisses to the losers and spank the winner? Had Alix omitted to tell her something, or had Silk just overlooked Takeshi, and made some agreement with Shaun to find him early on?

Silk was almost level with her, when Marianne launched herself at him. The buxom silversmith flung her arms around his chest, squashing her breasts up against him. Silk took a wary step back, only for her to step with him. She tilted her chin, and gazed longingly up into his handsome face, obviously expecting a kiss.

A burst of annoyance obliterated the warm glow Remy had succumbed to. This wasn't what she wanted to see. It was too ordinary, too heterosexual. It was wrecking her fantasy.

'You're supposed to wait to be found.' Silk gently tried to extract himself from Marianne's embrace by pushing on her shoulders.

'I thought I'd save time so we could be alone together.' She slid her hands down his flanks.

Silk closed his fingers over her hands. 'Why would we want to be alone? We're playing a game that involves everyone. It wouldn't be fair to keep everybody waiting.'

'They won't know.' Undeterred, she gave his delicious butt a firm squeeze. 'They'll just assume you're hunting elsewhere.' She moved her free hand to his upper thigh.

Silk's eyes narrowed in response, although the green glint of his irises still showed, making Remy suspect that Marianne was about to get herself chewed up and spat out. Didn't she realise that when a man was horny for you, he reciprocated your advances? He didn't try to push you away.

Marianne rubbed along the bulge of Silk's fly. 'It was good earlier. You need more.' She dropped to her knees and tried to bury her face in his lap.

'No.'

'You want me to, really.'

Silk watched her performance as if he were watching two snails mate, in a sort of vague appreciation of what was happening but without any real spark of interest. 'You're caught,' he said. 'Go up to the lounge. I'll see you there once I've found everybody.'

Marianne responded by pulling off her T-shirt.

Remy gave a squeak of surprise, which she hoped the trunk muffled. Marianne was wearing a black push-up bra, which she immediately unhooked, releasing her abundance of cleavage. 'Want to make them creamy?' She sucked coyly on her little finger.

Purr-lease! Remy's toes curled.

'No, thank you,' said Silk.

Marianne smoothed her palms down the sleek surface of her breasts then cupped their weight.

'Really. Tempting as the offer is . . .' He backed away. 'I don't think an encore would leave you with the right impression.'

'What impression would that be?'

'That what happened earlier was anything more than casual sex.'

'You came in my mouth!'

'You came on my fingers.'

Her face clouded, as if she'd just noticed that something didn't add up quite the way she wanted. 'So, you just fancied a quickie, and I happened to be convenient?'

'That's about it, yes.'

She raised her hand as if to slap him, then obviously changed her mind. 'Bastard!'

Silk shrugged. 'I suppose so. Now, can I get back to the game?'

'Sure.' She fastened her bra and snatched up her T-shirt. 'I hope you slip and break your fucking neck on the stairs. Arsehole!' She stormed out, her hand reaching for a door to slam. Sadly it was missing, assuming there'd ever been one there.

The moment she was gone, a shower of dust came pouring down the chimney, followed by a slightly sooty Alix.

'Ah,' said Silk. 'I thought so.' He crossed to Alix and dropped a kiss on to her forehead. 'Rules of the game, before you hit me.'

Alix shook out her fiery ringlets, but didn't even raise her voice, let alone her hand. 'Your business. Of course, if it was Remy or Chelsea, that'd be different.' She grabbed a handful of silky blond hair and tugged him down to her level. 'Muck with either of them and I'll fuck you up good.'

Silk winced at the grip on his hair. 'I'll bear that in mind. Chelsea's off-limits, anyway. Shaun's a mate. And isn't Remy already spoken for?'

'What, by Takeshi!' Alix's hands returned to her hips. 'That little punk thinks he's on a promise. She needs models. That's all.'

Remy had been about to emerge from the trunk, but decided to keep her head down after all. She'd known from the moment she'd set eyes on Silk that he was dangerous, but his dubious morality and flighty sexuality were a large part of his appeal. She understood that it wasn't malicious intent that drove him to sleep around. He was just out to satisfy himself, and women threw themselves at him. She could also see that letting Marianne down before she fell completely head over heels had a screwed-up kind of merit, and maybe even an ounce of kindness about it. Now, if he'd spent the weekend fucking her and lying to her only to walk away at the end, then he'd have been a real bastard.

But it wasn't Silk's comments that had kept her in hiding: it was Alix's. Prior to hearing her threaten Silk, Remy had never understood the extent to which her friend was warning off potential lovers. It certainly explained the number of dead certs she'd been with over the years, who'd suddenly backed off at the last minute.

'Thanks for telling me about Takeshi.' Silk turned to go. 'I'm going upstairs now.' He left with the same balletic grace with which he'd arrived.

'You can come out now,' said Alix, once the sound of his footsteps had died away.

Remy emerged from the trunk, and took a welcome gasp of cool air. She felt hot, and it wasn't just from being packed inside a trunk for the best part of twenty minutes. She pursed her lips and looked at Alix.

'What's that look for?'

'Did you think I couldn't hear inside the trunk? I don't need you to warn people off. And, for the record, I do like Takeshi. He's not just a convenience. He made me come really hard. So hard I couldn't get him out of my head until I called him.'

'I could make you come like that.'

Remy shook her head, making her red and black hair swing. 'No, Alix. You couldn't. What do I have to do to make you see that?'

'Give me a chance? How do you know it won't be good until you try it?'

'Right,' said Remy. She hated being baited like this, but there were limits to her patience. She wanted to be friends with Alix, without this constant niggly issue. If kissing her was the only way to prove Alix wrong, then a kiss it would be. Reluctantly, she allowed her breath to mingle with Alix's own as their mouths locked.

Alix's kiss was both soft and forceful. It was butterfly

83

light, dancing and darting, but also weighty like a lode-stone. Her arms snaked around Remy, squeezed too tight as she tried to coax her to love. The kiss was supposed to have been a distancer, but it was failing. Alix was too eager. Remy put her hand to her friend's chest and pushed her away, feeling coerced, resentful and manipu-lated. The kiss was poison. It wasn't going to cure any-thing. In fact, it had probably been a big mistake.

Alix took her by the hand and tried to rekindle the intimacy. 'No. That's it.' Remy sighed. 'It just doesn't get me off. I'm not into girls. I'm into guys. Preferably two of them, shagging each other. You should know that by now.'

Alix flushed, until her skin was as livid as her hair. 'Silk and Takeshi.'

Remy shrugged. 'In my dreams. Look, I'm sorry.'

'Forget it.'

Alix was trying to sound light-hearted, as if what had happened didn't matter, but it was obvious from the choked thickness to her words that she was hurting.

Remy bowed her head. 'Friends?'

'Yeah. You'd better go and find a new hiding place.'

'If I want to win my spanking, you mean.'

Alix licked her lips. 'I made that bit up. I knew he was heading this way, and I knew it'd make you hide. I didn't really want to watch you kiss.'

'Yeah, I didn't exactly enjoy watching him get groped by Marianne. So what does the winner get?'

Alix hooked her fingers through the belt loops of her cut-offs. 'A bottle of sake, a fig-leaf pendant, five lipsticks in assorted colours, a bottle of fake blood, a vegetarian haggis, a copy of *Exquisite Corpse* and whatever you throw in.'

'A spanking,' Remy suggested.

Alix had the grace to laugh.

7

There was nobody in the kitchen when Remy stuck her head round the door. Silk must have continued up the stairs. Remy cut across the vast dining area and ran up the back stairs instead. From Silk's comment to Marianne, anyone who'd been caught would be waiting in the lounge, so she avoided that room and kept going.

The stairs ended on a shallow landing with a door that led into the master bedroom. Chelsea's batwing coat was draped over a high-backed wicker chair in one corner. Remy went to the walk-in closet. It was bare except for an ironing board and an empty shoe rack. A further door led into a disused privy. Remy sat on the stone shelf and waited, listening to the sound of her own heavy breathing.

The cupboard was claustrophobic. The walls felt too close with so many thoughts swirling around inside her head. Silk and Marianne had been bad enough, without the scene with Alix. Remy hoped Alix had finally got the message. She couldn't pretend that there was any spark of attraction as they'd kissed, because there wasn't. Truthfully, her mind hadn't really been on Alix at all. Even now, her gaze kept straying towards the closet door. She rubbed her mouth, anticipating the brush of Silk's ruby lips.

Remy shuffled. The stone was making her bottom cold. At the same moment, a loud creak came from the room beyond. She sat a little more stiffly, bracing herself for discovery, but whoever it was didn't seem interested in her cubbyhole. Too restless to keep still, she inched forward, and eased the closet door open in time to see

Shaun's hand come down on Chelsea's rump, as her friend slithered beneath the big brass bed.

'Oi!' she squealed, and flailed blindly at him. Shaun easily avoided her feeble slap, and ducked beneath the bedstead. Their feet disappeared from view and the valance fell back into place.

Not a moment too soon, as Silk entered shortly after. He gave the room a cursory glance, then sat down on the bed.

Remy watched him brush a hand through his long hair, and then recline against the vast collection of cushions. He seemed less enthusiastic about the game than when she'd watched him slip into the workroom downstairs, before the double whammy of Marianne's come-on and Alix's threat. In fact, he looked in need of comfort. She briefly considered going to him and climbing on to the bed, but, even without Chelsea and Shaun beneath, she balked at such an obvious ploy. She'd never thrown herself at anyone in her life, and wasn't about to start now. Besides, she'd seen what happened to Marianne. Cute as he was, she wasn't going to fall into the trap of being anyone's plaything.

'Has he gone?' Chelsea's voice hissed from beneath the bed.

Above, Silk raised an eyebrow, but didn't stir.

'Shh!' Shaun stuck his nose out from beneath the sheet. 'Seems clear.'

Chelsea appeared alongside. 'Shall we stay here or find somewhere else?'

'Stay here and fuck.' Shaun optimistically wrapped an arm around her waist.

'Go to the lounge cause you're out.' Silk leant over the end of the bed, and grinned when the pair peered up at him. 'Poor performance, Shaun. I expected better.'

Chelsea scrambled out from the bed, while Silk rose to his feet. 'Where's my kiss?' She strained towards him on tiptoe.

Shaun scurried out and stood upright behind her.

'More than my life's worth.' Silk theatrically placed one hand across his heart. 'You'll have to wait till the wedding.'

'Too right,' growled Shaun.

Chelsea dug an elbow into Shaun's midriff. 'Give it a rest. All I want is a kiss. It's part of the game. Come on.' She took Silk by the hand. 'You can give Shaun one too. I won't mind.'

'Don't do it, man!'

Silk shook his head.

'Not even a teeny little one?' Chelsea grinned, then pressed her lips up against his.

The growl in Shaun's throat deepened. He tried to tug her away, but Chelsea merely held on to Silk and continued to enjoy the wet smooch, despite Silk's best efforts to resist.

A shadow streaked across the floor and nudged open the closet door, forcing Remy to back-step to avoid being caught. The cat brushed against her ankles, miaowing loudly. 'Not now,' Remy hissed. 'I'll feed you soon.' Luckily, Silk was too busy being groped by Chelsea to notice her lurking in the cupboard.

'Let's go.' Shaun finally tugged Chelsea away. 'You don't kiss him. I know where it leads.'

'Will you credit me with some self-control?'

'I know him. I know what happens.'

'Yeah, but I'm not trying to get into bed with him. I'm just enjoying a little bit of freedom before we tie the knot. Think you can handle that?'

Remy suspected the answer was no.

No sooner had Chelsea and Shaun vanished from sight than Silk was off down the corridor again to investigate the sound of a door slamming.

Remy followed him as far as the bedroom door, far enough to see him pulling aside a long tapestry that

Dolores was hiding behind. Apparently, nobody was trying very hard, but, with kisses as an incentive to get caught, that was hardly a surprise.

'Is that it?' she overheard Dolores say, after Silk barely brushed her shell-pink lips.

'Yes. What were you expecting, tongues?'

'Tonsils.'

Remy took several quick steps back. She didn't want to see another revolting come-fuck-me scene.

'Come and see me when you've finished playing games with the schoolgirls.' Dolores's voice echoed along the corridor. 'There's a lot to be said for age and experience.'

There's a lot to be said for taste and decency, as well, thought Remy, as she headed down the back stairs to the kitchen again. Frankly, Dolores's attempts to get laid at her daughter's wedding were deplorable. She just hoped Silk wasn't actually interested in sleeping with every woman in the castle, as Takeshi had predicted. If so, she'd lose interest pretty damn quick.

Severina and Eloise were heading into the lounge as she hurried back downstairs. That meant it was down to her, Takeshi and Lulu, which at least made all this dashing around worthwhile.

Takeshi came through the door from the main stairwell at the same time as she entered the kitchen from the back stairs. He grabbed her hand as they crossed paths near the dining table.

'You're playing?' he said. 'I wasn't sure. Where is he?'

'Just behind you, I think. He was with Dolores a minute ago, two floors up. There's only three of us left.'

Takeshi squeezed her fingers. 'Watch out for me and I'll make it worth your while.'

Remy frowned. Make it worth her while in what way exactly? Was he planning a reward for helping him to win, or something more immediate involving Silk? Her heart leapt at the thought of seeing them smooch, but Takeshi could forget it, if he thought it was a way of getting her into bed. This weekend was strictly business between them.

He gave her a cheeky grin as he headed into the tiny side room. Remy ran in the opposite direction and ducked behind the tall galley of kitchen units, heading for the pantry stairs with Shadow racing alongside. She'd just have to set him straight again later if he got any funny ideas.

The pantry steps were tight and steep. Remy took the first five a little fast, felt herself skidding on the worn stone, then Shadow was beneath her feet. She was aware of his tail swishing against her inner leg, then he was safely down and she was stumbling forward. She managed to grab the wall, but her ankle twisted painfully.

'Blasted cat!' she yelled, bringing Silk down the stairs behind her. 'Shit!'

Remy hobbled down the bottom three steps, gritting her teeth. She didn't think she'd done any serious damage, but that didn't stop the biting pain in her ankle each time she put pressure on it.

'Are you all right?' Silk caught hold of her upper arm and helped her towards the centre of the utility room.

'Fine. My damn cat's just trying to kill me in revenge for not feeding him.'

She nodded towards the empty cat bowl beside the washing machine. 'Suppose I deserved it. I guess I'm caught.'

Silk gave her an appraising look. It reminded Remy of the way he'd looked at her the first time they'd seen each other. There was something decidedly carnal about it.

She took a step back from him and snatched up the cat food. Of course, now she was caught they were supposed to kiss, but she didn't want to seem overeager, no matter that her heart was racing just from the way he was looking at her. She needed to appear different from the rest.

'Remy.' His hand closed over the foil pouch of cat food in her hand. 'You do know about the forfeits, right?'

Remy looked warily up into his green eyes. He was impossibly pretty, and she loved the way his high cheekbones and slender features added to his exotic fairy-tale appeal. 'Yes. I guess.' Her grip on the Whiskas pouch tightened. Silk gently extracted it from her grip and tossed it on to the dryer.

'May I?'

He rubbed his thumb back and forth over the surface of her lips a few times, coaxing them to part with the gentle caress. Remy watched him, mesmerised by the action. His eyes were so bright, like the cold green fire of absinthe.

Though what he tasted of was rum.

He breathed the dark warm burn into her open mouth, and somehow it seemed right that he should taste that way. The rum trade was as dark as the molasses from which it was made and Silk, for all his oceans of blond hair, was definitely dark. He tasted of the forbidden, of the sorts of pleasures gained only by the breaking of taboos. She wanted to wrap herself around him, squeeze tight, get naked, and feel his hair tickle her skin. She wanted to break some taboos. He was sure to be game. She wondered how he'd feel about going at it on the cold stone steps for starters.

Remy's fingers closed over his bottom. She stopped. He'd been groped to excess already tonight. Squeezing his arse wasn't going to make her memorable, but showing some restraint might. Besides, Takeshi was only at the top of the stairs. She didn't want him barging in. She let go of Silk, an image of the two men together in her mind.

Their eyes still connected, Silk leant in to renew the

kiss. Shadow thwarted him, sinking his claws into her foot.

'All right, already!' Remy reclaimed the cat food and bent to squeeze meaty chunks into the bowl.

'Later.' Silk was off again, his long plait sailing behind him like an exotic snake as he disappeared up the steps. Takeshi's at the top, her libido reminded her. She didn't want to miss out on that.

She squeezed faster, and thrust the bowl towards Shadow. 'Gotta dash.' The cat dived at the bowl. Remy urgently patted the fur between his silky ears, then hobbled towards the pantry steps. She took the stairs two at a time, despite her ankle's protest at the effort.

Takeshi was eight feet up when she re-entered the kitchen. He was perched in the old cannon emplacement she'd noticed at breakfast. How exactly he'd got up there she could only guess. Likewise, she didn't want to think too hard about how he'd get down.

Silk was at the end of the oak table, when she emerged from the kitchenette.

'Come down, you're out,' he called.

Takeshi swung his legs against the wall. Instead of coming down, he stood. 'Come and get me, if I'm out. I'm not officially caught until I've forfeited a kiss.'

'It's hide and seek, not kiss chase. You're in plain sight, therefore you're out.'

Takeshi gave him a wide smile. 'Frightened you can't get up, or of what'll happen when you do?'

Silk shook his head, making his long tail of hair whip about him. 'I thought we'd already exhausted the more tedious points of this dialogue.'

'So stop drawing it out and come on up.'

Silk ran with an easy grace. Just short of the wall, he leapt, caught the ledge and lifted himself into a sitting position beside Takeshi's feet. Remy raised her hand to applaud, but instead just pressed her palms together. Apparently, it didn't matter how cool you were, you could always rely on macho bullshit to initiate some action. Insinuate that they were anything less than top dog and men would go to any length to prove otherwise. Though why Silk cared what Takeshi thought, she didn't know.

Silk stood. There were only inches between the top of his head and the top of the cannon emplacement. 'Now you're caught.' He gazed down at the shorter man. There was a definite edge to his voice that left no doubt in Remy's mind who was king.

Takeshi bowed his head. Clearly, he'd realised it too. Except he grinned. But only the jester's allowed to mock the king. He caught her eyes as she stared up at them. 'This is for you,' he mouthed at her, his eyes seeming to add, Remember, I know what makes you tick.

So, he'd deliberately engineered this so that she could watch them kiss. Remy felt pinpricks of perspiration bursting across her chest and back. She shook her head, tempted to walk away. She didn't like the way Takeshi was pulling her strings. He probably thought that if he provided this little show she'd come running later. The problem was, he was right. The two men hadn't even touched yet and her knickers were sopping. She was more turned on now than when Silk had been kissing her, and that was saying something. Only willpower was stopping her rubbing her thighs together, or, worse, shoving her hand inside her fly and kneading her clit.

Seizing the advantage, Takeshi stroked his open palm across Silk's cheek. Tension immediately seeped into Silk's body language, straightening his back while loosening his limbs. He glanced down, as if contemplating whether to jump. Instead, he raised his arms defensively. Takeshi pushed aside the barrier and leant in close.

'You're trembling,' he said.

'I'm gonna fucking punch you if you don't let up,' Silk hissed into Takeshi's mouth as their lips touched.

Below, Remy gripped the table before her knees

buckled. She'd felt them both now, could imagine the sensation of both kisses. Silk's fire and Takeshi's sparkle. Dark and darker. Takeshi's kisses had lit fires inside her that wouldn't die down, and the aftereffects of Silk's were still washing through her bloodstream, causing a massive adrenaline high.

They broke apart too quickly.

She wanted so much more. Wanted to see them embrace and rock their hips together.

Silk's lips were thin and bloodless. His skin had flushed a delicate apple-blossom pink. Takeshi was staring at him. It looked like the end scene of a weekly drama. Any second the credits would roll and say to the audience, 'To be continued'. Except it was ultra-real.

Silk hurriedly stepped back from Takeshi, then slid off the ledge and landed in a crouch on the stone floor. He stood slowly.

Remy rushed towards him, then checked herself before they collided. 'There's only Lulu left in.' Just his nearness had her itching to press her lips hard over his to taste the imprint of Takeshi's kiss. She wanted to devour him, like some sex-hungry spider, but Silk didn't even seem to see her. His expression was stony. Without acknowledging her comment, he walked past her and out of the kitchen.

Takeshi climbed down the wall, finding foot- and handholds Remy couldn't even see.

'What the hell did you do to him?'

'Only what you saw.' A wide smile spread across his face. 'Can I help it if it was the most memorable kiss of the evening?'

'Watch it.'

'Oh, I know, he kissed you. You're not bad, but he's kissed women before.'

'How do you know he hasn't kissed men?'

Takeshi laughed. 'Because, Remy, he just walked out. He's gone off to sulk, because he enjoyed it.' He pulled her close, surrounding her with his embrace. 'I bet you did, too.'

Silk went straight up to his room and pulled on the coachman's coat that Remy had so carefully adjusted earlier that day. Up on the battlements, the night sky was clear and bright with pinpoints of fire and an iridescent streamer where the Milky Way stretched across the heavens. He pushed his hands deep into the coat pockets and stared sullenly at the gardens below. He felt soiled, invaded. It wasn't just because of Takeshi's impertinent kiss, either. The women had been groping him like some prize stud all evening. Of course, he'd brought most of that upon himself. He could never resist flirting when women hit on him. His lips curled into a grin. Then just as rapidly the smile slipped.

Chelsea had been a surprise. She'd never looked his way before. She'd always been loyal to Shaun. He wondered what had prompted the sudden shift. Last-minute nerves, perhaps. Whatever the reason, Shaun was probably in a monumental sulk, and he couldn't blame his oldest friend.

Silk put his back to the battlements and sat down. Irritably, he adjusted the hem of the coat, where one of the pins had just scratched his calf. He wouldn't think of Remy, even though his body sang with need for her. The woman had a static charge about her that made more than his hairs stand on end. The problem was, he wasn't the only one who appeared to feel that way. It was nice to have competition, but ultimately he liked to be sure he was going to win, and neither Takeshi nor Alix seemed the sort to back down easily.

He couldn't suss her out, either. She looked at him as if there were a connection, as though she liked what she saw, but when they'd kissed she'd seemed strangely hesitant. Maybe the relationship between her and Takeshi was more complex and advanced than Alix cared to admit. All this led him back to Takeshi, and his constant teasing. He really didn't like the way the other guy was constantly pushing him, but he was even more annoyed by the fact that Takeshi was always doing it for an audience. What the hell was his problem? The kiss had set his heart racing, but with anger, not desire. With some effort, he pushed them all from his thoughts.

Silk stood. He wondered whether the others had found Lucretia yet, or whether they were still hunting. If he was careful, he could probably make it back to his room unobserved. For tonight, he'd had enough of games. Sleep called, and the perspective that came with morning.

Back in the room he shared with Shaun, Silk stripped down to his pants in the dark and slipped beneath the old-fashioned array of sheets and blankets. With only forty-eight hours until the wedding, he guessed a little beauty sleep wouldn't do any harm.

Remy found Lulu curled up asleep in the bottom of the kitchen dresser, just after Silk left, while she was looking for a glass. She needed a drink to cool down. All she had to do was close her eyes and she could see the two men kissing and feel how each of them must have felt to each other.

She sneaked away, glass in hand, while Takeshi tried to persuade Lulu to go upstairs and let everyone know the game was over. Once in her turret room, she changed into the same striped over-knee socks and overlarge jumper she'd worn the previous night and lay on top of the covers. The air was cool, but not unpleasant.

The kiss! It felt as if she'd waited for ever to watch her two fantasy men get it on. She'd been to gay bars, seen men kiss before, but this was different. And the fact that Silk had left without a word afterwards only added to the effect. It was what every reluctant *uke* did. As Takeshi had said, they always questioned their feelings, and they always came back for more. The main problem was she just couldn't cast Silk in that role, when his every word and movement said *Seme*. She was never going to hear him longingly whisper, 'No, no, stop and let me go.' That was Takeshi's role. Wasn't it? Actually, she wasn't sure she could see him saying it either.

Remy rubbed the sweat from her brow, then pushed the same hand down towards the apex of her thighs. She needed to get the pair out of her head. The wedding outfits might be sorted, but she still had a catalogue to shoot, and an evening of posing nude for Alix to get through. Her clit responded with a dart of fire as she gently brushed its surface. The burn was good, so good. But the fantasy – she needed to tease it out, bring it to a conclusion. She wet her finger and rubbed. If only she'd brought the *manga* featuring the man so like Silk. Not that she needed any visual aid. The two men danced in her mind's eye, two exquisite marionettes, bound hopelessly together. They were emotionally connected, drawn to each other in a way that defied logic, rules and social mores. Slowly, their clothes melted away revealing skin tones of lily-white and pale bamboo.

'Please,' she murmured. She longed to see the kiss grow closer, their hips and thighs meet, crumpled sheets and Silk buffeted up against Takeshi's backside.

'Please, what?'

The voice came from the stairwell. A moment later Takeshi was watching her from the curtained archway. Remy's stomach gave an apprehensive lurch. He wasn't supposed to follow her up here. She watched his gaze follow the slick slide of her fingers between her thighs.

'Let me.' He covered her hand with his. His touch seemed to draw heat into her cunt, and waken other parts of her body that so far had remained unmoved. No matter how elaborate the fantasy, how immersing it became, masturbating herself never quite engaged her senses in the same way as being with a man, holding him and being held down.

'Were you thinking of us – Silk and me?' he coaxed. 'What do you imagine us doing, Remy? Do you have us lost in each other, or do you like to imagine one of us bound and unwilling? Are we reluctant lovers or enemies?'

'You're not anything.' She screwed her face up tight, despite the complex relationship she was still adding to in her head. Regardless of her fantasy, she didn't want to give in to him like this. But he knew he was turning her on. He knew the high she was floating on. He was planting images deliberately, in order to tease her over the edge.

His lips brushed the exposed skin of her stomach, causing butterflies where he made contact.

'I said it was strictly business.'

'And so it is. Strictly my business to get you off.'

'Futile promises.' She tried to sit up. Damn him for interfering. She was probably spiting herself, but she wasn't going to retract her promise, just because she was horny, *yaoi*-kiss drunk and had a beautiful man drawing his tongue across her clit.

'Oh, oh!' Her body sighed, as the soft lashes continued. 'Not fair.'

'That's right,' he said, and began sucking instead.

Remy feebly pushed at his head, his shoulders. 'We're not doing this.' Her voice was rising, as her resistance weakened.

'Oh, but we are.' He climbed on to the bed on top of her. 'Let me make this easy for you.' He grasped her wrists, pinning her to the narrow bed.

The feel of his cock bruising her thigh was too much. Why did he have to take control, and be so bloody composed about it?

'I don't want you: I want Silk.'

'No.' He breathed the denial into her mouth. 'You want me to have Silk.' He brushed her lips delicately, teased their seam with his tongue. 'Admit it. Would you like me to tell you what I'm going to do to him?' He kissed her chin, her neck.

'Yes,' she murmured, while shaking her head. 'No.'

'You're very indecisive tonight. Here, let me help you.' He let go of her wrist, and tilted to one side as he wrenched down his fly. His body covered her. They were hipbone to hipbone, skin to skin. Remy's free hand crept around him, and clasped the back of his bunched-up T-shirt. The minute she touched him to return his caress would be the point of no return. She knew that, knew it and accepted it as inevitable as the April rains. Still she hesitated, her fingers holding the cotton tight.

'*Onegai*,' he whispered. 'Please.' His tongue licked a teasing trail across her skin, following the line of the extended V of her sweater, while his erection speared between her thighs. He wasn't inside her yet, but, God, they were close! It was just like being back in the park.

Suddenly she *was* back in the testosterone-encrusted shack in the park, his fingers working her clit, his cock driving urgently between her thighs. Her body was literally shaking. She'd wanted him then, wanted him to come inside and fuck her until she couldn't get enough.

'Let me in, Remy.' His words were husky as he traced the curve of her ear with his tongue. 'I want you so very much.'

'I want you too,' she whispered. There were tears prickling in her eyes. Something about this was altogether too raw. She dug her nails into his skin.

'Yes,' he hissed. 'Do it again.'

Remy jerked her hand downward, scoring four thin lines across his skin, then clasped hold of his flank. 'No strings, OK?'

'Only little ones.'

'Shit! Don't you dare say it.'

'Ai shiteiru.'

She stopped her ears from hearing the words she feared above all else. No commitment. She'd been that route before and all it brought was heartache. His lips closed over hers again, and this time she couldn't help but kiss him back 'Tell me some more about the blond.' She pictured her graphic novel, although they both knew she was really talking about Silk. 'Tell me what happens next.'

8

Silk was conscious of the door opening. Splinters of light spilled around the frame. He had no idea how long he'd slept – maybe minutes, maybe hours. He guessed Shaun had finally decided to take his moping to bed. He closed his eyes again and feigned sleep. The last thing he wanted right now was a long dull conversation about infidelity and imagined slights. As far as Silk was concerned, a kiss was just that, but he knew that Shaun was far more territorial.

He listened for the other man stumbling about and shedding clothes, but the room was curiously quiet.

Silk risked a peek from beneath his eyelashes in time to see his sheet rise at the foot of the bed. The blankets rippled over him in a single wave, then settled to reveal the shocking-white faces of the Gorgons.

They'd daubed hot pink circles high on their cheekbones, making them look like Regency belles or perhaps geisha girls, and painted their lips a voluptuous blood red. They smiled at him in turn, revealing elongated canines that glinted in the light from the corridor. Silk groaned inwardly. Of course, to be truly authentic to the source, it should have been the moon, waxing opaque through an uncurtained window, but you couldn't have everything, and right now he wasn't sure he wanted any of it. He'd never been all that sold on Dracula.

Silk closed his eyes. He was tempted to pull the covers over his head and roll over, but he suspected they'd assume he was just play-acting and think it part of the game. He didn't want just to chase them out, either, so he guessed he was going to have to play along as Jonathan Harker.

'Go on! You first.' One of them said.

Silk peeped at them through his eyelashes again.

'He is young and strong; there are kisses for us all,' Lucretia added, as they urged Severina forward.

How long had they been practising this?

He lay still, anticipating the weight of her body on the bed beside him. She came forward slowly, while her sisters whispered and laughed in high silvery voices. It seemed an age before he felt her breath upon his face. Hell, they'd managed to whet his appetite with a little anticipation. Somehow, that seemed appropriate. Even Harker had found his visitors enthralling and intolerable.

Silk stared up at her. She'd coloured her eyelids a smudgy charcoal and emphasised them with seventies-style fake lashes, more Hammer Horror than Bram Stoker. However, true to her literary counterpart, Severina arched her long neck and licked her lips. They skimmed over the surface of his mouth and chin, descended to his throat, where she scented the air with her tongue tip, making the nearby skin tingle in expectation. He actually shivered.

Of course, this was the point where the count was supposed to walk in full of red-eyed, blood-curdling fury, turning the three bewitching ladies into three snarling bitches. Sadly, there wasn't any count resident at Castle D'Amon, only Shaun, who was missing his cue.

Silk swallowed. OK, he was warming to their presence, but unlike Shaun he didn't go in for bite marks and he didn't put it past them to draw blood. Hell, the Gorgons were crazy. He was perverse, but not that way. Drastic action was necessary.

He tore back the covers.

Severina yelped as he smothered her with the blankets. The other two gave delighted, out-of-character whoops at the sight of his near-naked body and strained over the footboard.

Lucretia ran her hand up his inner thigh, immediately targeting his concealed cock. Severina disentangled herself from the bedclothes and moved down to claim his nipples, while Eloise lifted her imitation Edwardian finery and straddled his head.

Her knees nudged his ears, while the split of her cotton bloomers revealed her muff. Silk could no longer see the other two, but he didn't need to. They were identical and he could feel them. Besides, Eloise was providing all the visual stimulation he could take as she rapidly unfastened her many-buttoned blouse to reveal a crimson corset from which her breasts were bursting.

'Jeeezuss!' he hissed.

Lucretia chose that moment to progress from nuzzling his cock through his black cotton slips to sucking on the tip. There was no stopping her, though. Eloise's sex covered his mouth. He gave a tentative lick, tasting her with just the darting tip of his tongue. Her muscles clenched, then responded with a gush of cream. Silk put his lips and tongue to work, and sank into a languorous ecstasy in which Remy, not Eloise, sat queening him. He couldn't wait to tip her velvet. He wanted to come, but not here, with these three. It was time to extract himself.

Silk grasped Eloise by the waist and lifted her. Luckily, she was so thin that it didn't take much effort to coax her upwards and backwards into her sister. Severina detached herself from his nipple. It took a little more persuasion to remove Lucretia from his groin.

'Enough.' He gathered them all together and pushed them towards Shaun's bed. 'It's time for one lucky lady to get what she deserves. Noses to the bed, girls, and bottoms high. Let's see if you're all as elegantly turned out as Eloise under these pretty dresses.'

They each bent and raised their long skirts to reveal

split bloomers. Silk fondled each of their upturned rears, squeezing and petting their cheeks through the cotton. He dipped his fingers through the slits and tasted their eagerness. It was nice to be this wanted. To be considered man enough to please them all at once. At least, he assumed that's why they were here together and not alone, although sisterly rivalry may have played a part too. He lowered their pants in turn, so the elastic formed a nice straight line across all their bottoms. If they'd been plumper, more rounded, he might have been tempted to give them what they wanted and screw them one after another. As it was, he contented himself with landing a few sharp smacks.

Tonight, he didn't want to be with anyone he didn't really want. The Gorgons and their reddened backsides were definitely not what he wanted. Nor was Takeshi. Absolutely not. The other man's image seemed to have fixed itself in his subconscious, and like a subliminal message it flashed up every time he tried to think of Remy. It wasn't as if he were even into guys, and that guy hadn't been all that great a kisser.

Silk rubbed his lips.

There hadn't been any depth to it, no fire or emotional attachment. Still, Takeshi's bitter-cherry, chocolate-coloured eyes filled his mind.

He gave Lucretia an extra-hard slap.

What he wanted was Remy, with her hard-edged bad-ass image and Catholic-girl turn of phrase. She was a curious dichotomy, and she had a beautifully shaped arse. He knew just where to find her, too. There weren't even any closed doors between them. This just left the small matter of the three waggling bottoms mooning him from Shaun's bed.

In the end, he set them masturbating, and simply walked out. Eventually, he supposed they'd notice he was gone.

* * *

The bats were screeching in the attic. Silk paused on the landing to pull on Remy's coachman's coat. He fastened a couple of buttons around the waist, leaving a sliver of bare chest exposed, and headed towards the ultrasonics. There was no light spilling down the narrow stairs from Remy's room. He hoped she wasn't already asleep. Now he'd left the Gorgons behind, he was far more aware of his body and his mood. The *Dracula* re-enactment may not have been his ideal choice but it had been simple escapism, something he desperately needed. He didn't know what it was about the castle but it seemed to be pushing his libido into overdrive and his nerves to breaking point.

The coat brushed at his calves and nipples as he walked, teasing his already frustrated nerve endings. He stuck his head under the arch. There was a scent to the air as he crept forward, keeping low so that he melded with the shadows. It was subtle, just a faint hint of spice and the sweet, intoxicating scent of woman. He slipped forward into the darkness, his senses reeling. His hand closed over the worn stone of the topmost step. He could see her now, from beneath the curtain, her image snapping into focus as his vision adjusted to the darkness.

He could see them both: Takeshi, naked and pale, moonlight spilling though the stained glass and painting his bare cheeks rose and blue; Remy in a black lace bra, her skin the molten silver of the waxing moon. She stretched her neck back, and opened her mouth to sigh. The opulent and magnificent carnality of it made his heart ache and his cock throb. He wanted to be in there with her, watching the subtle blush spread across her breast, cheeks and throat. He wanted to be burying himself deep, not lying against the cold stone steps, a silent witness to their passion.

Of course, Takeshi had invited him in.

Silk didn't move. He couldn't. The idea of the other man's lips burning against his shoulders, sweeping down his back to linger over his buttocks, held him rigid. He could almost feel Takeshi's bite. He clenched his muscles tight. This wasn't about sex with a man. He didn't want to compete tonight. It was about being with Remy, and only Remy.

He swallowed slowly, desperate for breath and perspective. Instead, desire rippled down his throat like some expensive liqueur. Only the thought of the other man's naked flesh touching his own kept him in the shadows. Silk stared at the base of Takeshi's spine, where a dragon emerged from between the cheeks of his bottom to flow across his back. The creature seemed to writhe with each movement Takeshi made, ready to propel itself off his back and strike with poisonous teeth. One bite was probably enough to have you reeling like a drunkard.

Remy wasn't reeling, but she certainly looked intoxicated. Takeshi hooked one of her legs over his arm, and there was a sound of wet sticky readiness as he slid his fingers into her cleft. Her nipples steepled in response; they were clear even through her bra. He wanted to suck and bite the two red treats, but there was something else to make his breath catch beside the vision of her breasts. Takeshi had turned slightly, enough for the light from the window to streak across his torso. His cock was hard and ready. Silk watched him roll a condom down his shaft while his insides squirmed. He wanted to be where Takeshi was. Ready to slide deep and feel Remy's heat around him. He wanted to be touching that cock.

Silk pulled back sharply, his fingers coming to his lips. He bit down hard on his fingertips, trying to blot out the image with pain. What was he thinking? He knew what he liked, and it wasn't other men.

He forced himself forward again, watched Takeshi's shaft disappear into the shadows at the apex of her thighs. That was a feeling he understood. He concentrated on the corresponding sensations, the way her body would envelop his, the fire that streaked down his shaft when he came. It made him hard but without the physical contact, which only served to increase his feelings of frustration. He kept his hands safely in his pockets. Bad enough risking being caught as a Peeping Tom, without being caught wanking, too. Besides, it was time for another walk.

Silk went out on to the roof. The night air soon dampened his ardour. It was hard to feel anything when there was a cold wind blowing around your balls and your feet were half frozen. He stood by the flagpole and let his hair billow out around him. Once he'd surrounded himself with ice, then he'd head back inside. He'd figure out in the morning how to approach Remy again.

Shaun stayed on the sofa before the parlour fire, brooding, when everyone else headed towards bed. He turned his cheek when Chelsea tried to kiss him goodnight. He knew everyone thought he was overreacting, but he'd also known Silk long enough to have lost more than a few girlfriends to him. Maybe it had just been a kiss, but she could've considered his feelings.

At least Silk had managed to look reluctant. Mind you, that didn't mean much. He often played hard to get just to reel the ladies in all the faster. Fuck it! They may be friends, but sometimes he really wanted to deck him.

He sat another half-hour, swigging port from the bottle and growing increasingly maudlin. Eventually, when he could no longer be bothered to bank coal on to the fire, he plodded along the corridor towards bed. Silk was probably off screwing someone, so at least he didn't have to psych himself up for a confrontation.

The bedroom door was partially open. Shaun gave it a shove, and it swung inwards, hitting the wall with a loud thud. The room had three occupants, none of whom, judging by the choice of underwear, was Silk. Two of them shrieked and fled on to the stairwell, which left the third.

Shaun continued across the threshold. She was face down on his bed, humping his pillow. He knew it was one of the triplets from her hair, but he had no idea which one. He watched her silently, as she alternately rubbed her clit and fucked herself with two curled fingers. Eventually, he resorted to a loud disgruntled cough.

It made no difference. Apparently, she was too far gone to worry about an observer. That or she already believed she was performing for an audience. She probably thought he was Silk.

Shaun looked around into the darkened corners. There was no sign of his best man but, presumably, he'd been here at some point. Girls didn't just walk in and frig themselves for no reason. Or did they?

The girl on his bed was now arching her back, while she rode her hand and pressed the other painfully into her groin. It didn't look comfortable to Shaun, but it seemed to be working for her. She was making ragged little grunts, loud enough and earnest enough to make his cock shudder to attention.

The moment he realised he was hard was the moment she turned over and spread her thighs. Her pubis was ruddy and glistening. It was slick with need. Inviting. He stared at her most intimate parts as if he were gazing at some exotic orchid. Damnation! He was about to get married and he was watching his cousin masturbate. He dragged his vision away from her, only for it to return to her sopping cunt a moment later.

'Bugger it!' Chelsea hadn't respected his wishes earlier. Instead, she'd made him watch while she'd tried to French-kiss Silk. For all he knew she was with him now, enacting some last-minute fantasy before they tied the knot.

Shaun unbuttoned, and slid down his zip. With one hand inside his fly, he edged around the bed and found a seat in the corner.

As he grasped his shaft and tugged, all the tension

and irascibility he was feeling seemed to flow into his cock and transform into raw hunger. He matched his pulls to the motion of Eloise's hand – he was sure it was Eloise – and let the mood take hold completely.

He didn't know when he started seeing her as the succubus of his dreams, but at some point she stopped being the Edwardian prostitute she resembled and became instead the leather-winged *Playboy* bunny of his most intimate fantasies.

Fangs glinted from between her succulent red lips. Her cruelly sharpened talons dug into his shaft leaving half-moon indents. Her breasts spilled from a leather basque, revealing two tiny mouths with sharpened teeth where there should have been nipples. And he knew that, beneath her ankle-length leather skirt, there was a prehensile tail that was good for all sorts of torture.

She was all soft curves, but as cold and cruel as the bleakest winter. She didn't need to tie him up. She could make him beg with a single tilt of her stubborn little chin.

'Chel-sea!' he whispered, not sure if he was calling the demon by name or praying for his saviour.

'Shaun,' she purred, and nipped his lip with her fangs. A single drop of blood rolled down his chin and splashed against his thigh. It was all it took to send him over the edge.

His orgasm streamed through his shaft like a ray of pure light. He felt as if he were giving birth to a rainbow. For a few moments, he felt ecstatic, drifting in a sea of colours. Then reality abruptly intruded.

There was a clap from the bed.

Shaun opened his eyes to find Eloise sitting, applauding him. She was still dishevelled, and, despite his stare, she made no attempt to put her tits back into her corset.

'Would you mind?' he said thickly, and pointed to the bedside table. His hands and lap were shiny with ejaculate.

Eloise chucked the box of tissues at him. 'Where'd the others go?'

'Your sisters left as I arrived.' He pulled out a handful of Mansize squares.

'Silk?'

'Haven't seen him.' He dabbed at his oversensitive cock tip. 'I take it you know that's my bed and not his.'

'I know.' She swung her legs over the side of the bed. 'I know who I came with, too.'

Shaun gaped at her as she took the box of tissues from him and knelt. He dared not flinch as she moped his cock and thighs, but he couldn't help clenching his stomach muscles. This seemed a little too intimate. Sure, they'd been looking at each other sideways on and off for years, but was his wedding weekend really the time to act upon it?

He caught her wrist as she dabbed the point of a tissue into his navel. 'I'm spoken for, remember.'

Eloise wet her lips. 'I guess it's goodnight, then.' She stood and finally straightened her clothing, then scooped her knickers off the floor. 'Shame. I could use some real action. You might have invited a few more of the boys to stay at the castle.'

'Chelsea sorted the guest lists.'

'That explains it. She's sorted. It's just the rest of us who are going to be forced into lesbianism if we want to get off.'

Shaun couldn't see that getting it on with the girls was much of a hardship. He suspected Eloise and her sisters would take on anyone who offered.

'Night,' he said avoiding her gaze.

'Night.'

The latch dropped. Shaun allowed himself a sigh of relief, before he stared at his exposed loins and shook his head. He hoped he hadn't just screwed himself in the arse.

9

'Remy. Time for you to rise and shine.' Alix bounded up the stairs to the cap house and into the darkened room. So much for making the most of the daylight, but what did she expect from a bunch of lazy goths? She was still amazed at how many of them had made it to breakfast the previous day. Maybe she'd have got a better turnout if she'd asked them to stay up all night.

Alix ignored the amorphous sleeping blob and crossed straight to the window. She knew exactly how to rouse Remy – she'd had plenty of practice while they were students. Remy had always insisted on waking ten minutes before her first lecture, which left just enough time to race across campus while slopping machine coffee over herself.

'Wakey, wakey.' She threw back the shutters. Cold, crisp light flooded the diamond-shaped chamber, licking everything with a dewy sheen. Outside, the morning mist was clinging to the lawn and the perimeter of the woods, reminding Alix of the sixties and seventies Hammer Horror flicks she'd been so enamoured of in her early teens. It was the perfectly atmospheric weather for snapping all those dress designs.

The smothered lump in the bed was just beginning to stir as she turned back from the window, remembering all the waiflike stars, their cleavages enhanced by tape, not silicone. It had been her fascination with their ephemeral grace, which had inspired her to pick up her first camera. Of course, her newly discovered sexuality had played a part too. Alix loved the slender silhouettes of those women, enhanced by flowing, soft, feminine dresses, and their heavily made-up eyes. She'd spent enough nights humping her pillow staring at the images coating her walls. Olinka Berova, Veronica Carlson, Julie Ege, Ingrid Pitt and of course the delectable Yutte Stensgaard. She'd loved them all, just as she loved Remy.

Alix perched herself on the foot of the bed, and rested her hand on a cocooned leg. Remy had the same shape as those women, the same heavily made-up eyes. The first time she'd seen her she'd been wearing a translucent calico mock-up of an evening gown. Time had frozen. Since then she'd nursed her through flu, seen her mascara smudged and still wanted her. She cherished her glimpses of Remy's deshabille, especially these early-morning moments when she was still a little bit grouchy. It was how the wake-up game had developed – from a desire to look and touch. The rules were simple: how far could she get her hand before Remy was up and ready to go. The sneaky caresses stopped the minute Remy opened her eyes.

It was Alix's fantasy that one day Remy would just lie there, pretending to be still asleep, looking every inch the Hammer starlet, while she stroked and loved her whole body through the sheet. She'd glimpsed her pubic curls and the rosy crinkled peaks of her nipples before now, feasted her eyes on the smooth expanse of creamy skin and spent the day distracted and disoriented by the vision. It had inspired more than one collection of nudes – but, hey, so had Kate Bush.

Alix trailed her fingertips along the smooth muscle of the calf beneath the coverlet. In her head she could hear Remy's breaths rising to sighs as her nerve endings came alight. She longed to tear away the shroud and sup the nectar from between her thighs, but she didn't dare do it now, not after the beautiful promise of last night had ended in the bitter taste of rejection. She couldn't face it again in daylight. Nighttime was for passion and adventure; daylight was for cold reality and hard work.

'Now, Remy. You heard me, up, up, up.'

She drew her hand up her covered leg to the curve of her bottom, gave a smack.

'Fuck!' Alix flew off the bed, and stepped straight back into the wardrobe door. Remy's butt was firm, but bouncy. She didn't have buns like iron.

Takeshi sat up. He squinted at her, clearly disoriented, and then looked over his shoulder at the space beside him. Seeing he was the sole occupant, he turned his attention back to Alix. 'Were you feeling me up?' He pulled a hand through his silver-blue hair so that it stood on end. His mouth curved into a dreamy smile. 'I thought I was getting a treat before breakfast.'

'No, I fucking wasn't.'

Takeshi lifted the pillows and propped them against the slender headboard. He peered thoughtfully at her. 'What's with the light? And what have you done with Remy?'

'I could ask the same.'

He gave her a mischievous grin. 'You wouldn't like the answer.' He yawned and stretched. 'Hey, are you room service?'

Alix scowled. There was something about this punk that irritated the hell out of her, but, strangely, he didn't scare her half as much as Silk. Takeshi wasn't about to break any hearts, except maybe his own. Sure, he was Remy's type, but not nearly as much her type as the super-smooth silver fox.

'What's up?' Takeshi looked down at his exposed chest. She was staring at him. 'Haven't you seen a naked man before? I can give you the full monty if you like.' He teasingly lifted the covers.

Alix slapped him hard across the thighs, wrenching the bedspread from his grasp. 'Save it for someone who'll appreciate it,' she snarled, and scrambled on to the stairs in a fiery haze of corkscrew curls. 'I know you're a prick without seeing the evidence.'

She reached the top landing and continued down. 'Uncool, Alix. Really uncool.' She'd known the pair were fucking, despite Remy's assertions to the contrary. It didn't make it any easier, though, being confronted with it like that. She should have checked whether Remy was up before heading in to wake her. At least she hadn't walked in on them actually shagging. Ick! Her stomach churned. She felt sick and the day had hardly started.

Several dozen steps later, Alix stomped past the open kitchen door, feeling exceedingly grizzly. Spring air and fashion photos, hah! She wanted to find a girl bar, and some lipstick lesbian she could pick up like a four-pack.

'Morning.' The three bridesmaids were huddled around the end of the counter, all looking pale and wan, two of them nursing glasses, the third, Lucretia, swigging tomato juice from the carton. 'We'll be down in ten minutes, once we've put some slap on,' Lucretia called.

Alix grunted an acknowledgement but didn't stop. Remy must be in the workroom. She wondered if she ought to go in, sod the consequences, and snog her brains out. Hell, if Remy could bed someone who slept with a doll, surely she could manage a charity shag for her best mate.

She wanted to break something.

Marianne was sitting at the bottom of the stairs. Alix brought herself to a shaky halt just short of a pile-up. 'Dammit! Are you trying to get bruised? Chairs are for sitting on. Stairs are for –'

She stopped as Marianne rose and turned. Her eyes were red-rimmed, and her bottom lip pushed out in a morose pout.

'What's up?' Alix glanced along the dark bottom corridor. There was no natural light, but a dull glow spilled from the workroom. 'Is Remy in there?'

'Not sure. Guess so.'

Alix stared at the Sisters of Mercy slogan across Marianne's ample bosom, seeing a transparent white lace dress. She blinked. It was obvious what was wrong – Silk. The surprise was that she felt she cared. Alix raised her gaze to meet Marianne's pale, whisky-gold eyes, and smiled at the dusting of pretty freckles across her nose. Everyone was makeup-free this morning, but, unlike the Gorgons, Marianne looked healthier, more vivacious for it, even with her puffy eyes.

'Aren't you supposed to be modelling corsets?'

'Yeah.' Her lip trembled. 'But I don't want to go in there. Not where I got dumped.'

Alix checked the urge to laugh. Dumped? You had to be an item first. The girl was living on a cloud. What she needed was plain talking, and Alix had never been one to mince words, especially when she was living with her own rejection. 'You fucked together, what, once?' she said bluntly. 'That hardly counts as a relationship.'

Marianne's bitten black-painted nails came to her mouth in shock. 'It does to me. How did you know?'

'I overheard. Do yourself a favour and write him off as a big mistake. You'll save yourself a lot of grief.'

Marianne stared at her, her eyes wide and bright. She rubbed her nose. 'Why are you being so mean?'

'Am I? OK, here's the abridged version. All men are bastards some of the time, and some men are bastards all of the time. Just accept that he wasn't interested in you as anything more than a temporary sheath for his cock. I know that's hard, but forget him and move on. There are loads of blokes coming to the wedding.'

'I don't want loads of blokes. I want him.'

Alix shook her head in dismay. 'Is anyone worth this much heartache?' She already knew the answer, and what a hypocrite she was being. Hell, she hadn't even had the quick shag and she couldn't manage to let go. No, her mind protested. It wasn't the same. Marianne was infatuated. She'd been in love a long time.

'Look, if you really don't want to go in there, I'll set up a camera in your room. She forced herself to speak gently. 'I can tell Remy what the deal is. She'll understand.'

'He wants her.' Marianne's voice rose a quavering octave. 'And she already has Takeshi. Is she going to play the two of them off?'

The snake of anger burst to the surface again. 'She's not after him, except as a model. It's just business with Takeshi.'

'Is that why he didn't sleep in his own bed last night?'

Alix closed her lips tightly for fear she might actually spit. There was bile in her throat. She wanted to strike. But what was the point?

Marianne obviously realised that she'd hit a nerve, because she petted Alix's hand. 'I've never seen him like this over a woman before. He's had the occasional crush on a bloke, but he never gives them his number. I think he's fallen for her.'

'No,' Alix protested. Don't tell me this, she thought. I don't want to know. She could scare him off, like others before. She could. Except that, in her heart, she knew this time it was different. Takeshi, beneath his foolish façade, was tenacious, determined and smart. He wasn't the sort to be put off easily. Strangely, that thought left her smiling. His desire for commitment would be his downfall. Remy didn't do commitment. She always played safe and planned her exit. Her mood bolstered by that thought, Alix left Marianne and headed into the workroom.

Three hours later, Remy was making the same journey along the bottom corridor laden with the outfits they'd just photographed. 'Bat shit!' she yelled. Lucretia had been saying it all morning, and she was rather taken with the phrase. She just hadn't anticipated having cause to use it quite so soon.

Remy lifted her foot carefully, but the sound of ripping cloth confirmed that the damage was already done. The stiletto heel of her boot had gone straight through the overskirt of the dress Eloise had just shed. Remy held the rest of the clothes high and made her way to the table in the workroom, where she dumped the load.

They'd been out since half-nine, in the morning mist, whose filmy tendrils wound around their bodies like ghostly arms, snapping off reels of film – she, the Gorgons and Alix, who was in such a rotten mood that Remy wanted to put it down to apathy, but suspected it was more to do with being rejected. Still, they'd snapped off reels, and now had all the shots of the women's wear she could possibly need. Except it might have been nice to have had a few scenes with the men. Silk had been a no-show, and she'd left Takeshi behind in her bed.

Hmm! She probably should have kicked him out of bed just to make a point, but he'd looked so peaceful, slumbering like the silver dragon upon his back. She wasn't sure what to make of the tattoo. Many people had them, but she was sure that in Japan they were still considered the mark of the *yakuza*. She felt certain he was connected, too, considering the *bosozoku* gang photos pinned to his noticeboard, and she'd read enough to know that the *yakuza* recruited from the Speed Tribes. No wonder he hadn't wanted to talk about it. Anyway, she couldn't believe she'd been so weak-willed. He'd set up one kiss with Silk and she'd happily fallen into bed with him. So much for asserting herself. At least the sex had been great, unlike with most of the men she'd known, right back to her first encounter with Duncan.

Remy shoved all the useless men back into her memory and returned her attention to the damaged dress. It had been one of the first pieces she'd made after deciding to quit being a wage slave and work for herself. The design was inspired by a foil chocolate wrapper and a bucket of chrysanthemums, and composed of layers of fiery organza over a bronze taffeta base. The fitted bodice laced at the back with silk ribbons, while the full skirt spilled to the floor. Each tiny movement the wearer made caused the fabric to shimmer, and crackle with threads of fire. It was dazzling in daylight, but by night, under the soft sheen of candlelight, it literally took your breath away.

Remy pressed the tear to her brow. She'd been considering wearing it to the wedding. She'd have to settle on something else now. Solemnly, she pulled a plastic sheath over it and stuck on a label marked 'damaged', then turned to hang it on the rail.

Silk was reclining upright against the wall in the empty fireplace, in his briefs. She stared at him, taking in the long lean thighs, the impossibly broad shoulders and the admirably defined crunch of stomach muscles, while heat suffused her groin, and swept up through her chest. Blood surged into her breasts, making them feel full and heavy. Her uplift bra felt like a medieval torture device. He looked incredible with his clothes on. Without . . . She was speechless.

He casually pushed himself off the wall, and stepped forward, displaying himself full on. Remy licked her dry lips. It was rude to stare, but she couldn't help it. Where else was she supposed to look when he just presented himself like that?

Her heart was thundering. 'Did someone steal your clothes?' Her words sounded throaty.

The soft orange glow of the overhead light made his pale skin seem peachy. He was virtually hairless, except for a fine smattering of golden hairs below his navel, which thickened softly towards his loins.

Remy dragged her gaze away from his body to the quarry tiles between them. She wanted him, wanted him desperately. It was taking all her willpower just to keep up a conversation.

'You said something about wanting to dress me.'

She had. 'I did!'

She felt crazily off balance. It wasn't fair of him to come here and shock her like this. Prickling desire like static fire crackled between triangular points of her nipples and clit. The whisper of cloth between her thighs was hopelessly inadequate and now sopping wet. Hell, her whole insides felt liquid.

'Are you going to?' He came out of the half-shadows into the central space.

Remy jerked her head upright to eye level. She was a professional. She'd seen plenty of naked flesh before while fitting clothes. It was just that none of her previous models had looked remotely like Silk.

Eye level wasn't so good a choice, either. She found herself looking straight into his eyes. If he leant in and kissed her now, she'd fall headfirst into their ocean depths.

'Erm, no. Yes. I mean yes.' Remy mentally pulled herself together. She could handle this. She didn't need to embarrass herself. Her gaze moved to his lips, which instantly released the memory of his warm taste on her tongue. That had been only last night, and he'd started it. She had a feeling he was going to start something now, too.

He touched her cheek with his index finger.

Remy jumped. A charge sparked at the point of contact, and raced down her neck to her already pointed nipples. She didn't dare look down. Not even her push-up bra and shirt would be able to disguise their peaks. Follow through, she silently willed him. Lean in and kiss me, before I'm forced to push you into the clothes racks and jump on you.

He traced the outline of her mouth.

Remy parted her lips and let her tongue slide over the top of his finger, then closed her mouth around it and sucked. Silk fed her a little more of the digit, then swapped fingers, until she'd moistened all five, finishing with his thumb.

She was trembling when he pulled it from her mouth, and drew it over her chin to the hollow at the base of her throat.

His hand swept lower, fingers disappearing beneath the black satin of her top and inside the lace of her bra. He circled the hardened point of her nipple, then cupped her breast.

Suddenly his lips were on her. Remy breathed into his mouth. Wild prickles of heat infused her throat, her senses. The crazy sensation ran straight into her cunt, and urged her to make skin contact. Her arms slipped around his naked back and her body pressed tightly to his.

'Well, excuse us!' Alix clunked her metal camera case on to the table by the door. Remy jolted to attention. The tempestuous red-head planted her hands on her hips. Takeshi appeared behind her. He'd dressed in a sheer grey T-shirt that clung to his wiry body, and black jeans. His hair was stuck up on end, a sign that he'd only just risen or he'd spent the last hour in the bathroom perfecting *manga* hair.

Suddenly the fact that she'd left him in her bed and was now down here copping off with someone else seemed terrible, the realisation made more poignant by his frozen expression. OK, so there wasn't any sort of exclusive agreement between them. It was supposed to be purely business, but she could see she'd just given him a hard slap in the face.

'Morning, Remy,' he said, his voice forcibly polite. 'Silk.'

Act normal, she thought. Remy turned to the clothes rail and snatched up an outfit. 'Here, try this.' She pressed the garments on Silk. 'I'll find some others I want photographing.'

'Why don't you let me do that? I know my size better than you do.' He gave his lips a nearly imperceptible lick. 'Maybe you could fix the coat.' He pointed to the coachman's coat draped over the back of a chair. The hem was still glittering with pins. Remy seized the excuse to focus on something practical. She supposed most people would be flattered to have three people in pursuit of them, but it was more than she could handle. The tension in the room was frightening, especially between Silk and Takeshi. Besides, she didn't want them fighting over her. She wanted to see another kind of action between them.

'I assume you're wanting to shoot some more.' Alix snatched a lens from Takeshi. 'Don't touch.'

'Yep.' Remy dashed over to the sewing machine. She checked the threads, then pushed the coat hem under the needle. Already the wool was beginning to smell of Silk. She breathed more deeply, letting his scent infuse her senses and distance her from the charged atmosphere. She'd be able to encase herself in this garment later and feel as if she were wrapped in his arms. The thought made her smile. Meanwhile, out of the corner of her eye she watched him select several of her favourites and dress himself.

Takeshi rifled through the rails alongside Silk. If they were going out shooting, he was going too. No way was he letting the pair of them out of his sight after seeing that clinch. He could hardly credit it after last night, but no, while he'd been tucked up in her bed, she was off canoodling. If he wanted to keep her, he was going to have to make a move on the competition. He didn't want things to get too far out of hand.

He watched Alix usher her out of the door, leaving him and Silk to follow once they'd picked up a few accessories. Silk was going through a box of gloves and cravats. Takeshi went into the corridor and relieved the suit of armour of its weapon. Somehow, the massive sword bolstered his confidence. He gave it a practice swing, then swirled it around his head in a victory pose. Yeah. He felt better.

He went back in to collect his outfits, still holding the metal two-hander. 'Didn't I see you in a film?' he asked Silk.

Silk gave him and the sword a wary look.

'Yeah, I remember. *Godzilla and the Golden Cockmonster.*' He laced his voice with sarcasm. 'Don't you ever get enough?'

Silk forced a smile. He rubbed his jaw. 'It's never enough.'

'Well, lay off, because she's already spoken for.'

Silk inclined his head a fraction, then shook it. 'Sorry, but the lady was enjoying it.'

Takeshi closed the gap between them. He wasn't prepared to lose over this one. 'Sex must be a constant source of disappointment to you.' He stroked a finger along the edge of Silk's lapel. 'So many women, so little satisfaction.'

Silk froze. Takeshi transferred his caress to his chest, where he circled around the button over Silk's breastbone. 'Maybe you should experiment a little.' He moved his hand rapidly downward, scissoring apart his index and middle fingers so that they stroked down either side of the bulge in Silk's trousers.

Silk shoved him squarely in the chest. 'Back off, yourself.'

It was Takeshi's turn to smirk. He'd found something he could use. 'If you think I'm lying, why are you hard?'

Silk glared at him, but didn't have an answer.

Remy followed Alix, carrying the tripod. She hoped she wasn't about to find herself at the centre of a three-way stand-off. She was apprehensive enough about having left the two boys alone together. She hadn't really wanted Takeshi to come out with them, but she couldn't very well tell him to bugger off. They needed to talk about their relationship, but not in public. Hmm, what relationship? Two one-night stands didn't count.

The Orangery was full of broken glass and tumbled ivy-covered statues with vacant eyes. It hadn't been used for over fifty years, according to Silk, who seemed to know the D'Amon estate rather well.

The moment she saw it, Remy fell in love with the place. It was still luscious in its decay, or maybe because of it. At its heart was a magnificent fountain topped by a dancing nymph, now cracked and dry with only a watermark as a testament to its former glory. Weeds had buckled the paved floor of the courtyard, and ivy interlaced the glittering metal skeleton overhead, filling the missing panes with greenery.

Alix arranged her tripod near the fountain so they could make use of the whole space, and Remy settled her stack of clothes before a gigantic stone urn with Cupid clinging to the base.

'This should be the last lot, apart from the actual wedding photos,' Alix said. She was using a combination of 35mm and digital. 'So, we can use tomorrow morning for your sitting, OK? Unless you've a burning urge to do it tonight?'

Remy gulped. 'No, tomorrow's good.' She suspected an evening session with Alix would involve far too many candles and too much massage oil. That, and she'd seen Alix's nudes before. They invariably featured close-ups of hand-span waists and wide flaring bottoms, or puckered nipples hung with liquid sweat. Such intense scrutiny was going to be hard to take even without the knowledge that Alix was likely to be getting a huge erotic kick out of seeing her naked.

The boys weren't speaking when they arrived. Somewhere en route they'd acquired props. Silk was wearing a Regency-inspired dress coat of bottle-blue velvet, one of Remy's favourites, and was carrying a silver-topped cane, which she guessed was his. Takeshi was wearing silk pyjamas, and carrying a fuck-off great sword. What he thought he was going to need it for, she couldn't imagine. Perhaps he'd just needed token proof of his virility while standing next to Silk, who looked so darn sexy, so radiant she wanted to eat him all up, using tiny nibbles.

They took turns to pose, starting with Silk atop a stone bench, with his arm outstretched, holding the silver-topped cane. Then Takeshi, reclining along the same bench in his silk pyjamas. Remy leant against a statue and watched the show, occasionally remarking upon some detail of the designs that she wanted highlighting. Alix took to grunting in response to her requests, so she figured she'd have to wait for the prints to see how much notice she'd taken.

It was well past midday when the green-tinted light in the Orangery began to fade. Beyond the ivy canopy, the sky was laden with thick grey clouds. 'What's left?' Alix slumped on to the stone bench. 'My stomach thinks my throat's been cut.'

'That was the last of my outfits.' Silk peeled his gloves from his hands.

'Takeshi?'

'Just the Spiderman pants.'

'Oh, please!' Alix clapped a hand to her brow in disgust. 'You seriously want me to photograph them? I thought they were a joke.'

'Not turned on by them?' Takeshi held open the dressing gown he was wearing and flashed the black and silver slips, complete with cobweb design.

'I dig girls.'

'Gee, so do I, but I still think these are hot.'

Alix scowled.

'What do you think, Silk?' He scooped the robe to one side and flashed his bum.

'They're a bit gay.'

Alix put the lens cover on her camera.

'No, wait, please.' Remy clasped her arm. 'I've been thinking about the cosplay thing Takeshi suggested, and

I don't think it's going to work because we don't actually have any character-specific costumes. But we could invent our own *manga* with its own set of characters, based around the outfits we do have.'

'Isn't that an awful lot of work?'

'Not really. We wouldn't actually have to write a story or anything, just come up with a title and some character profiles. She dropped her voice. If we go for the *yaoi* thing, we can make it work with just Silk and Takeshi, especially if we get them to undress a little and stage a bit of intimacy.'

Alix scowled. 'More pictures.'

'Think male burlesque with fake *anime* characters,' said Remy.

'If I must.'

'Let's do it.' Takeshi scooped up a pair of knee breeches. He gave Silk a sly wink, then pulled a baggy shirt over his head and began fumbling with a cravat.

'Great, now he looks like an Easter egg,' Alix sniped.

It was true. Takeshi did look rather pantomime, with his spiky silver-blue hair and baroque outfit.

He lifted the great sword, and practised a few swings. Alix shook her fiery locks. 'Maybe you ought to dress them, Remy, if you're actually serious about this idea.'

Remy rubbed her brow and tried to focus on costumes. Alix was becoming mutinous, partially due to hunger, and partially because she was sick of making her two rivals look good. Takeshi was cavalierly play-acting, and Silk – well, now! Dare she ask him to strip for the camera?

'Quit bloody obsessing, Remy,' Alix barked. 'Sort them out. I've been at this five fucking hours, you've got two minutes before I pack up and go in.'

It took less than thirty seconds to dress Silk. He looked like a *manga* character anyway. She just added the coachman's coat to the formal three-piece tail suit he was wearing, and asked him to braid his hair. She wanted him to tease it out as his clothes came off, until it swirled around him, dusting his bare calves. Takeshi took a bit longer, a fact Alix conveniently overlooked, despite a loudly rumbling stomach. They swapped the knee breeches for leather jeans, lost the shirt and added his own leather jacket with the picture of the girl, then a long duster coat. Somehow the contrast between the two men worked, although they began shooting most of the poses separately.

They'd been at it about twenty minutes. Silk was stripped down to shirt and trousers, and Takeshi to just his leathers. Remy had them posed like lovers, with Takeshi's hand upon Silk's shoulder, and their heads tilted towards one another. But the tension between them seemed to be running at an all-time high. Between shots, Silk seemed to be making it clear he was there under duress. Remy wondered if she was expected to feel obligated to him after this.

'Closer, and look into each other's eyes,' Remy demanded. Despite the pressure, she was enjoying herself immensely. 'It needs more intimacy.'

Takeshi leant forward and brushed his lips against Silk's.

Well, that was intimate!

Silk's lips parted in surprise. Takeshi snaked an arm around his waist and moulded their bodies together from hip to thigh. Silk retaliated by shoving Takeshi off his feet, followed by a wordless snarl of fury.

Remy's carefully constructed fantasy fell apart, although Alix gleefully continued snapping expressions. 'Yey, fight!' she cheered.

Takeshi snatched up the great sword and forced Silk back against the rim of the fountain. The tip of the metal beast pressed between the open edges of Silk's shirt, making cold contact with the skin.

'You've got to be fucking kidding!' Silk yelled.

'Stop it, stop it.' An icy shiver ran up Remy's spine.

She could see Takeshi's tattoo emblazoned like a warning across his back. She wished she knew more about him. He hadn't drawn blood, but he was pressing hard enough to force Silk over the viridescent bowl at his back. Takeshi tossed the sword aside and moved in, pressing two fingers to the impression he'd made in Silk's chest.

Unblinking, they waged a silent mind duel, while Silk fought for balance and Alix bobbed around the fountain's edge, still seeking out the best angles. 'Slowly,' she prompted, when Takeshi slid his palm down Silk's chest towards the half-opened zip of his fly. She leant in for a close-up of Silk's face. His expression was a combination of fury and bruised longing. Raw, but heart-meltingly beautiful. He snatched at Takeshi's hand.

Takeshi dipped his head instead, and poked his tongue rudely into Silk's navel, invoking an anguished cry.

Remy's insides clenched tight. She wanted to be able to see Takeshi's expression as well as Silk's, but she hardly dared move, let alone circle around for a clearer view. Faint 'oh!' noises were escaping her throat. Takeshi's tongue snaked along the golden line of hair across Silk's abdomen, and pressed a kiss to where, if he'd been erect and unconfined by clothing, his cock tip would surely lie.

Was Silk erect? He seemed to have lost all composure, unable or unwilling to escape. She could see him in her mind's eye, long and thick, creamy like the rest of his skin, apart from at the tip, which burned an exuberant plum red. If he'd still been zipped up, she'd have known how Takeshi's intimate kisses were affecting him. The trousers were cut tight across the hips, which meant they showed any bulges.

She saw the flick of Takeshi's tongue. Silk clenched his fists, so that his lacquered talons dug into his flesh.

She knew that sensation during sex. Takeshi had made her feel like that only last night. There were things that were so sensitive, so raw, so earth-shatteringly good, that all you could do was bite yourself, scratch yourself, stuff the pillow in your mouth in order to temper the sensations to a manageable level. Otherwise, orgasm came rushing up way too fast and the moment of explosion felt like crashing through a brick wall at forty.

Silk seemed immobilised by the whole experience, shocked into submission by the turn of events – or maybe at his own sudden arousal?

Alix kept taking pictures, gleefully snapping like a paparazzo on a window ledge.

Takeshi moved down and placed a kiss on Silk's inner thigh. Remy could picture Takeshi's next move, how he'd open the remainder of the zip and release Silk's cock, then slide his magic lips up and down the lily-white stem. It was so damn sexy she was rubbing herself against the fountain's edge. She'd never imagined Silk would turn out to be such a passive little *uke*. With her, he always seemed so dominant, so in control.

'Enough of this bollocks!' Silk rose abruptly to a sitting position, and his hand closed over the sword hilt. 'Get off me or I'll cut yer fucking nuts off! Got enough yet?' He directed the question at Alix.

'One more.' Alix snapped an extreme close-up of his face. If it came out in focus, it would show his green eyes to perfection, but Remy suspected she'd done it merely to wind him up a bit further.

Takeshi looked over his shoulder and caught her eye. He winked – a signal he'd used before to alert her to coming excitement. But surely the show was already over. Her body tensed in anticipation. Takeshi nuzzled against Silk's thigh, then bit down.

'Fuck! Fuck!' Silk was on his feet. He stumbled away from the fountain, and rubbed at the bite. 'I'm done.' He scooped up the coachman's coat and was out of the Orangery before she recovered enough wits to call after him.

Instead, balance recovered, she turned to Takeshi, who

grinned darkly at her. 'Done? We've barely started,' he mouthed.

Silk walked into the rising wind, until it threatened to make his eyes stream. Fuck! He was hard again. The little bastard had actually turned him on. Of course, being rubbed off provoked the same physical response regardless of who delivered it. The subtle whisper of breath across the skin fired the same nerves, coaxed the same synapses. So why was he feeling so emotional about it?

Because he'd been bitten? A more closeted part of his soul whispered that it was something else. Irritably, he pulled on a pair of gloves he'd stuffed into the coat pockets earlier, wrenching them the last half-inch with his teeth. This was supposed to be a relaxing few days of fun before the wedding, not a constant battle. He was sick of being wound up by that little prick. He'd had come-ons from other men before. He'd let them down gently, or politely told them to sod off. Why was this so difficult?

He thought again about the proposed threesome. Did Remy even know about it? Not that he intended to accept now. He didn't trust the bastard to keep his hands to himself, or worse still his cock, and he didn't need anyone's permission besides Remy's to seduce her. Judging by her reaction to him in the workroom earlier, he already had that.

A twig snapped behind him. Silk came to a sudden halt near the stile that led into the estate's arable fields and eventually to the lane. Perhaps it was Remy, come to apologise and persuade him back with soothing words and hands. That was worth waiting to let her catch up.

A hand slipped around his forearm. His elation vanished with the smell of perfume and nail polish. He knew it wasn't her, even before the acrylic nails dug into his thick woollen sleeve.

'Taking a stroll?' Dolores asked.

She wasn't an out-of-doors type – the stiletto heels proved that. She'd never make it among the horse-and-hounds crowd she so aspired to. This left only one reason why she'd be walking the grounds. She'd come specifically for him. She'd probably been watching the little fiasco in the Orangery from the comfort of the castle's upper storeys, and come out intent on pursuit and capture.

He turned towards her. The hunger and knowledge in her eyes convinced him his theory was correct.

Dolores slipped in close, pressed one slender thigh between his legs and up against the swell of his balls.

Release, they whispered. His erection jerked excitedly. Don't do it, said his head.

'Need some company?' Her voice was warm and syrupy as she tapped a shell-pink nail to his left nipple.

She wasn't his type. He'd told her so last night. It wasn't even to do with her age – she was old enough to be his mother – it was to do with her attitude, her reason for wanting him. To Dolores he was just a pretty toy, something she could flaunt like a costly diamond, but never love. A handsome diversion while she sought the rich old bugger of her dreams. Still, he knew she wouldn't give in without a fight.

'You know I'm not interested.'

She snuggled up closer, sandwiching his cock between their bodies. 'You seem interested enough to me.' She rocked their hips together while she traced one of his nipples through his shirt. The sensitive little swell tautened as she circled, until it mimicked the hardness of his cock.

Yes, yes, screamed his body, go with it. Ride her. No strings, no commitment, just sex. The ache in his loins became too much to withstand. He couldn't resist giving just the smallest rock of his hips. It was all the encouragement she needed. Her lips closed over the tiny swell she'd just raised, sucked until the fabric was damp and the wet cotton clung to his skin. Silk held on to her shoulders. He doubted drastic action on his part would lead anywhere good. How to extract himself? It wasn't often that he refused sex when offered. Could he really make this the third time in twenty-four hours?

The persuasive coaxing of her tongue was sending shivers down towards his thighs. Her hands were creeping lower too. They alighted at his waist.

'Do you need me to suck it for you?'

'No!' The word came out raspy, his throat closing over the vowel sound. 'No,' he repeated more forcefully.

She traced the length of his shaft with a fingernail, and peered slyly at him from beneath her heavily extended lashes. 'Did Takeshi turn you on?'

Bitch! screamed his inner self. Oh, yes, said his groin. 'I don't need sucking.' He grabbed her arm, only for her to press the point of her nail into his sensitive skin.

'Shame,' she murmured into his chest. 'I was looking forward to kissing it. Still, I guess you're ready for something a little more vigorous. Shall we stop making small talk?' She tugged down his zip. His cock was already poking at the elastic of his CKs. It was a relief when she stroked her hand against his blood-hardened skin, although the cold of her fingers was unanticipated.

The moment he felt her hand close around his shaft, he knew he was done for.

Dolores gave him a lip-gloss smile, and led him by the tail to the wooden stile. 'Let's get you dressed. I've brought some wet-weather gear.'

She rolled the condom down his shaft as if she were arranging one of her turtleneck sweaters. Dolores, he decided, would have enjoyed the days when sheaths had to be tied on with ribbons. She'd have fussed until everything was straight and neat.

'Mmm, you're so beautiful,' she purred in her fake cut-glass accent. 'All ready to come inside.'

Silk watched in amazement as she hoisted her tailored wool dress, and revealed long legs, lacy stocking tops, no pants and a blonde curling bush. She turned her back on him, and rested her elbows against the upper plank of the stile. 'Don't be shy now.' She gave him a wiggle.

He had to smile at that. Her bottom was tanned and more rounded than her slender nineties soap bitch image suggested, and it had a nice wobble to it. He gripped her hips with both hands, steadied her, then eased the tip of his cock along the channel between her cheeks. She jolted as he neared her anus, and gave a nervous giggle. Silk pushed into her sex and let her body suck him deep.

He'd forget Takeshi, forget Remy for the moment, just satisfy the itch he felt. He was beyond the point of doubts and regrets, lost in the irresistible warmth into which he eased his cock. His hips rolled of their own volition. Their pace built until his loins slapped against her soft bottom with a pleasing thwack. Her sighs became like music. They followed the rhythm, breathy and shallow one moment, wailing and wild the next. The repetition felt good. He could come quickly like this, but, now that he was here, he no longer felt the need to rush.

Silk slowed his pace, content to relax and enjoy a more leisurely fuck. The wind was rustling through the leaves in the treetops around them, and the air smelled of the coming rain. The sky was grey, but at least the sun wasn't burning his arse. More importantly, he didn't have to think any more. He just had to feel. And he felt good. He felt in control.

'I need your fingers,' she hissed.

Silk slipped a hand around her waist. It was awkward, considering his balance was dependent on his upright stance and her grip on the stile, but he was feeling magnanimous.

'No, silly. Not there! I can do that for myself.' She

knocked his palm aside, and pressed her own index finger to her nub. 'I meant in the out door.'

Silk regained his stance and gazed at her puckered rosebud. It was pink, with a delicate darker ring around the hole. Each time he thrust, it gaped a little, as if it were winking or inviting him to give it a kiss. The thought neither revolted him nor turned him on, but he could see what it was doing to her. Dolores was gagging for it.

'Did you bring the K-Y with you too?' He'd have to keep his gloves on for this: his nails were too sharp.

Dolores grasped the purse she still had looped diagonally across her, and produced a tin of Vaseline, which she'd probably bought as lip gloss.

'I know it's no good on rubber, but do it anyway.'

One-handed, Silk smeared the jelly over a leather-covered finger. Her body sucked greedily at his digit, pulling it into the tight furnace. He could feel the beat of her pulse; it was growing rapid and increasingly flighty. He wondered whether she asked this of all her lovers, or did she save it as a special request for those she didn't think would falter?

'All right?' he asked. 'Or would you like a little more? How many fingers do you really want, two, three – all five? How would you like me to push my whole fist in there?'

Her knees trembled. She grasped the stile tightly with one hand and rested her bust against the flat of the plank. Silk pushed his finger in as far as the knuckle, and drew it out quickly a few times, twisting as he moved. Dolores's musical sighs lapsed into incoherent grunts.

'Definitely two, I think.' He added a second lubed finger to the one already working her hole, and tickled the entrance with a third. He had a feeling Dolores was close to her perfect heaven. Not a bad result, since he wasn't actually trying.

'Use your cock.' The plea came out as a gasp.

'Say again.'

'Fuck me in the arse.'

'Tut, tut,' he teased. 'Nice girls aren't supposed to say such things.'

'My daughter will tell you I'm anything but nice.'

Silk laughed. He pulled out, then pushed into her rear between his scissoring fingers. It didn't matter to him where his cock lay, only that the channel was warm and tight. Was Chelsea like this in bed? he wondered. It would explain Shaun's extraordinary devotion. If she was, it was the only thing mother and daughter had in common.

Dolores sagged at the knees. Too much of a good thing and stiletto heels on grass just didn't mix. Silk pulled her upwards by the hips, stretching the muscles of her legs and forcing her on to her toes. 'Now hold steady.'

'Yes,' she murmured, like the perfect sub.

'Good girl.' He grabbed her plump derrière and rolled the soft mounds beneath his palms. Her heat was intense. It flooded his loins with majestic fire. 'That's good – so good. Faster now.' He could feel the coming swell deep in his balls.

'Yes,' she agreed. 'Yes. Oh, fuck!'

Perhaps she'd fit in with the horse-and-hound mob, after all, or at least with the pony club. He could just see her with a bit between her teeth and a bulbous horse-tail butt plug protruding from her pretty arse. He wondered how fast she could run. Despite her age, she still had surprisingly coltish legs.

Silk tossed his head back, and let his long hair stream out behind him. It caught the breeze and the light, scintillated with flashes of flax and gold. He forgot restraint, and penetrated her with smooth, easy, shallow strokes as he felt his seed build.

He sensed their arrival without knowing they were really there. But none of that mattered to his cock. It bucked, ready to fire. Dolores whimpered. Perhaps she sensed something too. Maybe she could see the coming storm.

'Mother!' Chelsea's shriek cut into the fog of bliss, but didn't stop the milking of his cock. Stars were exploding along his spine. Silk rode his orgasm until he'd truly come down. He saw no reason to cut himself short. They'd already realised what was going on. It was their prerogative if they wanted to turn away. It was clear, once he'd opened his eyes, that none of them had.

Dolores was still seeking Xanadu. Silk kept his cock in her bum and pinched her nipples hard. She came with a triumphant squawk.

There were five of them in total. All slack-jawed, all staring, while Dolores thrashed about and squealed. She looked like an ageing Barbie doll, which he guessed made him Action Man. (Everyone knew that Ken was gay.) Finally, she stopped twitching. The show was over.

'My mother.' Chelsea turned away in disgust. 'And the best man.'

The four gents each shook hands with Dolores, whose glistening pubic curls were still on display, and whose butt was obviously still full of cock. She seemed slightly dazed. The last man, a moustached tweedy sort in a flat cap, shook hands with Silk too. 'Good show, what?' His grin extended into his whiskers, and there was more than a simple appreciative gleam in his eyes. Silk tried hard not to laugh.

Chelsea acidly rounded up her party and ushered them off towards the castle. She looked back only long enough to give Dolores a particularly hateful scowl.

'Who were they?' Dolores asked, as he finally pulled out and tidied himself up.

'Shaun's dad, and his cronies.' He watched her smooth the wool dress down her thighs. 'The one with the flat cap is Major Cranthorpe, the neighbour. The last time I saw him, I was still young enough to be scrumping his apples.'

'All married? I suppose that's why they were all getting an eyeful. Not getting any at home.' She carefully realigned her jewellery, paying particular attention to her nonexistent wedding band.

'Cranthorpe's a confirmed bachelor.' And perfect for you, he thought but didn't say. Let Dolores work that out for herself.

'Are you going back to the castle now?' She held her hand out towards him. Silk ignored the invitation. He still wasn't going to play her game. He'd got what he wanted out of the encounter; now it was time to address his long-term desires, which meant finding a way of getting Remy alone again. It was so much easier to think when his cock wasn't demanding action.

'I need to change and grab some lunch before the rehearsal.'

'Oh, yes, that. Since when was it necessary to practise saying "I do"?'

'Since when were mothers so jealous?'

'Jealous!' she hissed, while extending her claws. 'I just think it's a waste of time. It's a wedding, not an opera.'

Clearly, she didn't know much about her daughter. But he let it go. Chelsea and Dolores were heading for a confrontation anyway. Nothing he said would make any difference.

'I suppose you're going to ignore me for the rest of the weekend now.' Instead of looking at him while awaiting his reply, she flipped open her compact – another treasure from her purse – and began touching up her foundation.

'I can be civil, if you can.'

'That's not what I meant.'

'I won't be visiting your bed, if that's what you mean.'

'No, of course.' She fixed a smile. 'From what I've seen you let the ladies come to you. Tell me, was Eloise as good as me?'

He knew the moment he hesitated that he'd made a

mistake. The problem was, he couldn't understand why she'd singled out Eloise. If she'd seen her then she'd surely seen her sisters. Suddenly, he wished he'd kicked all three girls out of his room when they'd first appeared.

'You can't answer, can you? I think I know more about pleasing a man than some teenage necrophiliac. Unless, of course, the reason you can't answer is that you don't know.'

Silk kept his expression neutral but his silence just made Dolores's mind work harder.

'She was with Shaun, wasn't she?'

'Don't be ridiculous. He's about to get married.' Where the hell was this going? His best friend had been stirred up over the damn kiss Chelsea had insisted upon, but not stirred up enough to jeopardise anything, surely. They'd probably just been talking.

'Yes, and I know men. Since when did marriage ever stop them?'

Bitter, venomous cow. She looked so bloody gleeful that she'd found a bit of shit she could stir. Her only daughter was about to get married and she was determined to wreck it for her.

'Are you sure you're not coming?' She extended an arm again, and flashed him a bitchy smile.

'No.' Regardless of anything else, he refused to be blackmailed. 'I'm going to find someone without an agenda to share lunch with.' And he hopped over the stile.

10

'I can't believe we need a rehearsal. All she has to do is walk down the bloody aisle.' This time the complainant was Severina. Remy rested her head against the back of the pew, and gazed at the angels on the chapel ceiling. This was the first bit of quiet time she'd had since the night she'd arrived.

The sky had grown darker as the afternoon progressed, the rain finally arriving as they crowded into the D'Amon family chapel. It was a fifteen-minute walk from the castle along squidgy dirt tracks, which bore interesting titles such as Castle Lane and Demon's Causeway. She'd ridden pillion on the back of Takeshi's bike, hanging on for dear life, although he claimed he'd barely made it out of second gear. Everyone else had walked over, and arrived a little windswept. They'd left a pile of muddy boots and umbrellas in the porch. Now they were mooching about in the inner sanctum, while Chelsea sorted through the various bits of paper intended as readings.

'Hey, look lively.' Alix slid on to the pew next to Remy, and gave her a sharp jab in the ribs. 'Lucretia's about to take the stage.'

Sev's face fell. 'Let me hide. I think I'll go see how the florist's doing.' She scuttled off towards the back, her velvet tailcoat flapping behind her.

'Isn't it a bit early for the flowers?' Remy asked.

'They're not doing flowers, just ribbons at the moment.'

'Can everybody hear me?' Lucretia bellowed through the pulpit microphone.

Remy sat up straight. She didn't do church any more, but nearly twenty years of forced attendance had taught her to look lively or get targeted when someone was preparing for a hellfire-and-damnation speech.

Alix laughed at her response and cuddled up to her arm. 'Easy there, it's just a crazy goth girl. How bad can it be?'

'Thank you for your attention.' Lucretia spread her hands wide and placed them on the lectern. 'I'd like to read you a poem of my own devising – for the bride and groom. I give you "Ashtaroth".'

'God help us!' Eloise's words carried across the rows from the choir stall.

> *'Where shall I seek my love?*
> *Where has the Voladora flown?*
> *From flesh-glazed shores of Quiddity*
> *Falling between bitter stars, alone.*
>
> *'In the green womb of Eden*
> *My vegetable love shall grow.*
> *Fat on the sap of Elohim*
> *Into the greener box, for show.'*

Suddenly, the patter of rain on the roof slate was extremely loud. It echoed like the marching of distant boots. Remy couldn't help imagining that really it was the marching of men in white coats come to wrap Lucretia in a nice huggy-jacket and take her somewhere safe and warm. Frankly, she wouldn't have minded their carrying *her* off, too. The surrealist nonsense delivered with a wide-eyed stare and much posturing had left her feeling as if she had a head full of puffer fish.

Chelsea began to clap. 'Thank you. It's great. Perfect.'

The rest of the audience remained absolutely silent.

Lucretia beamed. 'I've another two verses, but I'm saving them for the big day.'

Takeshi edged down the central aisle and leant in

over the edge of the pew. 'I'm heading back now. I've got some eBay listings that need checking, and the laptop battery's fried.' He brushed her cheek with his fingertips. Alix's hold on her arm tightened.

'OK. I guess that means I'm walking.' She hoped there was a spare umbrella. Then again, did they really need her? She was acting as a witness, but that just involved signing her name on a bit of paper. No way were they practising that. And she needed time to talk things over with Takeshi while there was no one else. 'Hang on, I'm coming with you.'

Remy rose, just as Dolores took to the podium. She balanced a pair of gold spectacles on her slender nose and began to read from the sheet.

'Stop it! Stop!' Chelsea came belting towards her, and up the altar steps. 'That's not what I asked you to read.' She snatched the verse from the lectern. 'What is that mush?'

'T S Eliot, dear. It's "The Love Song of J Alfred Prufrock".' There were loud guffaws from Shaun and Silk. Dolores ignored them. 'I thought your choice was a little sombre for a wedding. I think we could all do with something uplifting after the last piece.' She gave Lucretia a kindly look, as if the poor creature required pity for her terrible mental affliction. Lucretia flipped her the bird in return.

Dolores returned her attention to her daughter. 'Your whole ceremony's so dour, darling. There aren't even any hymns to wake people up.'

'We're saving the music for outside.' Chelsea's expression was stony. 'There's going to be a fiddler in the graveyard. He's highly respected. Besides, no one ever knows the words. Now stop interfering, and read what I asked you to or give it to someone else. Barney.'

The taller, gormless-looking one of the two ushers raised his hands as if to ward off the responsibility.

'OK, Wayne, then. Or Remy, you do it.'

It was only then that Remy realised her getaway driver had already got away.

'I think I'm entitled to a role in my own daughter's wedding.' Dolores strained over the pulpit wall, so she towered over Chelsea by a good two foot. But Remy had seen her friend talk down drunk horny roadies when they had forgotten that 'no' meant no. She wasn't about to be cowed by a little height or weight difference.

'Frankly, considering what happened earlier, you're lucky you still have an invite.'

Dolores blanched. 'Don't you threaten me. At least I came. Unlike someone else I could mention.'

'Broad daylight with the best man's cock up your arse. Sure, you *came* all right. Great introduction to the in-laws, Mum. You made a *fantastic* impression. They'll be talking about you for years.'

There were a few startled gasps. Shaun shook his head at Silk while drawing his finger across his throat.

'How was I supposed to know you were going to walk past?' Dolores said.

'You shouldn't have been screwing.' Chelsea directed an evil glare at Silk, who turned his away, apparently fascinated by the hidden image of the Green Man masquerading as St Francis of Assisi in the stained glass. 'And leave Dad out of this.'

'Why should I? Where is he? Fucking seventeen-year-olds? We both know he's not here because he can't bear the thought of giving away a daughter who's older than his latest tart.'

Chelsea bared her teeth.

'I know the lies he feeds you,' Dolores continued, 'and you believe him. But I lived with him for twenty years. He was always a lying, cheating wanker.'

'Why are you staring at Shaun?'

Dolores continued to stare, causing a pretty damson blush to wash over Shaun's cheekbones. All heads turned towards him.

'I haven't done anything,' he said, his kohl-lined eyes going wide.

'So you won't mind telling us why the chief bridesmaid was sneaking out of your room after midnight, looking like she'd just worked up a sweat.'

'You spiteful bitch,' hissed Eloise, before Shaun had a chance to respond. 'Nobody needed to know about that.'

The resulting silence was eerie. Remy resumed her seat and tried to sink as low as possible.

'It isn't what you think,' said Eloise and Shaun together.

Chelsea's fist closed on the papers in her hand, scrunching them mercilessly.

'It's my fault.' Silk strode towards Chelsea. 'They were with me.' He swept his arm in an arc that encompassed all three bridesmaids. Severina was still lurking at the back.

'Yeah,' said Lulu. 'We were doing the Dracula scene, but you –' she glared at Silk '– left us aces high and buggered off. Shaun burst in on us.'

'They are sharing a room.' Chelsea sucked on her bottom lip, while she stared half accusatorily and half full of desperate hope at Shaun.

'Yes, but that doesn't explain Eloise leaving late.' Dolores came down the pulpit steps. 'They had to be doing something, else why the fuss?'

'You're an evil cow,' Lulu muttered. 'They're about to get married and you're stirring. Can't you let them be happy?'

'I'm sorry.' Eloise pressed a hand to Chelsea's arm. 'Really, Shaun didn't do anything. I was in a world of my own. I didn't even realise he was there.'

'You were just talking, right?'

'Um ... not exactly.'

Chelsea's eyes were beginning to tear. Remy bowed her head against the pew back. This wasn't the time for a major fallout. There were only just over twenty-four hours to go until the wedding, and she'd just finished all the outfits. And, if there wasn't a wedding, bang went all her free promo material too. She wished she had a set of voodoo dolls so she could stick pins in Dolores.

'What were you doing?' Chelsea asked.

Suddenly Shaun was on his feet, with Silk behind him like a perversely pretty bodyguard. 'I watched her masturbate. I'm sorry, love. She was on my bed. I couldn't get her off.'

'Bastard,' Chelsea screeched, and slapped him across the face. Shaun put a hand to his cheek, then reached towards her. His fingers closed on empty space, as Chelsea swept past him and up the aisle. A moment later, the chapel door closed with a bang.

'Bad choice of words.' Silk clasped Shaun's shoulder. 'Go after her.'

'No,' said Alix. 'Let her calm down. I'll go after her, you go back to the castle.' She scooped up her leather gloves. 'And you –' she turned to Dolores '– are one very nasty lady. Chelsea hasn't said she wants you gone, so you're safe for now. But pull another stunt like that and I'll flay you.'

Marianne was trying on corsets when Takeshi got back from the church. She had several spread across the surface of his bed. He perched beside them, and carefully traced the boning of an exquisitely beaded velvet. Its shiny pile glistened in the half-light, the colour of clotted blood. 'Does Remy know you have these?' He flinched at the overlaid image his mind added of a girl trying to stem the crimson flow from her nose with her pale hand. His gaze settled on Marianne's curvaceous rear instead. Her plump curves were perfectly framed by a line of black lace along the top and a triangle disappearing into her cleft. The dark-eyed girl from his memory faded again, firmly into his past, where she belonged, along with the abusive boyfriend he'd subsequently beaten with a rusty exhaust. He had to move on, had to let go of these relics of his wild days. There was nothing he could do to change them. He'd left Japan knowing that. And he had Remy to think about.

'She said I could try them on. It's for the catalogue. Alix set up the camera. Look.' There was a tripod in the corner mounted with a digital camera. A long extension trailed from the back to a trigger clutched in Marianne's hand. 'Provided I stand between here and here.' She waved at the stage delineated by two lines of pillows. 'All I have to do is press, and hey presto!' She squeezed the trigger, setting off the flash and shutter.

'Bravo! How many nudes have you taken by mistake?'

'One or two.' Her lips plumped into a dour pout. 'It's sensitive.'

'Alix will be delighted. She might even frame you as art.'

'Quit teasing and tighten these laces.'

Takeshi shimmied across the bed, avoiding the rainbow of corsetry, and set to work on the lacings. 'Who's teasing? I'd pay for a nice black-and-white still of your bum. It's very shapely.'

'Can't you pull anyone else? I know you like skinny chicks like Remy.' She smoothed the corset front. 'I take it that's where you spent the night.'

'She's hardly skinny. The three goth princesses are skinny.'

'Whatever.'

'And, yes, I spent the night.'

Takeshi gave the ribbons a particularly vicious pull, which squeezed Marianne's generous midriff into a significantly more hourglass shape.

'Too tight,' she gasped.

'Not into breath play, or a little light S&M? I think I have some nipple clamps somewhere. That'd give Alix something to look at.'

'She wouldn't be interested. Alix is nice, not a pervert like you.'

'She's an artist. They're all perverts.'

Marianne squirmed, but failed to ease the knots. Takeshi smiled. He knew his knots, just as he knew the difference between a *yakuza* and an undercover cop. He didn't know why Osaka was so prominent in his mind again. Maybe because Remy reminded him so much of the girl he'd left behind. Not that Megumi had ever really been his. A mistake he wasn't about to repeat.

He got to his feet, feeling irritated, paced to the corner and jerked the pull for the lamp, on and off, on and off.

'Quit with the strobe, will you.' Marianne laid a soothing hand on his shoulder.

His desire to swear vehemently in two languages vanished with the touch, leaving behind the germs of a plan. 'How would you like to give your friend Alix a show?' There was a glint in his eyes, a sexual one that not even Marianne could fail to interpret.

'With you?' she screeched. 'No thanks.'

'Still hankering after Silk?'

She looked away.

Takeshi wet his lips. 'That wasn't exactly what I had in mind, anyway.'

'What, then?'

'Tifa.'

Her eyes went wide. For several moments her mouth opened but nothing emerged. Takeshi seized the opportunity to scoot around the bed and fetch Tifa from her favourite position by the window, staring out at the world she couldn't sense or feel. Someday sex dolls would be more than just toys. Her kind were already evolving. He brought her back to Marianne, and propped her up against the headboard.

'Don't you dream of being a film star? Why not do something risqué for a change and make some eyes pop?'

'You want me to ... With the doll!' Her words tumbled out.

'She's clean.' He couldn't help adding a smile.

'Why?'

Takeshi tapped his nose. 'Why not?' He swapped the memory card from the camera for one from his laptop case. 'Swap them back when you're finished.' He left Alix's card on the bedside table, and headed for the door with his laptop. There'd be a socket somewhere else he could use. 'Don't forget to dress her nicely. She looks good in white.'

'I'm not doing it. No way.'

'Suit yourself. It'll be your loss. She likes you, I can tell.'

'Yeah, but not like that.'

'Like that, Miss No-nerve Bi-curious.'

He closed the door, leaving Marianne to contemplate making her very own photostory porn. He had no guarantee she'd do it, just a gut feeling, and they normally paid off. Besides, he knew she fantasised about being a 1930s screen goddess, and this was probably the closest she'd get.

Remy lingered in the vine-covered chapel porch. The rain was coming down thick and fast, rapidly turning the dirt-track road into a filthy quagmire. She'd hoped to walk home with Silk, but he'd been consoling Shaun.

The outlook for the wedding seemed bleak. She was dismayed by Shaun's revelation, but she hoped that Chelsea would have the sense to forgive him once she'd got over the shock. It wasn't as if he'd really cheated. It was more as though he'd watched a porn movie. Only live. Porn theatre. Whatever.

She stared through drizzle at the grey sky. 'Don't you dare,' she threatened a particularly thunderous-looking cloud. Bravely, she stepped out from the shelter, but the drizzle turned to rain with a startling suddenness. Somehow, she didn't see Takeshi coming back for her, despite his attempts to woo her, so she was going to have to make a move for herself.

Her hair was soaked and clinging to her cheeks in seconds, but surprisingly she found herself smiling. Even the cold tickle as the rivulets found their way beneath her collar and rolled down her neck filled her with a positive charge. She hadn't realised it before, but being cooped up in the castle, constantly surrounded by so many competing characters, had drained her. Now the electricity in the air seemed to be coaxing her shrunken aura back to full strength.

A raindrop dripped off her nose. She shivered in her cropped jacket but trudged on, as images of the blond from her comic, of Silk and Takeshi, flitted through her mind. She smiled at the thought of seeing them streaking naked through the mud of the country lane, as they competed, Greek-style, in a sexual triathlon. Silk was long-limbed and agile, but Takeshi was swift and powerful. It would be a close race – too close to call. It would all come down to a bout of wrestling at the end.

About two-thirds of the way back, the sky went dark. Thunder rolled overhead, bringing with it the static charge of electricity and the smell of ozone. Finally, the novelty of being soaked wore off. She just wanted to get home to a bath.

The puddles were getting deeper. Remy tugged her collar up to her ears. The stretch ahead looked particularly treacherous – a muddy river churned up by the rest of the wedding party returning ahead of her, bordered on both sides by steep verges of wild flowers and high hedges. Tentatively, she eased a foot into the ooze, which squelched up to the top of the heel of her ankle boot. There was no alternative. Spray spattered her clothing with each subsequent step, until her trousers looked as if they were polka-dotted. One particularly large blob of mud landed on her knee. Remy paused to wipe it, but succeeded only in smearing it across her hand. She stared at the brown mark in disgust, hoping it was just mud and not anything even less pleasant, such as cow dung. There'd been hoof marks a little further back down the lane.

The rain continued to splash at her palm, washing away the ugly mark. Remy lifted her foot again and suddenly found her toes cold. She looked down to find her boot still firmly planted in the mud.

'Oh, arse!' She tried to poke her toes back in the top, but it was impossible without undoing the fastening. Awkwardly poised, she fumbled with the zip, overbalanced and came crashing to all fours.

Remy blew at a wet strand of hair, which clung stubbornly to her cheek. She didn't know whether to laugh or scream. She was just glad there was no one around to see her impersonation of a mud monster. Fashion designers were supposed to be immaculately turned out regardless of the weather. She hoped she'd be able to sneak back into the castle before anyone saw her. Maybe she should have accepted Lulu's offer of an umbrella.

A stream of bright poppy petals billowed across the path before her. Remy watched them skim across the mud until, too heavy to fly, they sank into its mire like discarded rubies. She wondered if anyone would think her a worthy enough gem to rescue, if they saw her here. She lifted her head. Fifty yards away, there was a pair of solid boots and the hem of a familiar coat.

Silk, she realised, and jerked backwards on to her knees. Why now, when she looked so grim?

The mud made a sucking noise as it released her hands. Remy wiped them down her mottled thighs. He smiled at her from beneath the shelter of his vast golfing umbrella, and let the last of the petals slip from between his fingers.

'Need a hand?'

A hand, a shot of brandy and a night watching him and Takeshi make out, she thought as he waded towards her, his free arm outstretched. She didn't like the idea of having to be rescued, but she guessed she'd already shattered the ice-maiden image with this ridiculous display.

Silk clasped her hand, and Remy gratefully rose on to her one booted foot. 'Take this.' He passed her the umbrella, then bent to release her other boot from the mud.

Remy pointed her toes towards him, feeling like Cinderella as he cleaned her skin with a tissue and slid the leather over her foot. 'Thanks. I think the other foot's stuck too.'

Silk grinned. 'Recite after me. Stiletto heels and mud don't mix. Stiletto heels and mud don't mix.'

Remy pursed her lips.

He shrugged. 'Guess we'll just have to do this the old-fashioned way.' He slid an arm around her back, one behind her thighs and scooped her up. 'Not too archaic for you, I hope.'

Remy shook her head. He might be a cad who slept with anything that moved – and she wasn't sure what to make of the fact that he'd fucked Dolores after coming on to her – but, apparently, he was also a gentleman. Modern men just didn't do this sort of thing, and modern women weren't supposed to approve. Bollocks to that. She wrapped an arm around his neck, and covered them both with the umbrella. If he wanted to treat her like a lady, she wasn't going to object.

Remy rested her head against his shoulder. His hair enveloped her in a silky cloud, blown around them by the wind. He smelled dewy from the rain, and warm. Nobody had carried her like this since she was a child. Delighted, she nestled closer, enjoying the movement of his body as he walked. She couldn't resist. She pressed a kiss to his neck.

Next thing she knew, the world spun past and she was on the floor.

Shocked, she floundered in the muddy pool, managed to turn on to her knees, while her bum protested the recent impact. Silk was flat on his back, staring skyward, with his hair fanned out around him over the surface of the puddle. 'Are you all right? What happened?' He must have slipped. She placed a muddy hand on his thigh, leaving a sticky print on the leather, and leant over his chest so that she could look down into his eyes. They weren't weirdly dilated or anything, just the beautiful evocative green she'd been bewitched by thirty-six hours ago. 'Silk?'

'Move that hand up any further and I'll be more than all right.'

Relieved, she poked him in the ribs. The umbrella was several metres down the lane, and speeding away at a rate of knots. But they were both so wet it didn't really matter any more.

Silk closed his hand around her arm. 'Why don't you come closer?' He tugged her towards him, so that her hands splashed down either side of his head and her breasts pressed against him. 'And finish what you just started.'

'Did I start something?' Her words brushed the surface of his lips.

'You know you did.' His arms entwined her, his hands going up into the back of her hair. Then his lips were on hers, and he tasted of the falling rain. Remy rubbed against him, heedless of the seeping mud. She felt she could lie here for ever with their tongues and bodies entwined, the thunder of her heart beating in her ears and his beating a second rhythm against her chest, but she wanted something else too. She wanted to get naked with him. Just once couldn't hurt the chances of her getting the two men together, surely.

Remy freed a hand and wrenched his waistband open. Her insides were liquefying. She had to feel him, had to touch him. His heat slid easily into her palm, causing her breath to catch.

'I'm yours if you want me.'

'You're all mine anyway, until you pay the cleaning bill on that coat. I don't remember saying you could swan about in it in all weather.'

'You're worried about a coat?'

Remy traced a finger over the sensitive eye of his cock.

'OK, I'll pay for it.' His eyes fluttered closed. 'Whatever you want.'

'Easy and cheap. You said it.' Remy threw her head back and laughed.

Silk bent his knees, causing her to slide forward until she straddled his hips, then propped himself up on his elbows. 'My turn.'

He undid the buttons of her jacket, and pushed his hands inside. Then his palms were over her breasts, supporting their weight and cupping them together. It wasn't enough. Off came the coat; off came the fitted shirt. The rain splashed against her skin, leaving cold spots that heightened her arousal, then continued as winding rivulets down her body. His gaze fastened on her bra. One finger traced the violet detailing, then he pushed it upwards, exposing her right breast, which spilled heavy and ripe into his waiting hand.

Remy moaned as little tendrils of electricity pulsed from her nipples to her belly. He wasn't going to rush it, though; he was caught up in the vision of her, just staring at the single droplet hanging from her red, perky nipple. Hell, she was in love with just the image of it. Where was Alix with her camera just now?

'Beautiful.'

Tiny hairs rose all over her body. Silk raised himself

from the muddy puddle and breathed hot air on to her skin. He sucked, teasing her darkening nipples into engorged points. Remy moaned. Her breasts had always been sensitive. Arousal echoed between her thighs, where the seam of her trousers was troubling her clit with a teasing, chafing caress.

'Silk ...'

They were rolling. Silk was above her, his hair tumbling around them, a cascade of gold and barley. He thrust a hand inside her trousers, pulled aside the damp scrap of cloth covering her and rubbed his fingers into the melt between her thighs.

Remy shoved his jeans down and clasped his firm arse.

Then light, blinding white, iridescent light.

'Shit!'

Silk tugged her on to her feet and up the steep embankment. They scuttled through a gap in the hedge, and landed on the grassy pasture of the field beyond, laughing and clutching their loosened clothing.

Through the leafy opening, they watched the tractor rattle past.

Silk stroked his fingers through her muddy hair. 'Shall we take this home?'

'Your room or mine?'

'How about the bathroom?'

Remy tugged on her wet clothes, and fastened her jacket tight. A long hot soak sounded like just the thing. She felt chilled now the heat of his body was no longer warming her.

A little further along, they found a gate that led back on to the lane, and, a few paces further, the mud track solidified into tarmac. 'Race you,' Remy screamed. She might not be able to wade puddles very well in her heels, but she could run in them. She'd proved that when she'd chased Takeshi across town. What was it with her, men and rainstorms? She wondered if her *bosozoku* bad boy had missed her yet. Was he waiting for her to get back? They still needed to talk. He had to understand that she didn't want to get all cosy and vanilla. She wanted to see him fuck Silk.

Silk caught her as they neared the front door. He clasped her around the waist as he wrestled a chunky iron key from his pocket. 'There are a few advantages to being Shaun's designated nursemaid.'

The door swung open, spilling them on to the stairs and a mottled collection of boots. Remy fell against the mail table causing it to rattle, though she managed to save Takeshi's helmet from rolling. She placed it back on top of his painted jacket, and steadfastly ignored the pangs in her conscience.

Silk pulled off his boots, then lifted her feet and tugged off hers. He chucked the sodden footwear behind him, as Remy clasped her arms around his neck and drew him into a full body embrace.

'I thought we agreed on the bathroom.'

Remy slid her hands inside his underwear and grasped his cheeks.

'Cold!' he squeaked. He tugged her down the steps to the ground-floor corridor and into darkness, past the glinting metal sentry and into the equally dark bathroom. He bolted the door behind them.

Remy squinted at him through the gloom. Even soaked and bedraggled, he looked perfectly scrumptious, just like her favourite *anime* character, Iason. There was moss in his long hair, and a muddy smear across one cheek. She reached up to wipe it away. 'Now what?'

'We get dirty – I mean clean.'

The hot tap sputtered into life, sending swirls of steam upwards towards the arched ceiling. Remy clutched his lapels from behind and drew the great coat off his shoulders. She wasn't going to stand around while he made everything perfect. The dripping wool collapsed between them, forming a soggy puddle. Remy nuzzled against Silk's back, and pressed a line of kisses down his spine. She reached the top of his trousers and wrenched the shirt loose, then began her line of kisses again, this time working upwards against his bare skin, while she massaged his muscular stomach.

Silk trembled as she teased the downy hairs along his backbone. 'Patience, princess.' He clasped her hand and moved it towards his trouser fastening.

'Patience yourself.' Remy slipped his button, while he rummaged through the collection of shampoo and bath-foam miniatures on the shelf above the tub. A moment later, he produced a bath bomb and tossed it into the peaty water, where it fizzed maniacally. Remy watched it spin and dive. It was out of control, a little like her love life.

Silk found some matches and lit candles at either end of the shelf, then turned to face her.

Remy looked into his eyes. The pupils were deep and dark, like slivers of onyx or inky pools. She wanted to fall into his gaze, forget her responsibilities and lose herself for a while in the dark heart of his soul.

'Wet things off.'

'You could kiss me first.' Remy strained forward on tiptoe to reach his lips, even trampling on the sodden coat for extra height. 'You kiss everyone else.'

'Not entirely everyone else.'

'Marianne, the Gorgons, Dolores – Takeshi.'

He tilted his head and sucked his lower lip. 'OK, you win. But *he* kissed *me*.' He pressed in close, and rudely poked his tongue between her lips. Remy was tempted to laugh. Was he really splitting hairs over Takeshi? Actually, that didn't say much for her chances of seeing them getting it on. Maybe she was going to have to start working with Takeshi on this one. See if she could persuade him to go in for some real seduction instead of the annoying tease and torture he'd pursued so far. She suspected he was teasing her as much as Silk.

Silk started with the top buttons of her coat, Remy with the bottom. Somewhere in the middle, they met and he peeled the sleeves from her arms. Her top rapidly followed.

Remy grabbed the back of his baggy shirt and sent it skimming across the tiled floor. If she had to resort to a threesome to get the two men into bed together, it just wouldn't be the same. No, she'd tie Silk down on false pretensions before it got to that.

Silk pulled down her trousers and pants and blew on her skin. 'Let's get you warm, my mermaid.' He scooped her up as he rose, then carefully lowered her into the bath.

The water was like a silver cocoon. Effervescent bubbles tickled the back of her neck as they rose to the surface like sparkling beads. The warmth prickled across her skin, finding its zenith in her cheeks. She hadn't realised just how cold she'd been. Now the water was enveloping her, soothing away the chill, and heightening her desire at the same time. Remy plunged beneath the surface, then rose again, and wiped the droplets from her eyes.

Silk leant over her, reaching for the soap.

Remy raised her hand. 'Not yet. Get naked and get in.'

He hooked his thumbs into his waistband in response and looked coyly down, drawing her gaze to his loins and the sight of her muddy handprints across his thighs.

Remy chuckled. He wasn't about to fool her with a coy pout. 'Quit the theatrics and strip.'

'Yes, ma'am.'

The flickering candlelight painted rich shadows across his musculature as he stepped out of his leather trousers and underwear. She'd seen him near-naked before, but this was different. The dim light gave everything a black-and-while movie glamour, highlighted the brilliant opalescence of his pale skin. And of course she'd never seen his cock before. Yet here it was, as proud as the rest of him.

His cock was beautiful, long and porcelain white, with faint splashes of blue where the veins were visible through the skin. The tip was ruddy though, ripe and tight. She couldn't help it. Her whole body felt plump and eager. Remy gripped the side of the bath and pulled herself on to her knees. She leant forward to him, briefly bypassing his cock to brush her lips to the tiny fleshy point below his navel. She nipped. Silk jumped, but he couldn't go anywhere because her hand had clasped the base of his cock. Then with one glorious mouthful she encompassed his shaft.

Shivers of excitement raced down her throat as he filled her mouth. Remy sucked, but she wanted to be closer than this. She wanted their genitals locked together. She wanted rough, frantic, pounding, thrusting joy. She wanted to be experiencing the heady rush towards orgasm.

Silk's loins arched towards her, pushing more of his shaft into her mouth. Remy released him with a sharp hiss.

'Get in.' She smacked her hand through the surface of the water.

Silk stepped into the water behind her. Remy immediately twisted around, and sought his mouth.

Their bodies slithered and slipped together. His hands tangled in the red and black strands of her hair. Remy forced his legs together and straddled him, forcing him lower into the water. His cock butted against her bum. She raised herself on to her knees and sank on to his erection.

Which was exactly what she needed.

'Like to be on top, do you?' Silk laughed.

'Got a problem with being on the bottom?' She raised her hands up through her hair, elevating her bust into the bargain.

Silk immediately rose up and latched on to a nipple. 'No problem at all.' His breath was hot. The lap of his tongue was exquisite. His cock felt so good inside her. She just needed a little extra bit of coaxing. She pushed him back down, and drew his fingers to her clit.

Silk coaxed the little nubbin with a delicate flick. Like a touchpaper in her womb, the buzz was instant and intense. Remy mashed his fingers harder into her heat. Easy, he might be, but she defied anyone to experience this and not want more. Hell, she wanted more and they'd barely started. It wasn't often she came more than once, but with Silk she thought she might. Her body was dancing to its universal rhythm. Her clit was pulsing; everything was slowing, building to that final epic release.

Then the buzz fell into the background.

Surprised and hungry for the bittersweet release, Remy swivelled her hips, faster, slower, as she tried to break through the plateau, but nothing made any difference. 'Come on, come on.' The pad of Silk's finger buffeted her tightly swollen nub. It was perfect, perfect, but the threads of fire didn't seem to be reaching anywhere. Remy bit her lip. Maybe she was just too eager. She looked down at his face, his chiselled cheekbones, luminous-green eyes and long feathery eyelashes. He was the most perfect man she'd ever been with, so why wasn't it happening?

Why? She wanted to scream. Instead, she watched his pupils dilate, his mouth open and his brows furrow. 'It's coming.' He reached towards the base of his cock as if to stop it, but his stomach muscles clenched in a tight ripple that flowed out across his groin and caused his hips to buck, once, twice ... He was soaring. Three times. He collapsed, hissing through his teeth. 'Shit! Sorry.'

Remy dragged her hands across her face, rose so that he slipped out, then turned and sat with a splash. Why hadn't she come? Everything was just right. She was so turned on, and he'd been pressing all the right buttons.

It should have been easy. Instead, it had felt as though she'd hit a brick wall.

Silk wrapped his arms around her and pulled her back down into the water. 'Hush.' His hair stuck to her skin like living vines, camouflaging her arms and breasts. Remy traced the path of one lengthy strand across her stomach, and fought the urge to cry. She stared up at the twin candles, hovering like will-o'-the-wisps overhead. She couldn't understand it. What was wrong with her?

Silk lifted the soap. 'Hey.' His lips teased the ring of her ear, as he slid the green bar over her breasts. 'You can't rush these things.'

Remy wriggled. 'I hope that's unscented. I've got sensitive skin.'

Silk brought the bar to his nose and sniffed. 'Soap flavour with a hint of watermelon.'

'You can really smell that?'

His teasing caress moved to her earlobe and from there to her neck. 'Yeah, of course.' His breath whispered over the curve of her collarbone. He drew the soap down her torso in a slippery line and circled back up under her breast. 'What do you dream of, Remy?' He passed the soap to his other hand, and circled it around her tummy button. 'The Gorgons like their vampires, Dolores longs to be somebody's pet and Shaun has his bondage fairy fantasy.' He grinned. 'It's all he talks about when he's drunk. But what about you? I know you get turned on by clothes, but what else?'

The soap reached her pubic curls, where he worked up a thick lather. Remy tried to find words. She still needed to come, and she didn't want to walk away from him just to go to her room and masturbate while thinking of the two men together. But what to say?

He edged the soap down between her thighs, where it slid, smooth as satin, back and forth over her clit. Little jolts of interest leapt upwards towards her nipples, which he tweaked with his free hand.

Remy closed her eyes. What if he was horrified? He'd been uncomfortable enough about the mention of that kiss. Then again, wasn't this a perfect opportunity to find out just where his boundaries lay? 'You,' she said huskily. 'And Takeshi – together.'

The circular motion of his hand stopped abruptly. Beneath her, she felt his stomach muscles clench again. Slowly he forced them to relax, and the delightful slip of the soap, back and forth across her clit, began again.

'Go on. I want to hear it.'

Remy raised her knees. The water suddenly felt too hot. 'You're both naked,' she began, uncertainly, 'and you have Takeshi pinned against the wall in some back alley, with his hands above his head. You're holding him there with just one hand; your other is wrapped around his cock. He's whimpering, and there's sweat upon his brow, and across his pecs. He's loving every second of what you're doing to him, but he's hating you at the same time. He wants you to stop, but he also wants so badly for you to make him come.

'Then you're on the bed together, and the covers are gone.'

Remy sank into the fantasy, until the images played out before her closed eyelids. Silk's hand was still working the watermelon bar over her clit in a soapy dance, but in her mind she was inside Takeshi's skin. She was the *uke* being made to come against her will.

Her hands clasped at the bottom sheet over the mattress, to which her flaming cheek was pressed. Silk was on his knees behind her. He was going to do it this time. He was going to take her all the way. His hair tickled as it brushed softly against her back. She felt his cock tip brush her anus. Her own cock was hard, virtually bursting.

'You're mine,' he whispered. 'For now, and for ever.'

She shook her head, her breaths coming hard and fast against the rumpled linen. 'Nothing lasts for ever.'

Suddenly his tongue was dabbing against her anus, rimming her until she was panting, begging incoherently.

'Are you doubting me?' A finger wriggled inside. Soon it would be his cock.

'No! Please! No! Let go!'

'Always the theatrics.' His hips rolled against her bottom. 'Why don't you just admit it for once, and say yes?'

Remy's powers of description failed her. Her head echoed with the sounds of her own breathing. Her clit was erect, poking heavenward like a ruby bead. She was on fire, burning up. She stretched her neck, opening her mouth to a strangled cry. Her vocal cords no longer seemed to be working. Her body jerked as her orgasm shattered, sending her hurtling through the brick wall into a spiralling wheel of icy fire.

For a moment, she lay still, pulling her atoms back together. Her aura seemed to have expanded to the size of the room. Silk released the soap and it dropped like a stone to the bottom of the bath.

'Better?' he asked.

Remy blew out her next breath, and nodded. Not just better – glorious.

11

Remy sat on the bath mat, wrapped in four fluffy aubergine towels, with her back pressed to the side of the tub.
She felt satiated and curiously content just to remain
where she was, watching the subtle movements of Silk's
body and the play of light across his skin as he brushed
his hair. After her explosive orgasm, they'd relaxed and
cuddled in the water. Silk had washed her hair, massag-
ing her scalp as he worked up a foam. She'd felt like a
child again as he created soapy spikes and kiss curls. His
own hair he'd left until they both got out, and then he'd
rinsed it with cup upon cup of tepid water, while leaning
over the tub.

Silk pulled a bristle brush through the long wet
strands of his hair, carefully working loose the knots and
tangles. It fell like a sheet of golden taffeta, shot through
with a multitude of tones and shades, from the palest
ash blond to the deepest amber. She'd never seen anyone
pay such luxurious attention to their hair before. Hers
rarely received more than a quick once-over with a hot
brush. Even when she went to a salon, it was never as
sensual as this. The long strands danced and shimmered.
Remy curled her toes into the thick pile of the bath mat,
and hugged the towel to her face. He really was exquisite. She couldn't wait to see the photos Alix had taken.

'You're staring,' he said. 'Can I get you something?'

Remy shook her head. He'd already dried her and
liberally dowsed her in talcum powder. 'I need a drink. It
can wait.'

'I can run up to the kitchen.'

'No.'

'Really. I'll be two minutes.'

Bath sheet loosely tied around his middle, Silk unlatched the door and left her in the candlelight.

Remy stared at the door, amazed. Was he like this with everyone? The evidence said otherwise. There were a few points to clear up with him now, as well as Takeshi. First, she needed him to realise that, while this was fun, it wasn't about to turn into anything more deep and meaningful.

She gulped, recoiling from the thought. How was it that all her interactions with men seemed to lead towards relationships? Sticky, convoluted, difficult relationships. Couldn't they be attracted to each other, have sex when they felt like it and cut the crappy emotional-baggage part out? She didn't need the binds and expectations, and she was sure they didn't, either. For the first time, she wondered if she used the complex relationships of her *manga* books to experience vicariously the pains of separations. The fatal flaw was that she was already emotionally hung up on both men. But that still didn't mean she wanted to be in a relationship with either of them. Besides, she was still more interested in their relationship with each other.

Silk hadn't commented on her fantasy, and she felt weirdly embarrassed about asking him if it had turned him on. Maybe she'd spilled a few too many intimate details.

'Dark thoughts?' he asked, when he returned a few minutes later carrying two mugs of frothy chocolate topped with marshmallows, and a plateful of biscuits.

Remy looked up at him from under her fringe, but didn't move her head from her knees. 'Pitch black.'

'The best kind.' He passed over a mug and sat beside her. 'There's no sign of life up there. I hope everything's sorted out. The weekend's going to be a bit of a nonevent if Shaun and Chelsea aren't talking.'

'You don't think they'll call it off, do you?' Bugger. In

all this excitement, that particular hitch had flown her mind. She wondered if Alix had talked sense into Chelsea yet.

'No.' Silk didn't sound too certain. 'Chelsea will realise her mother was just being a bitch. She knows Shaun's worst habit is his jealousy.'

'Nicked a few of his girlfriends, have you?'

'They were never his girlfriends. No matter what he thought.'

Remy tried not to smirk as she lifted a marshmallow from her drink and sucked the chocolate from its surface. 'What do you expect me to think? You did bed all three bridesmaids last night.'

'Actually, they jumped me while I was asleep.'

'Yeah, right.' She swallowed the marshmallow. Just as it was *Takeshi* who'd kissed *him*.

'I walked out, remember? I'm not interested in them, Remy.' He stroked a finger across her brow, and the knot in her stomach transformed into a flutter of panic. 'I'd rather have you.'

'Takeshi,' she hissed. He was supposed to fall for him, not her.

Silk's eyes narrowed. 'Oh, yes, your boyfriend. I forgot.'

He hadn't really forgotten Takeshi, not for moment. It was impossible when she dragged him into the heart of every conversation, and every intimate caress. What was it about the guy that made him so pervasive? Did he feel guilty for trying to poach her? No, he didn't. The only person who thought they were an item was Takeshi.

Silk watched the muscles of her calves flex as she climbed the steps ahead of him. They were the colour of buttermilk, creamy and smooth. She had beautiful legs. He'd loved the feel of them as she'd sat astride him in the bath. The way she'd so casually draped them over the side, so he could soap her clit. Damn! It had blown him away. He wanted her again now. Just watching the pitter-patter of her bare feet on the stairs was threatening to tent the towel tied around his waist. But part of him was deeply suspicious about getting too close. Was he being set up? Just thinking about her fantasy of him and Takeshi gave him acid heartburn, or butterflies of lust. He wasn't sure which, maybe a touch of both. But he definitely wasn't interested in getting physical with him. Hell, he wasn't interested in their becoming any more than passing acquaintances.

Remy paused by the door to the second-floor corridor and turned towards him. His eyes were level with her breasts, which looked full and bouncy, tugged tightly together by the knotted towel. He lifted his gaze, determined not to stare.

'I'm going up,' she said. 'Need to find some clothes. Guess you do too.'

He nodded, and suppressed a smile when he noticed that she was also having trouble deciding where to look. Her gaze was lingering around his navel, where the towel skimmed over his hips and highlighted the action-man lines on both sides of his abdomen. Maybe they should forget clothes. Maybe he ought to loop her hands around the rope banister, slide up the aubergine towel and take her from behind. He felt his cock rising at the picture of her creamy backside, and her pert cheeks dusted honey-gold by the fake torchlight.

'Silk.' She leant towards him, so that her toes curled around the lip of the step.

No. He pulled back from her, the uncontrolled lust in his throat convincing him that it was time for some separation. He wanted to spend the night with her. They could curl up on a sheepskin rug before a roaring fire, or luxuriate in a sumptuous four-poster bed. But he needed to catch his breath, and it was also time he checked up on Shaun.

'Later. I ought to make sure the wedding's still on.' He briefly brushed his lips to her cheek, then watched her continue up the stairs until she disappeared around the bend.

Silk crossed the hall to his room. Shaun wasn't there, but he hadn't really expected him to be. Silk pulled on a pair of navy lounge pants, and headed along the corridor to the living room, where he found Shaun sitting in the dark before the fire.

He watched his friend stare morosely into the flames for a moment, before crouching on the rug beside him. 'No sign of Chelsea?'

'Nope. Haven't seen her. No one has.' Shaun's gaze never moved from the blaze.

'Have you tried her room?'

He turned his cheek towards Silk. 'I'm not completely stupid. I've tried it five times in the last hour. It's locked, and I can't just let myself in because the dress might be on the bed or something. It's bad luck for me to see it.'

'Still thinking positive thoughts, then?'

Shaun scowled and produced a bottle from between his thighs, where he'd been cradling it. He took a liberal swig.

'OK, bad joke. But this won't help.' Silk snatched the bottle from his grasp. 'How much have you had?' He held up the bottle to the light, so the contents glowed like venom. Shaun shrugged. It was about a quarter gone. 'Keep it up and the only girl you'll see is the green fairy.'

'I'm drowning my sorrows. Mates are supposed to help.'

Silk took a swig, winced and shivered as the angry green pixie juice scorched its way down his throat. 'I'll get us some glasses, shall I?'

Shaun closed his fist around the neck of the bottle. 'Waste of time. Where've you been? You could have stuck around to help me sort things out. I had to walk back with the Gorgons. The three of them just kept apologising.'

'I, um, had to wash my hair.' He ran his fingers through the damp strands.'

'You've been fucking. I'm pissed, not stupid. It wasn't Dolores again, was it?'

'As if.' Silk swallowed a second draft of the liquid, more as a show of solidarity than out of any real desire. He'd never drunk remotely as much as Shaun did. Normally, he was too preoccupied with other pleasures, and he liked to keep his wits about him. 'Why do we drink this stuff? It tastes like the venomous squeezed liver of an alcoholic sweetshop owner.'

'It's the romantic drink of poets.'

'Shaun! It's head-fuck juice. It causes sane men to do crazy things, and it's probably the closest thing we have to the Pan-Galactic Gargle-Blaster.' He held it at arm's length. 'And it tastes like cold fire.'

'It's fucking great, yeah?'

Silk shook his head. 'Yeah, it's fucking great. Now, what are you going to do about sorting things out with Chelsea?'

'Dunno. Sleep on it.'

'And face it in the morning, with a hangover, I suppose?'

'It's a plan.'

'It's a dumb plan. The wedding's tomorrow.'

Silk pulled his hands through his long hair again and let it fall through his fingers. Judging by Shaun's glazed expression, it was already too late to hope for sense tonight. He should have got here earlier, and someone other than Alix should have gone after Chelsea in the church. He trusted the fiery dyke to be neutral about men as much as he trusted the blue-haired biker not to touch. Everything was screwed up.

Remy headed up the eight steps to her garret, to find Takeshi sitting cross-legged on her bed.

'Everybody else came back ages ago,' he said gruffly. 'Where've you been?'

'I thought that was obvious.' She dropped the towel and padded nude across the room. The floorboards creaked as she neared the bed. She could feel Takeshi watching her, although she avoided making eye contact. They needed to have this conversation, but she didn't really want to start it. Remy snatched up her sloppy jumper and pulled it over her head. She should have woken him first thing and set things straight, not left it until she'd been with Silk. She stared at his boots a moment, mildly annoyed that he had them on her bed, then turned her back on him and snatched up a perfume bottle. Why did things always have to be so convoluted? Other people had simple relationships, didn't they? So why did she have Alix, Silk and Takeshi all after a piece of her? Irritably, Remy spritzed the perfume. Men, fucking men – and lesbians! Did she really need any of them?

'You still reek of him.'

Remy twisted around on the spot. 'What?'

'Silk. I can smell him on you.'

A hard lump of indignation formed in her throat, but all she could do was stare. There was no way he could smell Silk on her skin. He was guessing, or he'd seen them return. Still, at least it meant she wasn't going to have to break it to him.

'Good, was it?'

'None of your fucking business.'

'Isn't it?' He got off the bed. 'I thought we had something, Remy, you and I. We do have something.'

Remy backed away from him, until her backside made contact with the rough-hewn wall below the window. Something about his stance, the way his shoulders were squared and his feet were planted, spelt trouble – the sort of head-on-collision trouble you couldn't easily side-step. She'd thought he was predominantly about fun, but somewhere behind the *anime* mask was rage and sorrow. She could see it in the dark smudges beneath his eyes and the tension in his jaw. Why had she never noticed the vengeful fire in his eyes?

He seized her wrist, sniffed the fingertips, then softly bit the pad of her thumb. Alarmed, Remy snatched her hand away, bringing her elbow back hard against the wooden shutter in the process. 'Ow!'

The light in his eyes was black. He took her hand again and kissed the palm, worked upwards towards her bruised elbow, so that his tongue tip trailed over the skin, raising the sensitive hairs.

A tremor ran up her arm and down her spine. 'Stop it! Yes, I've been with him. So what? You don't own me.'

His mouth closed over the fleshy crease of her inner elbow. 'Takeshi!' She snatched her arm free of his grasp and put both behind her back. A wash of colour and heat seeped across her skin from her cheeks down to her already awakening clit. 'Get off me! I invited you here to model, not to play at being my boyfriend. I made it plain before you agreed to come.'

'And then you broke the agreement.' He grasped her shoulders, pressed up close.

'You came to me last night.'

'And you invited me in. You could have told me to go.' He nudged her chin upwards with the side of his fist. I love you, said the light in his blazing eyes.

'Jesus! Shit!' Remy dragged a hand through her damp hair. This was all crazy, and way too intense. Takeshi's hands closed over hers, and laced with her fingers and hair. He drew their hands free of the strands, and held them like a barrier between them.

'We could've had him together.' He forced her palms to her sides, then on to his hips.

His lips closed over hers, pulling her into the mire of his lust – a swirling, burning space of heat and lava. It was easy to get drunk on his kisses. There was something about them, something mysterious and appealing that tugged the strings of her psyche. They had such a bitter-sweet tang. But, she wouldn't play his game. She had to be in control.

Remy turned her head away, and pushed him back one step. 'Stop it! Stop it now.'

'We're good together. You came so hard you could barely breathe.'

'I was thinking of him.'

Takeshi's eyes turned inky black. 'Of me with him. What's this all about, Remy? Are you going to play us off until the only solace we can find is in each other's arms, just so you can then get off on watching us? What happens when we both walk away?'

'You're the one playing cat and mouse.'

'Guess that makes you the dog.'

She slapped his face. She looked at her stinging palm. Her mouth was dry, and her pulse was pounding in her ears.

Takeshi grabbed her and sent her sprawling across the bed. He covered her with his body, grabbed her wrists and pinned her down. 'That hurt!'

His breath was hot against her face.

His cock was hard against her thigh.

'What are you going to do, fuck me into submission? It still won't make me your girl.'

He released her more violently than he'd grabbed her. For a split second, he stood by the bedside looking down at her, his face deathly white and his eyes full of ghosts.

Remy sat. 'Takeshi?'

He jerked away from her, and fled down the stairs.

'What the hell!' Remy launched herself on to her feet, dragging the bedclothes with her. What was that all about? One minute he's coming on way too strong. The next, he's seen a phantom.

She scampered down the stairs after him, too late. The reverberated thud of the front door being slammed echoed up the spiral. Remy raced into the kitchen and wrenched open the nearest set of shutters. She lifted the sash window and stuck her head out. The sky was black with just a flash of light on the horizon, as if someone had drawn zigzags across the sky with a neon-pink highlighter.

'Takeshi!'

He was on the drive below. He pulled his helmet on in response to her voice. Remy watched him straddle his bike and rev the engine. The back wheel spun and he sped off in a shower of gravel.

Buggery bollocks! She hadn't meant to chase him off. She just wanted him to understand that this wasn't about anything deep. It wasn't that she had anything against him. They could still be friends. She just had other plans for him and Silk. Was that selfish?

'What's up, baby doll?' Alix clamped a hand on her shoulder. Her smile vanished the moment she saw Remy's face. 'No, really. What's up? What's happened? Has Chelsea called everything off?'

Remy took a breath and exhaled slowly, trying to calm her frantic heart rate. 'I need your help.'

'Anything, babe, you know.'

'Go after Takeshi for me, and bring him back. He's taken his bike.'

'Remy.' A deep furrow creased Alix's brow.

'Please.' She guided Alix towards the stairs.

'Wait. What happened? Have you fallen out?' Alix planted her feet, but Remy urged her forward.

'Quick, or you'll never catch him.'

Remy watched impatiently from the castle door as Alix pulled on her boots and zipped and buckled her jacket. There were times – this being one of them – when a driving licence and vehicle would be really darn useful.

What had she said to make him scarper like that?

Takeshi zipped up his jacket, and pulled on his helmet. The cloud cover was making a mockery of the twilight.

The sky was black and creepy. He wished for the city, for the screaming neon and multi-tonal traffic signals. He wasn't even sure there were cats' eyes on the main roads out here. He knocked the bike lights on, creating a beacon for all the flying insects to descend upon. A stray moth landed on the speedo dial. Disgusted, he flicked it away. The bike sputtered, then roared into life towards the gloomy dip between the rock faces that supported the rickety bridge. He'd taken an instant dislike to that spot on arrival. It reminded him of someplace else. He kept expecting someone to leap from it – dive into his headlight as he sped below. He didn't want to look up at it, either, just in case there was a corpse hanging. Over-active imagination? Perhaps!

It was too quiet. He needed noise beyond the whistling wind and growling engine to drown out the roaring inside his head. Takeshi reached for the CD player that wasn't there. He'd left his customised bike back in Japan, had started over with a Honda Fireblade. It was cool, with its sleek *manga*-like lines in black and silver. The kind of bike Cloud Strife rode out of Shinra HQ, but it wasn't the same as his old fantasy piece, even if it did, as one reviewer put it, 'accelerate like a scalded cat'.

Out past the gate, the lanes were waterlogged. Mud splattered his leathers as he revved the engine and chugged through. Standing water wasn't going to stop him tonight. He needed to be out of the castle, away from Remy and her emotional constipation, away from the blond demon whom he both wanted and hated.

Low-hanging branches reached towards him like skeletal hands. One scratched along the side of his helmet, and a shiver went up his spine. The iridescent flare of another light caught his attention in his mirrors. Someone was coming up behind him, and, considering they were just off private property, it was probably someone come to take him back. If it was Remy, he'd be flattered. He might even forgive her choice of words. She couldn't know what she'd said, what unpleasant memory she'd dredged up.

Of course it wasn't Remy. She didn't have a licence. It was Alix, he realised, recognising her old Ducati. Remy had sent her wannabe lover after him, as if that were going to charm him into coming back before he was ready. He wanted to stay out. Wanted to tear up the world with his noise, until all around him was nothing more than a rushing blur of colour and he was numb with exhaustion. He didn't want to think. He didn't want to think at all. And he definitely didn't want to talk to Alix.

He'd spent his youth in senseless chases. If he could outmanoeuvre a squad of police cars, he could race her, even down country lanes. And the Monster had always been a twitchy ride, prone to giving your ass a good thwacking at any kind of speed.

Takeshi opened the throttle, and idly watched the speedo climb. He went into the next corner hard, hitting the back break as he hit the apex of the curve. The back wheel slid sideways. He opened the throttle and shot away. It was a crazy move to do at dusk when the sky seemed to be full of moths and the lanes were sodden and unfamiliar, but he was feeling reckless.

The road filtered on to a slip lane at that point, taking him on to a stretch of dual carriageway. Takeshi leant closer to the chassis, and kicked the bike up a few gears. He was cruising at an easy ninety, but a quick glance in his mirrors confirmed she was still on his tail. He didn't fancy taking this as far as the motorway, so he took the next exit, only to find himself taking several sharp corners before ending up on a bumpy lane, heading towards some heritage site. Takeshi dropped the power off a bit and followed the gravel strip down the middle of the lane. He'd lost sight of Alix, but that didn't mean she wasn't still behind.

Rather abruptly, the road funnelled through a wooden

gate into a deserted picnic area surrounded by a copse of trees. A pair of squirrels were wrestling over a half-eaten chocolate bar. Faced with lights and noise, they both ran. The one hampered by the chocolate trophy headed straight for him. Takeshi automatically hit the front brakes, causing the bike to judder, before he remembered to release the throttle. The squirrel froze. Takeshi swerved, sending the bike into a power slide across the blanket of wet leaves.

The next thing he was aware of was putting his hands out to save himself, then burning heat in his palms, despite his gloves. The Blade skidded over the wet grass, finally landing with a thump against a gnarled tree root.

Takeshi shook off the adrenaline blur and shock and rolled on to his left side to investigate the damage. He'd given himself a few nice bruises by the feel of it, and muddied up his leathers, but otherwise he was intact, cushioned by the grass and leaf litter. He turned on to his front, and looked morosely at his bike. The engine was still chugging. He doubted there was any damage, but even so . . .

Alix's headlight illuminated his prone form. Takeshi squinted. Life just kept getting better. She stopped a few yards away, released her auburn corkscrew curls, and after an ungainly dismount dropped her helmet on the bench of a nearby picnic table. 'You fucking idiot. It's dark, wet and you're going for the ton. Do you have a frigging death wish, or what?' She looked down at him disdainfully, where he was lying in the mulch. 'So what have you broken?'

He wished he could pull the leaves over his head like a blanket and hide. Instead, he got to his knees, pulled off his gloves and flipped up his visor. 'I've skinned my leathers saving a squirrel, and I wouldn't have done that if I hadn't been trying to lose you. Should have remembered, though.' He tugged off his helmet. 'You're not too hot on taking hints. I mean, you've been best friends with a girl for eight years, and you still haven't figured out she's never going to let you screw her.' He was on the offensive, determined that, since she'd caught him, he wasn't going to take any crap.

'Hey, Romeo,' she planted her hands on her tiny hips, 'You're walking a thin line with me already, so quit with the snide remarks and listen up. Remy asked me to find you, so I'm here. She'd like you to come back.'

'Too busy screwing Silk again to come herself, is she?' He turned his back and hauled the heavy bike upright. Aside from a layer of mulch, it too appeared to have escaped unscathed. The mirror had folded back on its springs. He flicked down the stand, and straightened the handlebars. '*Kuso!*' The impact had forced them against the engine cover, creating a dent.

Takeshi ran his finger along the gouge, then kicked a pile of leaves, sending them swirling into the air. Alix was still watching him. Why couldn't she just take the hint? He stared at the bark of the nearby tree, deliberately trying to blank her. There was moss growing like a green beard around a bulbous stump that if you squinted formed a nose, and above that two gnarled branches formed eyebrows over sunken pits.

Her hand closed around his shoulder, the grip strong without being too imposing. She'd removed her gloves. 'Takeshi. I didn't know it was about Silk, OK?' She stroked the side of his neck, just below his hairline. 'If I had ... Well, I don't know. I suppose it was kind of inevitable. He is her type. Oceans of blond hair, big eyes, broad shoulders. Back at uni, a guy with long hair just had to walk past her and she'd be all over him.'

'Will you fuck the hell off and leave me alone!' Takeshi swallowed. He could already feel his barriers crumbling. Inside he was shaking. '*Kudasai!*' He closed his eyes, but that only brought everything into sharper focus. There was no distraction on the blank canvas of his eyelids, no patterns to make in the dark. Why that precise phrase? Why had she used a set of words he never wanted to hear again? The fact that she'd said it in a different language didn't change the meaning.

The scene opened like a cinema reel across the canvas of his mind. Osaka by night: a place of wet gliding tarmac. A neon dream of lipstick-pink and *idoru* curves. Tight boyish arse and schoolgirl bangs. She blinked, looked straight at him. Blew his name to him as if it were a kiss. Megumi, the cutest, most infuriating brat he'd ever known. At twelve, she'd stolen his ride and trashed his bodywork in a race by scraping the whole bike along an alley wall. Then she'd hit fifteen, and flowered. By the time he quit high school, she was heading for a career as a barrister, an unusual choice for a *bosozoku*, who spent more than a little time fleeing the wrath of the law. But her first love was still her bike, though Takeshi thought he ran a close second. That was until the day Ryuji turned up. He remembered the bike throbbing between his thighs as he watched them kissing on a street corner, acting as if he didn't care, when inside his heart was corroding.

She'd got into the whole cosplay thing in addition to the bikes by then. She'd been with her girlfriends that night, the group of them all painted up like *anime* dolls. His cock had been hard from the purring motor and seeing the arch of her slender white neck, and the sheer length of her legs. She rarely wore a skirt, let alone one so short. But she'd done it for Ryuji.

So nonchalant, so blasé, so hopelessly affected and naïve. In turmoil, he'd French-kissed her friend, Yukie, who'd taken him to the *kabuki* to watch a rendition of *Benten Kozô*. Takeshi had fallen in lust, sneaked backstage, deserting his date, and smeared the greasepaint of the *kumadori* star. He'd finished the night with his first stage-door encounter. He'd never seen the girl again, but the show and the star he'd gone back to, until, drowned in red and white kisses, he thought he could face Megumi and Ryuji again. Of course, he'd been wrong, so very wrong. And, when he'd pinned her down and tried to get her to see sense, she'd flung that little gem at him. No matter what he did, he couldn't change the fact that she was in love with someone else.

Alix rested her forehead against the space between his shoulder blades. Takeshi clamped his lips together. The words he wanted to speak, wanted so desperately to share, made his tongue feel swollen. Was this the time and place? Was he going to give up his past to a woman with a parallel agenda?

'I thought it was an act,' she whispered, 'but I realise now that you're actually in love with her.'

For a moment, he was confused over whom they were talking about, before the present flooded his emotions again, leaving him tasting bile. He kicked a stone. It bounded over several hummocks, and into the long grass. Remy made him feel the same way Megumi had: alive and free, although, to begin with, she'd just made him feel. Before she'd chased him to the park, sex had become mechanical, a rubbing, jerking motion he engaged in twice a week with strangers, whose names he learned only so he could add them to a list on the wall. Remy had opened his heart to the possibility of something more than that again. Hell, they'd already shared more than that. He'd spent last night in her bed sharing intimate fantasies. He'd lost Megumi, but he wasn't going to lose Remy, especially not to an arrogant fool like Silk.

Alix squeezed the knots of tension at the back of his neck. 'Don't give up. He may be pretty but he's still a vain bastard with no regard for anyone else, and who'll drop her the minute another pretty girl walks by.'

Takeshi dragged his hand through his sweat-dampened hair. 'So why are you rooting for me all of a sudden?'

Her hand crept forward around the edge of his collar,

then traced the metal river of his zip. 'Well, I'm not exactly getting anywhere.'

He eyed her cautiously, dubious of the hand of friendship she seemed to be extending. She had no reason to like him, had done little more than tolerate him since they'd met. Maybe she was just being sympathetic because she'd already decided that, like her, he didn't stand a chance, or maybe it was just a ruse. Did he care?

She pressed a single finger to his chest. 'So what if she's had Silk, it's only what you said you were going to do.'

Takeshi stared at her finger. 'It's not just about him. It's not even about her. She just said the wrong thing, OK?' He pulled his keys from the ignition, and scrambled up the bank of gnarled tree roots.

The woodland was dark and uninviting. It looked oppressing. What he needed was space, time to think things over and develop a strategy.

'What did she say?' Alix pulled herself up the bank behind him.

'Forget it.' His past was his, and it wasn't something he was prepared to dissect with a stranger. Alix took his hand, but even that didn't persuade him. He didn't want to get maudlin. He just needed some perspective. Admittedly, it was the sort of perspective that imagined Silk trussed up like a suckling pig, with a ball gag in his mouth and a huge dildo up his arse, but what the heck!

'Come back with me.'

Takeshi rubbed a hand through his silver-blue hair. 'OK,' he agreed, 'but don't expect me to sit and talk it out over a nice cup of tea.'

An hour had passed since Silk had sat down with Shaun, although it felt like two, and, beyond an apology, they still didn't have a plan for how to patch things up with

Chelsea. Eventually the absinthe blacked out Shaun's moroseness and dropped him head first on to the carpet. Silk peeled his friend off the floor and half-steered, half-carried him along the corridor to their room, where he bundled him into bed fully clothed apart from his socks, which he thoughtfully pulled off. Worn socks equalled cold feet, cold feet meant a restless night, and the groom still needed some decent rest to look presentable at his wedding. Which reminded him. He rummaged through Shaun's makeup on the nightstand, found his black lipstick and replaced it with the more fetching shade of plum Chelsea preferred. The wedding would go ahead, he convinced himself. Shaun and Chelsea were too good together for it not to. He was just going to have to motivate Romeo big time in the morning.

Silk climbed beneath the covers of his own bed and settled down. He was still wearing the jersey pants he'd pulled on after his bath with Remy, and now, away from the fire, he was feeling a little goose-bumped and irritable again. It wasn't supposed to be like this now that he'd been with her, he was supposed to be relaxed, calmer. Silk looked across the dark divide between the bed at Shaun, who was noisily fly catching, his head crooked painfully to one side. He guessed he should prod him, but somehow he doubted it would raise anything more than a grunt. Instead, he shuffled further down his own bed and turned his vision upward, seeing a montage of images imposed upon the ceiling: Remy in the rain with her eye makeup smudged and rivulets running across her naked breasts; the soft weight of her breasts bouncing as she rocked up and down on his cock; Takeshi's cock dipping between her parted thighs, while the glistening silver dragon on his back writhed and danced, until it grew close enough to him – their uninvited observer – to surround his body totally and squeeze him tight.

Serpentine eyes met his gaze, widened into the hollow dark of Takeshi's pupils. The way he'd seen them when they'd first kissed.

Hell, that made it sound really bad, as if he expected there to be many more kisses to follow.

The thought of the other man's lips upon his own was all it took to make him writhe. Silk rolled over, trapping his erection between his body and the mattress as he steadfastly tried to ignore it.

It was happening again. Every time he thought of Remy, Takeshi took over. He'd thought it would be different after what they'd shared earlier. Clearly, the blue-haired bug was going to be harder to dislodge than he'd anticipated. He was just too persistent, like the excitement centred on his groin. Denying its presence was pointless, but how to deal with it? He was just hot for Remy again, he decided. That was all.

Except it was the idea of Takeshi's hand, not hers, brushing along his shaft that was turning him on.

Silk turned on to his side.

Shaun's drunken snores were growing louder, each irritating wheeze now punctuated by an almighty grunt. Silk pulled the pillow over his head. Unfortunately, the lack of oxygen made his head swim even faster.

Admit it. You want him, his conscience whispered. You want to feel his lips, the way his kiss touched your throat and darted down to your cock. You want to feel him nuzzle up against your groin again. Accept it, you want him.

Silk pictured Takeshi's dark, dark eyes with their beautiful almond shape, his dark eyelashes and a stray lock of silver-blue hair. Suddenly, his lips felt swollen. They parted apprehensively as the imaginary Takeshi leant in to deliver a kiss. Yum! his body sighed, as his lips brushed against the pillow. Ack, no! said his brain. I'm heterosexual. I'm normal, whatever that is. I'm not into guys. I'm not into guys.

He threw off the pillow, which landed across Shaun's chest. He couldn't carry on like this, naked and hungry in the dark. Besides, any more snores and there wouldn't be a wedding, because he'd have murdered the groom.

Silk padded back to the dark lounge and heaped more coal on to the dying fire. He sat in Shaun's former spot, prodding at the embers until the poker became too hot. Dropping that, he lifted the empty absinthe bottle. It too was hot, the dregs condensing around the neck.

He palmed the matches next, struck one after another, and watched them burn until he almost singed his fingers. Down to the last two, he lifted the spirit bottle again, unscrewed the lid and dropped a flame into the vapour-filled inside. It flared, blue with an orange heart, then vanished with a scream, leaving the dead match in the bottom. He wished that all ghosts were so easily dispersed.

The last match he held between his index fingers. There was a tightening in his stomach like exam nerves. He could live in denial or he could try to sort this mess out.

He put the match back in the box. They'd need it to light the fire in the morning. Besides, what he needed now was a catharsis, not pyromania.

Silk shuffled back to rest his head against the sofa, and allowed his palm to close over his aching erection. If he was going to sleep tonight, he needed to get off. At least he could keep his thoughts private.

He slid his hand inside his pants and stretched out his toes.

12

Remy was sitting in the dark before the kitchen stove with Shadow in her lap, when Alix returned. 'Thank God!' She bounded to her feet, dislodging Shadow, despite his attempts to cling to her trousers. 'Did you catch up with him? Did he come back with you? What happened?'

Alix backed away from the questions, and began spooning chocolate powder into a mug. Her nose and cheeks were an ice-blasted pink, which made her ringlets seem wilder than ever. Remy glared at her. She'd been waiting for ages. She needed answers. 'Alix!'

The photographer splashed milk on top of the chocolate powder and whisked the mixture. 'He's outside on the gravel, giving his bike a rubdown.'

Remy frowned. Rubdowns were what you gave horses, weren't they? 'Did he say why he stormed off?'

'Not exactly.' Alix picked up the kettle and poured boiling water into her mug, causing the chocolate to froth. 'You'd better ask him yourself, but I think sleeping with Silk is probably the crux of it. Honestly, Remy, do you never think about anybody's feelings?'

'I didn't plan it, you know. It just sort of happened.' Besides, Takeshi's reason for leaving had to be more complex than that. He'd been upset, but that didn't explain why he'd gone from hot to cold in the space of a breath.

Alix put her back to the workbench, and cradled her steaming mug. 'Forget it. I don't need to know. Just don't involve me in any more of your lovers' tiffs. It's hard enough knowing you're screwing someone else without having to mediate 'cause you can't decide which guy you want to be with.'

'I'm sorry,' Remy bowed her head. Now she'd managed to alienate Alix too.

'Whatever.' Alix turned her back.

'Remy!' The shout echoed up the stairwell. A moment later Eloise barrelled through the wooden door. 'Remy! I don't know what happened. Everything's trashed, and Chelsea's lost it. You've got to come quick.'

Trashed! The word flashed across her vision like a lightning strike. If this was a joke, it was in seriously bad taste. She sprinted down the stairs, jumping the last four in her haste to reach the workroom. She could hear Alix and Eloise behind her.

'Sev managed to winkle her out of her room about forty minutes ago,' Eloise was saying, 'but she's well out of it. I mean, it's not as if Shaun and I actually did anything. It was all me. He just wanted to get some kip, and he was murmuring her name the whole time.'

'Too much info.' Alix raised her hand to ward her off. 'Until I'm getting some too, I don't want to know the sordid details of everyone else's sexploits.'

Remy stopped abruptly just inside the workroom. There were clothes everywhere. Her entire stock had been flung around like jumble, and at the centre of the devastation sat Chelsea, her flaxen hair falling like a sheet of gold across her back, clutching a coat.

Remy picked her way cautiously over the sea of delicate fabrics, Shadow padding lightly behind her. He slipped inside the flared sleeve of a dress as she reached Chelsea, and eyed the bride-to-be suspiciously. Remy grasped Chelsea's shoulder. 'What the hell happened?' Chelsea pulled the back panel of the coat out taut. Someone had painted the word 'wanker' across the brocade.

'Shit!' Remy tore the morning coat from her grasp.

'And this.' Severina emerged from the shadows by the

chimney, and threw the remains of a shirt at Remy. It had a heart-shaped piece cut from it. 'Whose is it?'

'It's Shaun's,' bubbled Chelsea.

'It could be Silk's.' Severina looked optimistically at Remy.

Remy shook her head. The outfits were very similar, but Silk had kept his after the fitting. This had to be Shaun's. She turned the coat over, and the curved front immediately confirmed it. Silk's coat was cut straight. 'Who found this?'

'We did.' Sev pointed at herself and Chelsea.

'What were you doing down here?'

'It wasn't me,' Chelsea blurted. She grabbed at the coat sleeves and attempted to pull it from Remy's grasp.

'I never thought it was.' Remy let the fabric go, but her eyebrows rose in alarm when her friend crushed the fabric to her cheek.

'We came down to take another look at the dress. Chelsea kept muttering some rubbish about seeing it for the last time. She seems to think Shaun's about to run off with my sister.'

'Which is complete bollocks.' Eloise ventured into the room to join the huddle. 'Honestly, Chelsea. He's only got eyes for you. And besides –' she nervously paced from one foot to the other '– he wears far too much makeup. We'd look like the gothic ugly sisters together.'

Chelsea lashed out from her seated position, and caught Eloise hard across the knee. The bridesmaid crumpled into the pile of clothing.

'Ow! I'm sorry. Nothing happened between us.' She crossed her arms in front of her face. 'I'd just been queening Silk and I was totally revved up. I've been fantasising about him since I was fourteen. It wasn't supposed to involve Shaun. He just walked in on me.'

Chelsea looked at her for a long moment, her face suffused with a mixture of misery and fury. Eloise must have thought she was going to lash out again.

'Don't hit me,' she pleaded.

But Chelsea willed her internal turmoil to subside some – albeit with difficulty. After another moment her expression softened and she offered her hand. Startled, Eloise took it. Then they were both hugging, and sniffling into each other's shoulder.

'Glad that's sorted,' muttered Alix. 'It's like a soap opera around here.'

Chelsea drew back from the embrace. Some of the shadows had already washed from her face. She gave Remy a watery smile, then stiffened. 'My dress! Shit, Remy, my dress!'

Remy searched the floor, scooped up the black and purple taffeta, and began to give it a once-over.

'It's fine, no panic.' Remy completed her check. 'I'll have to press it again, though. You should take it up to your room once I'm done.' She found a hanger. 'Now, when are you going to talk to Shaun?'

Chelsea shook her head. 'You can dress him in something else, can't you?'

'Does that mean the wedding's still on?'

Chelsea shrugged her shoulders.

Remy looked around at the piles of clothing. 'I reckon I can find something. Assuming nothing else is damaged.'

'Doesn't look like it.' Alix lifted several garments. 'Just crumpled. Who do you think is responsible?'

'My mother.' Chelsea rose to her feet. 'She's been a complete bitch since she arrived. Mind you, she's been totally screwy ever since Dad left.'

Severina found a perch on an empty trunk. 'Yeah, but actual sabotage? Besides, I don't think it could have been. Shaun's dad phoned a while ago to say he'd seen her in the village. Apparently, she's booked herself into the Hog's Head.'

'Yeah,' Eloise agreed. 'And she'd hardly walk all the way back here just to mess up some clothes, when she'd have to knock to get in.'

Remy sucked hard on her tongue. Silk hadn't locked the door behind them, and it had been unlocked the whole time Takeshi and Alix had been out. Alix was giving her looks that suggested she was thinking along the same lines. Still, she wasn't convinced. Chelsea's mother was no walker, and tossing clothes around didn't seem her style. Besides, her outfit was on the floor too.

'Well, I assume it wasn't any of you lot.' Chelsea turned her head to look at each of them in turn. 'And I don't think it was Silk or Shaun.'

'Or Takeshi,' Remy added.

'That only leaves Lulu and Marianne.'

It was only then that Remy noticed the absence of the third bridesmaid. 'Where is Lulu?'

'Out howling at the moon or something.' Sev flicked her gaze upwards. 'But it wasn't her. No way.'

'I'll go find Marianne and have a quiet word.' Alix planted her hands on her hips. 'Chelsea, wash your face, then get to bed if you don't want to spend the next forty years looking at pictures of yourself with puffy eyes.'

Chelsea nodded. 'I think there's some cucumber in the fridge.' She turned to Remy. 'You still think I should marry him, don't you.'

'Sure. Forgive and forget, right.'

Alix raised her eyebrows. 'Don't you stay up all night either. I want you fresh as a daisy by eight, so I can catch the light in your room. Payment shoot,' she added when Remy stared at her blankly.

'Yeah, sure.' Remy sighed and contemplated camera sabotage as a get-out clause. She wanted her butt plastered over art gallery walls about as much as she wanted an intimate candlelit supper with Takeshi, Alix and Silk, but a deal was a deal.

'What happened between you and Takeshi?' Severina asked, once Alix had left.

Remy shrugged. 'I got naked with Silk.'

'Bitch! The whole way?' Severina turned on her, eyes blazing.

Remy apprehensively nodded.

'There's a waiting list. You can't just jump in.'

'Didn't know.' Remy bowed her head and started picking up the clothes. Whoever heard of a waiting list for a bloke? Actually, the thought was repulsive. She thought about Takeshi. She guessed she hadn't really considered his feelings. She'd best go up to his room and find him once she'd finished putting this lot away, and try to make some peace.

Up in the lounge, Silk was oblivious of the commotion. The shrieks of outrage and distress didn't reach him. The only sounds were the crackle of the fire and the slick swish of his hand moving back and forth along his shaft. The stress was seeping from his body; all the mixed emotions that were clouding his thoughts were dispersing. In his head, he was outside again, watching raindrops scintillate like tears in Remy's eyelashes, and remembering the weight of her astride his hips.

Silk drew his tongue over his lips. He'd tasted her heat in the sweat and perfume of her body. She'd looked so perfect with her clothes soaked and her makeup smeared. He'd wanted to take her right there in the muddy puddle, where the ozone charge in the air magnified the result of every caress and made his senses tingle.

The fire before him crackled, and the coals collapsed in a shower of embers. Silk watched them flare orange and white. He felt calmer now. Each tug intensified the erotic burn and smoothed away the dilemmas he felt over Takeshi. He closed his eyes, and eased his thumb over the top of his slit as he tried to picture Remy and Takeshi together in his bed. He couldn't escape the draw of the silver-blue snake, but maybe he could make things more palatable for himself.

Yet there was a shadow on the edge of his conscience. His eyes fluttered open to find Takeshi's silhouette highlighted against the backdrop of the stairwell. The shock of discovery stilled the motion of his lungs, but his cock leapt. Their eyes locked. Takeshi's lip curled in amusement. 'Need some help with that?' he asked.

Silk's next breath came out sharp. It hissed between his teeth, as emotional as it was voluble. He couldn't stop himself. His balls felt high and hard and the feeling in his cock was divine. He was almost there, but he wouldn't let himself come looking the guy in the face. That connection wasn't there. They weren't lovers, and they never would be.

Silk let his head loll back against the sofa, but the scenario's potential continued to play out inside his head.

Takeshi walked over and knelt down by his thighs. His pink tongue flickered over his lips, obscenely suggestive and sweet with promise. His mouth closed over Silk's cock and engulfed him to where his own thumb and forefinger were curled around his shaft. Then a hand covered his own and began to dictate the rhythm of the strokes. The rough caresses were too much to resist. Bitter pleasure coiled in his balls and up his shaft. He was going to come in the guy's mouth.

Give it up to me, the voice inside his head coaxed. Takeshi's voice. You can't resist, can you, blondie?

He could resist this. He fought for an image of Remy, but all he got was a sense of her watching them from the periphery.

A digit touched his anus. Needle-sharp, his orgasm poured through his shaft, leaving the sticky splatter of his seed across his thighs.

Silk raised his head. The door on to the back stairs

was swinging open, but there was no sign of any figure. His mind was playing tricks on him. It was late. His need for pleasure was gone, but he'd come with the other man's name on his tongue.

The bedroom was dark when Alix went in. She'd knocked twice and got no response. The corsets Marianne had been given to dress in earlier were all neatly piled on the chair beside the tripod she'd set up, but there was no sign of the buxom jeweller.

Alix turned on the camera and briefly reviewed the first twenty or so images. There was nothing she considered perfectly framed among them, but, with four hundred plus pictures on the card, there was bound to be something they could use for the catalogue.

She switched the camera off again and swept her gaze over the furniture, seeking inspiration as to where the girl might be. The room was a twin, much like the one she was supposed to be sharing with Dolores. At least now the bitch had moved to the village, she'd be able to rest in an atmosphere that wasn't drowning in spite. Assuming she ever got any sleep, considering what had gone down tonight.

She spotted Takeshi's doll sitting by the window. Alix nonchalantly sauntered over. She couldn't resist giving the lump of moulded silicone a vicious prod. He'd just started to grow on her, but it was hard to feel sympathy for a man who'd spent this much on a sex doll. What was wrong with a real woman? It was sad, really, and sadder for the fact that he'd brought her to a wedding as if she were on the guest list. What woman was going to be impressed by that? Not Remy, she was sure. She wasn't even interested in live girls.

She guessed she was going to let go and put her firmly in the past.

Alix glanced around nervously. She'd left the door

open a crack, but not enough for anyone to see in from the corridor. The doll's hair felt real. The silky tresses slipped between her fingers.

Why was it that the only two women she'd ever really wanted were both in this building, but neither of them wanted her? Chelsea had Shaun, and Remy, well – it wasn't fair that she should lose out to a doll-owning maniac and Lord Übergoth.

She prodded the fleshy rubber again in morbid fascination, then upended the doll and lifted its skirt, just as she'd done to every Barbie doll she'd ever held. Unlike most of them, Tifa was wearing underwear. Delicate white lace tangas, with a floral pattern woven into the fabric.

Alix sat her back up, and peeked under her blouse, to find a matching lace bra supporting a heavy bust. It couldn't rival Marianne's, but it was considerably more ample than Alix's own. It was the work of mere moments to scoop one breast out of the lace to hold in her palm. There was no life in the flesh, but the texture and weight were reasonable approximations. She squeezed the nut-brown nipple, then lifted the skirt again and probed beneath the pants. She had hair.

She had hair!

Barbie was always clean-shaven. Mind, she'd never had any genitals, either.

Alix pulled the wispy pants aside and stared incredulously at the doll's triangle of dark-brown curls, her perfectly cast pudenda, and pearl-like clit. Laughter brewed inside her throat. OK, he was Japanese. Everyone knew they were weird when it came to sex, but pubic hair on a sex doll!

Alix shook her head, then stuck a finger between the doll's nether lips. The attention to detail extended to the inner workings too. She wondered which porn star she was modelled on. One with a plastic smile and considerably less pubic hair, she imagined.

She curled her finger, pressed the tip into the doll's lovingly recreated G-spot. Hey, she could practise her technique. She dabbed at the spongy bit of flesh, imagining it was Remy she was finger-fucking and not a lump of lifeless plastic.

She wiggled another two fingers inside, followed by a fourth, something she'd rarely managed with a partner. Of course, there was no lubrication and the fake flesh was clingy. Alix frowned in concentration, pushed in her thumb to make a fist, feeling a deep thrill of satisfaction. He may have fucked Remy – she wasn't going to fight the truth any more – but she'd fisted his doll. Of course, Remy had already moved on to Silk, and Takeshi was languishing like her, but in some convoluted, screwed-up way it still felt good. And they weren't really friends, just pretend ones. She'd merely done what was necessary to bring him back for Remy.

Except that it wasn't that simple.

She'd genuinely felt something for him out at the picnic spot. She'd sensed a loss that was far deeper than his affection for Remy, or even her own regrets. 'Issues, that boy,' she murmured to herself.

The bedroom door swung inwards. Alix blinked rapidly in confusion as the shaft of light from the corridor reached her by the window. The head of Takeshi's shadow drew level with her toes. 'Having fun?' he asked, holding his phone aloft to capture her image.

Alix jerked her hand from the doll. 'What are you doing here?'

He looked left and right. 'It's my room, unless I've got myself lost, and you're trying to turn my doll into a lesbian. What are you doing here, or did you really sneak in to molest Tifa?'

Alix hastily drew the shirt across the doll's exposed breast. 'I'm looking for Marianne. Someone's cut a hole in Shaun's wedding outfit and written "wanker" across his coat.'

'So, why do you want Marianne?'

Alix shrugged cagily. 'To eliminate her.'

'You think she did it? I thought she was hot in pursuit of Silk, not Shaun?'

'Maybe she thought it was Silk's.' Alix turned slowly as Takeshi circled around her. 'What are you thinking?'

He licked his lips. 'It could be her. She likes to be melodramatic, and Silk is a wanker.' He glanced at his phone. 'But, as you can see, she's not here.'

'No, guess not.' Alix carefully sat the doll upright, while Takeshi continued to circle her. 'What?'

He opened his hand to reveal a memory card sandwiched between his index and middle fingers.

'What is it?'

'Marianne's screen test.' He nodded towards the camera.

Alix slotted in the card. The first image showed a corseted Marianne straddling the bound and gagged doll, the next showed them sixty-nineing, her mouth glinting with saliva, and her eyes full of hunger. Alix gave a tiny gasp, then clamped her lips closed to prevent anything more revealing coming out. The girl looked delicious with all those pretty freckles, and the sassy S-shape the corset gave her. It emphasised her dramatic bust and the fleshy peachiness of her bum. It made her look so fuckable that Alix wanted to smack her lips in anticipation.

'She knew I was going to show you.' Takeshi lowered his gaze.

'Is this a bribe or a consolation prize?'

'It's a way forward. She wants someone to admire and appreciate her, and you want someone to cuddle.'

'Life isn't that simple.'

He shrugged, and drew a finger affectionately across Tifa's cheek. 'It is if you want it to be. Close the door on the way out.'

* * *

Marianne was nowhere in the castle, not even the bat-infested attics, but her old Mini was still parked on the drive, so Alix took her search outside. She wasn't even sure why she was trying so hard to find her, except that it made her feel as if she had some purpose in being here, and she couldn't get the explicit photographs out of her head.

The night had lost the hazy quality of twilight and now lay in a dismal blackness. The clouds were blotting out the stars and all but a sliver of the Beltane moon. Alix followed the line of lanterns as far as the gravel drive, then circled the castle until she was standing on the lawn, not far from where they'd taken the first catalogue photos of Takeshi.

The grey stone shimmered in the moonlight. Alix carefully followed the path that wound into the woods and eventually to the Dower House. At the threshold of the forest, she paused, hand on the bark of a sturdy oak. A torch would have been bloody useful. As it was, she wasn't going back just to come out again, so her night vision would have to suffice.

The woodland floor was still thick with decaying leaf mulch from the previous autumn. Everything smelled damp. 'Who is it?' she hissed, startled by a nearby howl. 'Who's there?' Hadn't someone said that Lulu was out here too? 'Lulu? Lulu? Lucretia!'

A white figure shot across the path.

'Stop! Wait!' Alix dashed after her into the depths of the dewy undergrowth. 'Lulu.' Brambles snagged at her clothing. The ground was rough and sloped gently downwards. Looking back, she could no longer see the path, but she was gaining on the crazy bridesmaid.

Alix charged headlong into a small clearing, to find Lulu naked and dirt-streaked, pawing at the side of an old fairy-tale well. Thick ivy trailed over the roof and the stonework Marianne was precariously clinging to.

Alix stared at the pair, unable to express her incredulity. 'What the bloody hell are you doing?'

'We're consulting Myfanwy, the Lady of the Well,' Marianne said, as if that were perfectly apparent.

'Right. OK.' As if that explained cavorting in the woods, on May eve, skyclad and barmy.

'If you petition her and anoint yourself with water from her well, she'll help you gain your heart's desire. Lulu said so. But the bucket's stuck.' Marianne gave the frayed rope a vigorous pull, making the bucket clatter against the stone shaft.

'And you believe her?' Alix slapped her brow. 'What are you, stupid? Mi-van-wee. That's Welsh! We're nowhere near bloody Wales. Why would she have a sacred well here?'

Alix looked back and forth between the two women, wondering which one to drown first. Marianne would make the more satisfying splash, but she'd probably float considering her vast bust, presently squeezed into a transparent white negligée, and offset by a pendant of St Sebastian. The moonlight played across her skin, reminding her of the sliver of light illuminating the half-undressed doll as she'd cradled her breast.

Lulu, on the other hand, she felt like holding under just for suggesting this nonsense. The girl was currently cleaning her fingers with her tongue.

'What's she been doing, nibbling mushrooms?'

'No. I don't think so. Maybe.' Marianne slipped forward on the stones. 'Yeep!' she squealed, scratching loose a chunk of moss. She clung to the rope until Alix went over and helped her regain safety.

'So, which one of you idiots trashed the clothes?'

Lulu continued to clean herself, moving on to her upper arm, and then her breast. Marianne looked sour, and guilty. 'It was just Silk's stuff, and we didn't plan it. We just went in to get the pendant.' She clasped the silver effigy. 'Lulu said it would work as a focus, but then we heard them next door – Silk and Remy – sharing fantasies, giggling and splashing, and him howling like he'd just been shot through with darts. Well, he is a wanker,' she concluded. 'I gave him everything he asked. I even swallowed.'

'Too much detail again.' Alix straightened her face. Merely knowing that Silk existed and slept around was enough information. She didn't need to hear about which crevices he'd relieved himself in. Besides, she didn't want to be thinking of Silk if she managed to coax her into bed later.

Had it come to that? Yes, she realised. She was going to take Takeshi's advice.

She gave Marianne her best schoolmistress glare. 'Quit basking in self-pity. You knew he wasn't for keeps.'

Marianne's lip trembled.

'And next time you decide to get snip-happy with the scissors, check you've got the right outfit first. You trashed Shaun's outfit, not Silk's, and now Chelsea's distraught.'

'But Dolores described it.'

Alix sighed. Why wasn't it a surprise that superbitch was involved? Dolores was spreading evil even from afar. She pressed her fingertips into her sinuses. Gothic weddings, pah! She'd be sticking to quickies down at the register office from now on. They were a lot less stressful.

Marianne had begun to sniffle. Alix took her hand and helped her down from the well edge. 'Come inside and we'll talk. Remy's sorting the clothes, it'll be fine.' She wasn't entirely sure that was honest, as both Chelsea and Remy would likely be after blood, but it stopped the snivelling. Besides, serial comforter seemed to be her role for the weekend. She'd be glad when it was over and she could go back to offering support in a nice stress-free environment, maybe as a helpline counsellor for Biker Dykes Anonymous.

'What about Lulu?' Marianne asked.

The girl stopped licking and entwined herself around Marianne's thigh in response. 'Don't give up. He's yours for the asking.' She stretched towards the moon, displaying her skinny figure in all its black and white glory. 'Oh, Lady Myfanwy, most blessed and fair, in whose watery depths the Moon doth tremble –'

Alix grabbed a handful of hair and pulled. 'Quit acting like a lunatic. It's too cold. We're going in.' Lulu flapped wildly, careened into a crop of nettles and sat with an almighty screech.

For a moment, they stood together hand in hand watching her flail, then waded in and hauled her out.

Once the clothes were back on the rails, Remy pressed Chelsea's and the bridesmaids' dresses. Everything else made do with a shake. She didn't have the time or the materials to replace the back panels of Shaun's coat, or to make him a new shirt, so she sifted the collection again for an alternative outfit. Most of her shirts were based on a loose-fitting design *circa* 1800, so that was easily replaced. The coat was trickier, as he had to match Silk. In the end, she went for a velvet version of the original with a marginally fuller skirt. That also had the advantage of a deep velvet pile to add an extra touch of glamour. With luck, it would pull some of the guests' attentions back to the groom instead of their being entirely glued to the best man. Suddenly there seemed a major risk that Silk might outdazzle the bride, particularly as Chelsea wasn't exactly looking her best. They'd have to work on that tomorrow. Brides were supposed to have a radiant glow, not look as though they'd come for a funeral.

She took time out for a coffee laced with rum after the ironing. A little Dutch courage before she faced Takeshi again.

He was lying on the bed when she went in, having

ignored her knocks. He lifted his head, then let it loll back down uninterestedly. Remy stared at his prone form. He was tucked beneath the bedspread with his back to her and his head resting on Tifa's lap.

'Can I come in?'

She tiptoed to the bed, where she rocked uncomfortably on the balls of her feet awaiting a response. 'I'm sorry.' She tried. 'I could have handled it better earlier. I never meant to hurt you, or for you to get the wrong idea.'

'Which wrong idea was that?' He rolled over and propped himself up on one elbow.

'Well, erm, that it was serious. Anything more than fun.'

'Fun,' he said slowly, as if weighing the word's meaning. 'Yes, it was fun, but it was more than just a novelty fuck. We had a connection, Remy, a real connection. We spent the night in an extremely narrow bed.'

'What's that supposed to prove?'

Takeshi whipped his head back violently. His blue hair flicked over his face, masking his eyes. 'Right now, it proves that you're a selfish bitch. How would you feel if I'd gone off straightaway and shagged Lulu, or Alix, and then flaunted it in front of you?'

'I didn't want you to hear it from someone else.'

He sat abruptly. Remy jerked backwards in response, recalling how he'd grabbed her earlier.

'Is that supposed to make it better?'

'You were going to sleep with him.'

He nodded. 'Yeah, I'd have made sure you were involved.'

Remy sucked on her lips. She wanted to challenge his statement, but in her heart she knew it was true. He knew how turned on she got by the idea of seeing him and Silk together. The thing was, she still wasn't convinced that was what had made him storm out.

'Why did you run off? It wasn't because of Silk.'

'Why did you send your fan club after me instead of coming yourself?'

'I don't drive, and I didn't think of riding pillion until after she'd gone. Now you.'

'Old ghosts.' He pulled the covers around himself. Remy followed his eyes as he dipped his head, but she couldn't decipher him.

'Go on.' She made a space for herself on the bed beside him and risked rejection by clasping his hand.

Takeshi stared at their intertwined fingers. 'It's old history. You just jogged an unpleasant memory. Let's leave it as that and talk about something else.' He stroked his thumb against her palm in a slow spiral, then tugged her closer. Boy, did he know how to play her emotions! His palms slipped up her arms until he'd clasped her in a cradling embrace. 'Tell me why you're so scared of commitment.' He breathed into her ear.

Remy shivered, anticipating his next move. 'I'm not.'

'Sure, you're not.' His lips touched her earlobe. Remy rubbed her thighs together as the pleasure shot diamond sparks through her limbs. His kiss went lower, pressed into the sensitive spot above her jugular.

'Not fair,' she squeaked. Feebly, she tried to push him away. It had taken every ounce of strength she'd had to break free of her family, dump Duncan and go it alone at fashion college. Keeping out of the serious commitment zone had kept her focused and free. But it did sometimes get lonely, and she did like Takeshi. He could also help her business, and he'd already helped her live out her fantasies. In her mind's eye she saw him and Silk lying like spoons on a bed, then standing, their bodies two pale silhouettes against the blackness of a bedroom, before her fantasies moved on to future possibilities. Would he allow her to watch him with strangers he'd picked up in the park, or men they'd found together online?

Would she ever be able to escape the lull of his kiss?

Was he taking care not to mark her? Her dress for the wedding was cut low, and the last mark he'd given her had only just faded.

His hand was inside her jumper, teasing a nipple. 'Come to bed.'

'Can't we just be friends who get intimate occasionally?'

'Uh-uh.' His kiss crept across her jaw to her lips. Then his body covered her and smothered all thoughts of resistance.

It was too easy to lie still and let him bring her pleasure. Too easy to drift, to disregard the statement she was making by staying. Too easy to come, too easy to lie in his arms, warm and safe and sink into welcoming oblivion.

Takeshi's dreams were uneasy. A shadow with a sharp set of claws raked across his back like a multi-needled sewing machine. There were specks on the periphery of his vision, dark shapes whose presence made him uneasy, and a white fox darting around the furniture of his subconscious.

There was something missing. Something he'd misplaced.

Blindly, he reached out, seeking the comfort of its tactile form, and his hand closed over the curve of a flank. She was still there, warm beside him, snuggled into his embrace.

'Megumi,' he murmured, and tugged the blankets around them both. It didn't matter that she was still partially clothed, only that they were together, and she'd spent the night.

13

Daylight had formed a bright margin around the edge of the curtains when Remy woke. She stretched in Takeshi's arms, then turned over so that their noses pressed together. He looked incredibly peaceful, still sleeping or else doing a good job of faking it. She tilted her chin and pressed a kiss to his nose. For once, she didn't feel like running. Maybe it was time to let a few of her barriers fall. They were still going to have to talk over the Silk situation, though. She wasn't prepared to give up that fantasy yet.

The alarm clock was flashing 10:20 to her in fire-engine red as she rubbed the sleep from her eyes. It was a miracle that Alix hadn't already come looking for her. She lay very still, anticipating a knock on the door. She owed her friend, but she didn't really want to move or pose.

Eventually, she sat up, dragging the covers down in the process. Takeshi rolled on to his stomach and pressed into the warm space she'd just vacated.

He looked so boyish, so uncomplicated in the brassy half-light.

She ran a finger along the ridge of his nose, explored the contours of his brow and cheekbones. He might not have Silk's fallen-angel radiance, but Takeshi was still beautiful. This morning he was the most beautiful she'd ever seen him.

Her caress lingered over his collarbone. The dragon on his back tormented her. Ever since she'd first seen the tattoo, it had fed her questions about who he really was. Now it seemed out of place, as if it belonged to a different man. A man of secrets, not the innocent boy beside her now.

She dropped a kiss on to his shoulder where her fingers had been, and her breath stirred his hair. Sleepily, he swatted at the irritation. Remy continued her tease. Following the flow of the dragon, she licked her way down his back, to where the winged creature emerged from between his cheeks.

The pattern was intricate, coloured with different shades of inky blue. He squirmed when she traced his anus and again when she poked her tongue possessively inside.

He yawned languorously, and rolled on to his side a little to give his erection space. His eyes were closed, but his smile showed he was awake.

Remy traced his balls, insistently, making his legs part.

Half hidden on his thigh she found a second tattoo, composed of small wobbly Japanese characters, probably self-inflicted, if that was the right term, and intriguingly intimate. 'What's this say?'

'Nothing. Don't stop.'

Remy rose on to her haunches. 'Sorry. I've got to move. I'm late for Alix.'

'So be late.'

'Can't. I owe her.'

He rolled over and got off the bed, suddenly full of boundless energy. 'Don't move.'

Remy watched him cross to the tripod still set up in the corner. He switched on the digital camera, shifted the apparatus right a foot, then adjusted the angle and focus of the lens. Remy squinted as the flash briefly penetrated the darkness.

'She'll kill you.'

'She'll thank me. This'll be far more intimate than a few bottom shots. Besides, she won't notice until she gets home.'

He returned to the bed, trailing the trigger lead, and sporting a serious morning glory.

'What if I don't want to play?' Remy tugged the bedspread up to her chin so it formed a patchwork wall.

'Don't be mean.' He tore down the barrier, and hoisted her on to her feet. 'Let's see that heart-shaped bum.' He lifted her sweater, the only garment she was wearing, and bent her over the bed.

'Ever been spanked?'

'No.'

'Oh, well. First time for everything. Beautiful.' His palm came down hard against her rear.

'Ouch!'

'Gorgeous.'

'Ow!'

'And lucky red.'

A glowing behind definitely wasn't her thing, she decided, wincing at each successive blow. It was just making her vexed. Remy turned before he could land another, and left her own handprint across his stomach. 'Oi!'

Takeshi stared at the mark, somewhat taken aback.

'Not so keen to take it, are you, Tokyo boy?' she snarled. 'How about you bend over and I spank your behind?'

'Actually, I'm from Osaka.' He winked, not even trying to disguise his mirth. 'Spank away.' He turned and wiggled his bare rear.

The sting in her hand surprised her. After only a few smacks her palm burned redder than his cheeks, and rather than being irritated or angered, Takeshi was squirming against the bed in obvious pleasure.

She tried swapping hands, but that started hurting too, so, after a farewell swat, she resorted to rubbing circles into the heated skin.

'Oh, yes!' he sighed as her nails scored angry flames

across the peachy surface. 'Oh, yes!' he said again, as her tongue licked at the top of the channel between his cheeks.

Remy drew her tongue around his hole in concentric circles, teasing, but never delivering. She could see how much he wanted it from the sweat starting to bead across the backs of his thighs. 'Was there something?' she asked, pausing for breath.

'Bitch! Don't tease.'

She breathed hot air over his winking rosebud, then swirled her tongue around the band of nerves just inside the dark hole.

Takeshi's legs buckled. He flopped on to the bed, shaking. 'Oh, God! I want to fuck.'

Remy straightened, ready to flop on to the bed beside him. He caught her hand. 'No.' His voice was desperate. 'Don't stop – it's fantastic. Remy, please.'

She lapped again at the shadowy entrance.

Takeshi humped the bed in response, his arms flailing wildly, until his left hand closed over something more solid than the sheets.

He'd grabbed an arm. The doll!

No! He wasn't going to. He couldn't.

All along, Remy had believed deep down that she was just for show. Now it seemed that her gut reaction was wrong – very wrong. Part of her was revolted by the thought; part of her turned on. Which was making her squirm the more? She wasn't really sure, but she knew she wanted to stand up and watch, not strain her tongue and her neck trying to get the best angle.

He'd manoeuvred the toy so that her legs were gaping, clearly displaying her black thatch. Remy watched him lick across Tifa's cunt, leaving the fleshy lips shiny. His breathing was urgent and excited. 'You've stopped again.' He lifted slightly as he slid the doll beneath his hips.

'I want to see.'

His next exhalation was harsh, borderline exasperated. 'So, use your fingers instead of your tongue.'

Remy kneaded his buttocks as he sank full length into the doll and began to buck madly.

'Remy!' He grasped her hand and sucked her thumb into his mouth, only to release it coated in saliva a moment later. 'Now, do me.'

Obligingly, she circled the slippery digit around his anus and over the hole. She'd slipped a guy a finger before, but never like this. It had always been her taking the initiative. The experience had always brought her partners pleasure, but the aftermath had always soured things. Men had such trouble accepting that nerve endings responded in the same way, regardless of whether you were gay or straight.

Takeshi's body offered no resistance to the penetration. It swallowed up her digit to the knuckle and clasped it in a powerful heat. Remy wriggled her thumb in a teasing circle, and wondered what it would be like with a strap-on or some beads. Maybe she'd pick up a paddle too. Would he help her shop for such things? She'd always been intrigued by them.

Grinning, she straddled one of his outstretched legs and rubbed her sex up against his thigh, desperate for some friction. This was getting seriously kinky. Maybe she could design herself an outfit too. What would Alix think of that? Or Duncan?

For once, the thought of her former fiancé didn't revolt her. Maybe she was finally over that bastard. She'd realised something else, too, something she'd known deep down since their first brief encounter. She could be happy with Takeshi. He was willing to share her fantasies, if only she'd share his. You couldn't ask for more than that.

Remy worked her thumb a little harder, determined to give him what he needed. She just hoped he wasn't going to fall into a stupor after this, because she needed some attention herself. Her clit was just begging for a touch. Dammit! She braced her leg against the bed and pushed her free hand into the molten heat at the top of her thighs. The resulting pleasure was intense and immediate.

Takeshi groaned. His hips worked faster, and his cheeks began to clench in sync with the shallow thrusts of her thumb. 'Remy. Oh, Remy.' His gasp oozed with emotion. Then he stiffened as a shiver ran up his spine and his cock jerked.

Remy didn't remember their sagging on to the floor, only that she'd ended up on her back, with his musky taste thick in her mouth and her hand working desperately over her clit. Moments later, he was between her thighs, his hot breath whispering over her mound and his greedy kisses bringing her off.

A floor above the hammering bedsprings, Alix poked her head from the covers of two pushed-together singles. Her left arm and shoulder were dead. Groggily, she raised her head. The daylight was blistering. They'd forgotten to close the curtains last night, worse luck.

Beside her, Lulu grunted and rolled over, allowing some circulation to return to her arm. Alix straightened her legs, dislodging Marianne from her hip.

'What time is it?'

Marianne unglued her panda eyes, and looked around for a clock. 'Too early. Midday?'

Alix stared at her smudged mascara, which had left spider's-leg streaks over her pretty dusting of freckles. After they'd come back from the woods, all nettled and green with dock-leaf juice, they'd settled in the kitchen. Alix had been determined to talk sense, but Lulu was acting as dotty as ever. She'd suggested an experiment in the middle of one crucial sentence, then disappeared into the night, only to return holding a nettle.

Alix stroked the hair of the gently breathing girl. Stupid bitch. Nettle carefully pinched between forefinger and thumb, she'd perched herself on the edge of an armchair, still naked, and stung her clit. After she'd leapt around shrieking for several minutes, she'd done it again, squealing something about invoking Cleopatra's spirit, without compromising her vegetarian tendencies with needless cruelty to bees.

Then, of course, they'd had to wrestle the green prickly frond from her, by which time they were all pretty intimate, and Lulu had given herself an itch only a tongue bath could cure – a pleasure immediately reciprocated. It had been easy for them both to turn on Marianne, who'd watched, up to that point, with eyes like saucers.

Alix grinned, recalling how they'd raced up the staircase naked and shoved the beds together, before collapsing on to them and starting a fumbling, caressing, licking, sucking, finger-fucking lust quest. And she hadn't thought of Remy once.

Shit, Remy! She was supposed to be snapping her naked.

Alix freed the rest of her limbs and staggered bandy-legged to her suitcase. She pulled on jeans and a velvet, bottle-green sweater, fluffed her ringlets and bobbed barefoot to the door.

'Breakfast?' Marianne enquired hopefully.

'Remy.'

'Oh!'

'Don't worry. I won't be long.' The pictures wouldn't take much above forty minutes, maybe less considering how appealing bed was at the moment. Except that the cap house was empty, and a quick look at the travel clock by Remy's bed confirmed she was over three hours late.

Alix padded back down the cold stairs. She'd waited years for the chance to photograph Remy, but, surprisingly, she didn't feel any urge to go and find her. All she could really think about were the two sleepyheads in her bed.

'Told you I'd be quick,' she said as she bounded through the doorway, then pulled up sharp. Lulu and Marianne were cowering side by side in the bed, while Dolores was framed by the light streaming through the bay window, resplendent in a Barbie-pink suit.

'Hello, Alexandra.' She stretched her fingers over the leather of her matching handbag. 'Where's my daughter?'

'Not here.' Alix gave a shrug. She wasn't going to let Dolores wreck her mood. In fact, she was tempted to snog Marianne in front of her, just to see if they could scare her off.

'She's not in her room.' Her hand moved from the bag to her waist.

Alix mimicked the pose 'She's probably with Shaun.'

'They've made up?'

'Course.' She had no idea if that was true, but she didn't want to give Dolores any further satisfaction. She'd have to find Chelsea and warn her that her mother was back.

'Good, good,' Dolores said, bringing Alix's thoughts to a halt. 'I need to have a chat with her about the bouquet.'

When Silk woke, he found Shaun facing him, perched among his crumpled sheets, and hugging his toes. He looked surprisingly sober this morning, if a little red-rimmed beneath the eyeliner. He wished his own head seemed that clear. He'd been dreaming of Takeshi, of being butt-fucked among falling cherry blossom. He was cracking up. There was no other explanation for it. Best to forget it for now, along with the fellatio fantasy he'd constructed the night before. He had Shaun to sort out. That's what the best man was supposed to do, wasn't it? Be around to smooth things over so the groom didn't have to do anything other than recite a few lines. As if you could forget to say 'I do.' Besides, he wasn't sure this was something he could fix. He could only make suggestions.

'I've completely bollocksed things up,' Shaun said, once he realised Silk was awake. 'We're getting married, and I don't even know if she's speaking to me.'

Silk pushed himself into a sitting position. His brain would work better that way. 'So, quit moping, and go apologise.' He was through with hand holding. 'And don't take no for an answer.'

Shaun hitched his knees and bowed his head so that it was resting on them. 'You know I'm crap at standing up to her. Just one look and I lose my bottle.'

'Shaun, I really think you need to handle this one yourself, because you don't want me to do it.'

'Oh – no.' Shaun was suddenly alert and upright. 'You're right. I don't. You're supposed to stick to the bridesmaids.'

'And you're supposed to stick to the bride.'

Silk ducked as the pillow he'd thrown at Shaun last night was returned with interest. 'Hey, do you want my help or not?'

'Probably need it.' Shaun sniffed at his clothes. 'Hmm, need new clothes too.' He slipped out of his black ensemble and pulled on another, equally black.

'A flash of colour wouldn't hurt.'

Bewildered, Shaun searched among his possessions, and eventually found a violet scarf, which he pulled through a hole in his black jeans so that it dangled like a tail. 'Now what?'

Silk leant out of bed and took a roll of Velcro from the top drawer of the bedside cabinet. 'You might find this useful.' He tossed the roll to Shaun, who eyed it sceptically.

'How's this supposed to help?'

Silk snuggled back down and tugged the covers over his head. 'Use your imagination, Shaun.'

'But we're supposed to be abstaining.'

'Fine, if you want to play at being a virgin. But wouldn't you rather see her walk down the aisle knowing she's got your come dripping down her thighs?'

Shaun lashed him across the thigh. 'You know, for all those angelic looks, you're actually a filthy beast.'

'No shit, Sherlock!' Silk said from beneath the covers. 'Now, go bang her and leave me alone.'

Remy snuggled against Takeshi's smooth chest. They'd both cleaned up in the bathroom and were now enjoying a quiet cuddle, but time was against them today. Much as Remy wanted to stay and learn a little more about him, she had far too much to do. She had no idea whether Chelsea and Shaun were speaking yet, and she needed to try Shaun's new outfit on him just to check the fit. Then there was Alix to appease, and she had no idea how she was supposed to behave around Silk, or whether Takeshi would even discuss it.

'What's on your mind?' he asked.

Remy lifted her head so she could see his face. 'Wedding preparations mostly, plus you and Silk. I can't pretend yesterday didn't happen. I need to work out where we all stand.'

Takeshi defensively stroked his finger down his nose. 'Tell him it was a one-off. I'm not sharing you.'

She cocked her head to one side and eyed him thoughtfully. 'This from the man who's been chasing him all weekend and who just fucked a doll.'

'Consider him dropped, and Tifa too. I want you to myself, Remy.'

Remy pushed herself on to her haunches. It was a pretty ideal, all monogamous and cosy, but that wasn't what attracted him to her. And she still didn't like the idea of monogamy. She wanted to live on the edge with him, plan some horny little games and live out some fantasies. That's what they'd been doing so far. It's why she couldn't help coming back for more. As he'd said that first time in the park, 'Who else are you going to indulge your *yaoi* fantasies with?' Who else indeed?

'I think I prefer it when you're hot on the chase. Where's the advantage in dating if it means the end of the show?'

He rolled on to his front, and pressed his head into the pillow. 'That was ending regardless. It couldn't carry on after what happened yesterday afternoon.'

'Why does me and Silk having sex affect anything?'

He pressed his face into the linen. 'It just does.'

Remy stared at the back of his head. It didn't make any sense to her. 'What's wrong?' She teased the back of his neck with her tongue. 'Are you just jealous I had him first?'

'No,' he said petulantly.

Remy licked across his shoulder, while slithering up his body. She found his ear and traced her tongue around the curve of the lobe, caught it between her teeth. 'We were thinking of you. I told him all about what I want to see you two doing together. All about how I want to see him fuck you.'

'He hasn't got the strength.' Takeshi shrugged her off. He met her gaze, his face hard set, so that his lips were drawn back in a sneer that showed his teeth. 'I'm no tame little *uke* for him to use.'

'He's taller than you,' Remy goaded.

'He'd still be the bottom.'

'Prove it.'

'Drop it, will you? I've had enough of games. If you want to watch me fuck guys, you can come to the park with me sometime.'

'I don't want to watch you fuck guys.' That wasn't true. Just the idea of spying on him as he picked up other men was causing a warming thrill in her chest. But the thought of him with Silk was an even bigger thrill. 'I want to see you fuck him.' She reached out to touch his face, but Takeshi turned away. 'Come on.' She snuggled against his back. 'I'm sorry I upset you, but he is gorgeous, and it just happened. If you'd been about, I'd have involved you.'

'No, you wouldn't.'

'Please, Takeshi. You looked so damn hot in the Orangery during the shoot. And I know you want him. You've been teasing him all along.'

'Stop it, will you.' He thumped the headboard, forcing it against the wall where it drove a notch into the plaster. 'I'm pissed off, OK? He thought we were an item but he still made a move on you. What kind of bastard does that?'

'One who knows he can get away with it.'

Takeshi grunted.

'So teach him a lesson.'

'Maybe.'

They lay in silence for a while. Remy stared at the knots of tension in his shoulders. It made no sense that he'd get so worked up about it when he'd been proposing threesomes behind her back. She still didn't know much about him, though. It was possible that he was always this mutable and screwed-up. Maybe that was why he hooked up with strangers in the park.

'Who are you?' she wondered aloud, while she drew circles on his shoulders to try to ease away the tension. 'Tell me about yourself. I mean, you could be anybody. A former *yakuza* hit man for all I know. You've got the tattoo.'

Takeshi half turned his upper body and peeked at her over his shoulder from beneath his spiky fringe. 'Intriguing, isn't it?'

Remy felt the thud of her own pulse. The way he was looking at her made her feel exposed to her very toes.

There was something about him at that moment that seemed edgy and dangerous. She couldn't exactly say what. It was just a sense that he'd seen things, and been places that only bad boys went, and somehow it was all tied up in why he was so annoyed about Silk.

He turned to face her fully. 'It's just a tattoo.' He cracked a half-smile. 'People don't just walk away from a life in the *yakuza*, Remy. You read enough *manga* to know that. I just like tattoos.'

He eyed the lily-white skin of her shoulder contemplatively.

'Don't get any ideas.' Nobody was coming near *her* with a needle.

'Why not?' He grinned, so she elbowed him in the ribs, nearly knocking him out of the narrow bed. 'OK.' He turned onto his stomach and dug a soft spot in the pillow. He looked away sharply, leaving an impression of pain and tears.

'I did run a few errands,' he said, 'but they're not very nice people, and I don't deal with authority very well.'

Confused, Remy tentatively pressed a fingertip to the head of the twisted dragon. The sheer magic of its detailed scales must have taken hours of work. Had he winced and teared up then, too? 'Takeshi?'

He breathed noisily into the pillow. 'Japan's not an easy place to grow up. You're expected to excel, and I was never much good at anything.'

'So you say.' She stroked a line down his body, following the same path as earlier until she reached the wobbly blue doodle on his inner thigh. 'What does this bit of rebellion say?' She knew several people with Oriental characters tattooed on to their bodies, but he was the first who was also familiar with the language. The others could have had 'Five-Yen Super Whore' or 'Chop Suey Tuesday' or worse inked on to their skin and they'd have been none the wiser. They just accepted that their 'Love',

'Fortune' or 'Whatever' tattoo said what the artist said it did.

'It says, "Mind your own business".'

Remy kissed his butt, determined not to let him sink back into his pit. 'Bet it doesn't.'

'All right, it says "Megumi", if you must know.'

'Me-goo-me,' she practised, while redrawing the character on his skin. 'Intriguing. Sounds like a first love.'

She slithered over his back, sandwiching them together so that her nipples brushed his skin. 'Bet she looked just like Tifa.'

Takeshi rolled over, crushing her with his body. 'No. She had pink streaked hair, a heart-shaped face and a death wish. Brilliant, though. You remind me of her. Same hair. Different colour. Same up-for-it attitude.'

He grabbed her hands, pinned her to the bed and pressed several hungry kisses to her lips, as if by devouring her he could take the edge off whatever pain had wet his cheeks. Remy struggled beneath him, the taste of his hot salt tears making her feel claustrophobic. At last, he eased off, although he drew out the final kiss by holding her lip captive. 'I love you, Remy.' He turned his head so their cheeks brushed.

Remy held her breath. The moment seemed to demand a mushy response of her own. 'Were you in love with her too?' she asked instead.

His head came up again, but his expression was glazed. 'She was one of the best bikers I've ever known. The Osaka Speed Queen, they called her. Some of the risks, some of the crazy stunts she pulled – they'd take your breath away.' He pressed his fingertips to his lips, his thoughts falling in on themselves.

'Go on.'

Takeshi merely shook his silver-blue locks. When he eventually spoke, his voice was cut with a lignocaine slur. 'She fell in love with a stupid bastard who had to be macho and had her riding pillion in fishnets on her own fucking bike. She came off during a high-speed police chase. Took so much skin off her arms and thighs they didn't have enough left for all the grafts they needed.' He lowered his head, severing the eye contact between them. 'She lived. But he really messed her up.'

Remy pushed her hand through the curtain of hair between them. Was he talking about himself? She wasn't sure, but it seemed strangely insensitive to ask.

'Fucking Ryuji. That's why I left. I had to, before I killed him. Bastard walked away from the crash with a manly scar and a caution, after he'd totally wrecked her looks and her self-esteem.' He swallowed hard. 'I was there. I didn't see her come off the bike, but I saw the aftermath. Him lying there whimpering and her with blood running down her face. So much goddamn blood.'

Remy traced the contours of his face with her fingertips, and brushed away the saltwater streaks. 'Did she even know how you felt?'

Takeshi shook his head, then looked up. 'I don't know. Maybe, but we never spoke about it. We were never lovers or anything, even after the accident. She was still with him. Still thought he was her shining knight. When really he was a Grade A prick.'

'I'm sorry,' Remy whispered. What else was there to say? She wrapped her arms around him and squeezed tight. The few traumas she'd suffered with her family seemed minor in comparison. There was still something she could share, though. 'Hey, did I ever tell you about my former fiancé Duncan? He was a prick too. He punished me for dumping him by marrying my sister.'

'For real?' Takeshi pulled her on to his lap.

'For real. Every Christmas, he turns up in a Santa sweater and tries to get frisky with me under the mistletoe.'

'Guess he's turned on by your tight black outfits and jingling charm belts.'

Remy pursed her lips. Takeshi raised his hand in surrender. 'Hey, they work for me. I'd like to see you naked apart from that belt.' He rocked his hips. 'Maybe I should send you to fetch it. Have you do a belly dance.'

Someone rattled the doorknob.

'Do Silk, and maybe I'll do it.'

Takeshi bit his lip.

'Sorry to interrupt.' Marianne marched in, pointedly staring at any other part of the room. She was dressed in Alix's 'Leda' dressing gown, an item Remy had made for her back in college. 'Got to get my case – need some clothes.' She sashayed over to the other bed, and hoisted a purple holdall on to the patchwork.

Still pressed together, they watched her rake through the faded contents and pull out a grey Concrete Blonde T-shirt and an embroidered skirt.

'Oh, by the way, Remy,' she said, her voice muffled by the T-shirt as it went over her head. 'Message from Alix. "The session's cancelled, but it'd be a real help if you could get your butt out of bed, stop groping whichever bloke you're with and sort out Chelsea and Shaun." Dolores is back, and she means business.'

Remy pulled the bedspread around her shoulders and slid off Takeshi's lap, leaving him to snatch up the sheet to hide his modesty. If Dolores was stirring people up, her workload for the day had probably tripled. She had no choice but to move. She tugged on her socks, pants and jumper. 'Any idea where Chelsea is?'

'Out, I think.' Marianne turned to face her. 'We've been all over the castle, except Shaun and Silk's room, but I saw the catering van pull up a few minutes back so she might be sorting them out. Erm, isn't that jumper a little skimpy for daywear?'

Remy looked down at herself. She was showing a fair portion of thigh between the top of her over-knee socks and the bottom of her jumper, which was just below C level, but did it really matter? It was mostly women in the place apart from Silk, Takeshi and Shaun, and two of them had already seen a darn sight more of her than a stretch of thigh. 'I think I'll do. You should try some V-necks: they'd flatter your shape more,' she added, unable to stop herself retaliating just a little. The girl was probably responsible for Shaun's slashed outfit. Overall, she was lucky to be getting off so lightly.

'Ladies.' Takeshi put his arms over his head and ducked. Remy kissed him on the back of the head and left before Marianne could voice a response.

She found Chelsea in the marquee that had been set up on the lawn. Rather than the traditional white affair, the canvas was a velvety black with purple and silver trim, like something out of a Gothic fairy tale. Remy crept inside. Despite the sharp crisp daylight, inside was dark as midnight. Strands of twinkling fairy lights mimicked the sky, looped between the lofty ridge poles and encircling the two massive uprights. A multitude of tables were dressed in black transparent voile, and scattered with delicate silver stars. Chelsea bustled between them, fussing over minutiae. As far as Remy could tell, everything was already perfect.

She wound her way through the tables until she reached the bride. 'What are you doing out here? You should be pampering yourself.'

Chelsea gave a hysterical squawk. 'No – oh! Can't sit down, the whole thing's going to be a disaster. I've got to get these right.'

'Chelsea, they're perfect.' The centrepieces, exotic twisted candelabra of nymphs and wicked fairies, had already been expertly framed with wispy bunches of baby's breath by the florist. 'Leave them. You need to go in and talk to Shaun.'

'What about?'

Remy folded her arms. Chelsea was stubborn and obsessive; she could handle that, but she wasn't going to put up with petulance – not today. 'About getting married and what happened about –'

'Screwing my chief bridesmaid.' She gave another high-pitched cackle. 'Yeah, I really want to talk about that. Say, we could discuss how my mother's made herself the favourite topic of conversation in the village, and how some vindictive little bitch has trashed the outfits, too.'

'He didn't screw anybody. They didn't even touch.'

'It was still sex.'

'Was it sex when you got frisky with that male stripper on your twenty-fifth?'

Chelsea shook her head, causing her tresses to fall across her face. 'That was different.'

'How?'

'And it's only according to Eloise that nothing happened, who, let's face it, is the next biggest slut around after Silk, and he's screwed ninety per cent of the castle so far this weekend.' She tugged at the veil of golden strands. 'Wish he'd come here and screw me.'

Chelsea was babbling. Remy backed her into a spindly chair. 'Now you're getting hysterical.' The thought of Silk with another woman made her feel spiny too. 'Besides, you don't really mean it.'

'Don't I? I'm not immune just because I'm engaged. The guy's drop-dead, and I hear he fucks like a god.'

'You're in love with Shaun. You know the cookie? Badly dressed king of the castle? The guy with the smudged eyeliner and the cute dimply smile that you're always going on about?'

Chelsea ground her canines, but the fire was fading from her eyes, leaving them a washed-out cornflower blue. She slumped back in the chair. 'I suppose I'm going to have to forgive the silly sod.'

'Sounds like a plan.'

'I really hope so.' They both turned to find Shaun standing in the canvas doorway. 'Would you leave us,

Remy? We've got a few things to work through.' He strode towards them with a coil of something black looped between his hands.

'Hey, that's my missing Velcro.'

'Take it up with Silk.' Shaun's gaze never left Chelsea, whose eyes were transfixed on the binding. 'Now, what was that I heard about you wanting Silk?'

A ruby sheen washed across Chelsea's cheeks. 'You weren't supposed to hear that. I was just –'

'Pissed off? Jealous?' he suggested.

She nodded, slack-jawed.

'And you wanted to get back at me?' Shaun shook his head solemnly, then grabbed her wrists and hoisted her off the chair. 'I'm sorry about what happened. I should have walked out as soon as I saw her. But I was tired and annoyed about you kissing Silk. There's only you that means anything to me.'

'I once snogged a stripper,' Chelsea said.

'Uh-huh!' Shaun curled his lip meaningfully and then tore apart the Velcro hooks.

Remy made for the nearest exit. She didn't need to see what he was planning to do with it. She could imagine, even without Chelsea's litany of protests.

'No, Shaun. Not the tables, they're all set.

There was the sound of scattering cutlery, which briefly drew her attention back, but by then Shaun had manoeuvred Chelsea away from the tables and had her backed up against one of supporting poles. 'After tonight, I'm your slave,' she heard him say, 'but just this once, you're mine, pussy cat.'

Outside the marquee, Remy smiled to herself. That was that sorted. She just hoped there were no more disasters ahead.

'Remy, darling.' Dolores was waiting by the front door of the castle. 'I hear there's been a problem with the outfits.'

'Yes, but it's all sorted.'

'Oh, good,' said the older woman, giving her best toothpaste-advert grin. 'Because I just need your help on a few aspects of mine.'

Helping Dolores was the last thing she wanted to do, but if she had to run interference long enough for Chelsea and Shaun to fuck in peace, so be it. 'Let's go to the workroom and discuss it.'

14

Takeshi got out of bed shortly after Remy had left. For all Marianne's talk of urgency, she seemed content to bustle about doing very little. She was probably waiting for him to ask where she'd spent the night, not realising he'd had a hand in it, but he didn't want to listen to that. He was glad she seemed less Gothic today, but right now he wanted some space to work through his feelings.

He'd never told anybody how he'd felt about Megumi before, had never really said anything to her. Not after the first time, when she'd flung it back in his face. If he had, maybe he could've stopped it all. Maybe she wouldn't have been with Ryuji that night, riding pillion wearing fishnets and a miniskirt. Regrets? They were pointless. He couldn't change ancient history. But he could fight the future. And he was determined not to let Silk snatch Remy from him.

He wished she weren't so determined to see them together. But she was right: he had enjoyed teasing Silk. Actually, he fancied him a little more than he really cared to admit. That hair, those eyes, and all that creamy butterscotch skin. Takeshi touched his lips, reliving the sensation of the brief kiss they'd shared. He'd done it for her, but he'd also done it for himself.

No – he stopped his train of thought. It was taking an emotionally dangerous track. One of them could get seriously hurt, probably him. He felt fragile enough. Silk was a loose cannon, an arrogant, cocksure libertine. He wasn't sure he could face losing out to one again, not when he'd become so attached to Remy. It was best if he just avoided the other man. There'd be other opportunities to play to her fantasies with less threatening men.

Could he really walk away now? He thought of how Silk had reacted to his touch, the way he'd fought to mask his responsiveness to the merest trace of fingertips playing across his stomach. He could see him now, writhing, arching his back, with his long golden hair fanned out around his shoulders and falling in cascades across the bedclothes. He was so beautiful. How would he respond to a warm mouth closed around his prick?

Takeshi bit his lip. He'd promised himself at the start of the weekend that he'd have them both, Silk and Remy, by the time it was over. Was he really going to pass up on that now, when he could make it happen so easily? Well, maybe not that easily. He wasn't exactly sure how he was going to work Remy into things, since seducing the other man was going to rely on a fair amount of luck.

Takeshi pulled on a pair of 501s, leaving the buttons undone. This was stupid. He was letting his mind wander. He needed to think about something else.

'Hey, where you going?' Marianne called.

He stepped into his trainers. 'To work.'

She scowled, but he ignored her and snatched up his laptop and mobile instead. In the corridor, he struggled into a clingy raglan T-shirt he'd picked up on the way out of the door, only to find it had ketchup down the front. Sod it, he thought, rubbing at the mark. He wasn't trying to impress anyone. He was going to bury his head in the sand, or at least the Internet, and stay out of trouble for a while. Just this once the world could drift by.

Velcro. Who'd have thought that something so simple could be so effective at bonding people together? Shaun ripped the soft fuzz from the hooks, releasing Chelsea's wrist from a supporting pole. He didn't think he'd respond to that innocent sound in quite the same way ever again. He hugged Chelsea to his side, and wondered if he could cultivate a fetish for the stuff. He'd start by not returning this roll.

Chelsea tucked her hand into his back pocket and gave his bum a sly pinch. 'The day's a-wasting,' she said jovially, 'and I ought to go find someone to fix the table you wrecked.'

'Couldn't we fix it?' He followed her to the exit.

'Do you know how to fold a napkin?'

'Nope.'

The sky was clear and bright, and the air smelt of spring flowers. He wanted to take Chelsea down to the woods, away from the stress of preparations, and give her a green gown. It wouldn't be long until they were swept up in the actual ceremony. Now, he wanted to spend a little time remembering why they were doing it.

The bank would be full of bluebells, and quiet. His gazed drifted towards the forest, in time to catch Silk darting into cover. What was he doing out here?

Shaun scratched his brow in concern. Last night was a bit of a blur, but he could vaguely remember that his friend had seemed a bit odd, not quite himself. He'd been a bit off earlier, too.

'Hey, dreamer.' Chelsea tugged him towards the castle.

'Do you mind if I excuse myself for a few minutes? I need to sort something out.'

Chelsea pursed her lips. 'OK. It won't take long, will it?'

Not sure, he thought. It was hard to tell with Silk. He generally kept his own counsel, which meant getting him to open up could be akin to pulling teeth.

'Well, just remember: Remy needs to check the fit of your new outfit.'

'Sure.'

Shaun followed Silk into the woodland. There was no sign of him, but he had a fair idea where he'd be.

Although he'd have been horrified by the observation, Silk was predictable when it came to being moody. He had a few favourite spots around the estate from their teenage days, including what Shaun had dubbed his suicide spot.

Shaun reached the rickety bridge that spanned the castle driveway. By nightfall, the road below would be packed with cars. Now, it was empty and peaceful. He pushed past the branches laden with catkins and stepped out on to the boards.

Silk was leaning over the splintered wooden railing, his face hidden behind his billowing golden hair. Shaun carefully picked his way across, while the bridge creaked painfully with each step.

'I'm supposed to be the one with pre-wedding nerves,' he said lightly.

Silk's head sagged a little further.

'Come on, mate.' He pressed a hand to Silk's shoulder. 'Tell me what's bothering you.'

'It's nothing, Shaun. Shouldn't you be with Chelsea?'

'We're sweet. But you look grim.'

The wind blew a halo of blossom around their heads. Silk put his hand through it, scattering the virginal petals. The next gust shook the bridge, causing Shaun to blanch visibly.

'Can we get off this damn bridge – please?'

Silk peered into the middle distance, seemingly oblivious of Shaun's whitening knuckles gripping the handrail.

'Is she getting to you?' Shaun guessed. He had no idea which 'she' it might be, but Silk and girl trouble were synonymous. Most of the time his friend had a *carpe florem* attitude. He kept aloof except when he was out to charm, but, just occasionally, one of them would reach inside and touch a part of his heart. Then, boy, could he brood!

'You can leave any time. I can find my own way back.'

'It's not the way back I'm bothered about.'

Silk straightened. He pressed a taloned finger to Shaun's plum lips. 'It's nothing. I'm fine.'

'If it was nothing, you wouldn't be out here.'

Golden tresses fell like a waterfall as Silk bowed his head. He closed his eyes so that his long eyelashes dusted his cheeks. Shaun shook his head. 'Sort it out, Silk. I don't want you moping on my wedding pictures. The other ghouls, yeah, but not you. You're supposed to be the pretty one. The fucking contrast. You're not supposed to look like a tortured soul.'

'Sorry.' Silk raised his head a fraction, enough for Shaun to see a faint smile tweak his lips. 'Aren't goths tortured?'

'Only the sad ones.' Shaun gripped his friend's arm. 'Just go fuck whoever's causing the problem. That'll fix it.'

Silk shook his head. 'If only it was that simple.'

'Damn it, Silk. With you, it's always that simple.'

Silk left his friend on the bridge and wandered back to the castle the long way round, through the wood. Maybe Shaun was right. Maybe it *was* that simple. The only person he was hurting was himself. Of course, he still half suspected that Takeshi was just jerking him about. But there was only one way to find out.

He paused in a fading patch of sunlight. Row upon row of dapper bluebells surrounded him, all chiming him a silent lullaby. He didn't want to go back to the castle. The Jacobean edifice felt like a prison, with its solid, regimented lines of bricks and mortar. But nor did he want to alienate his best friend on his wedding day.

The thought of seeking out the blue-haired biker terrified him. He didn't like to be in a position where he wasn't in control.

What was he supposed to say, anyway? I'm obsessed with you? I want you?

He didn't hurry back, although he took the direct

route. As he slipped through the front door, he heard voices along the bottom corridor – Severina and Eloise, he thought, starting the preening process that would encompass bubble baths, full-body massages, hairdressers and makeup artists specially hired for the day, before Remy carefully moulded them into their frocks. He supposed he'd have to think about getting himself groomed at some point.

Someone had left a tray of glasses and a sherry decanter on the stairs by the kitchen door.

The door itself bore a handwritten 'Fuck off, I'm working' note, signed by Takeshi. He guessed he'd found him. Silk pondered the sign. He had to go in. If he didn't, he knew he wouldn't summon the courage again. He didn't even have a plan. How did you tell another man you wanted to fuck him? And that you were sorry you'd shagged his girlfriend in the mistaken belief that it was her you really wanted? He'd probably get punched.

Yeah, that'd please Shaun. A best man sporting a nice black and purple shiner.

Silk bent down and poured himself two glasses of sherry, which he downed in two gulps. OK, he was set.

The kitchen was in darkness; all the shutters were drawn. Instinctively, he reached for the light switch, then paused. There were three orange pockets of light surrounding thick church candles, evenly spaced along the oak table, and Takeshi was sitting at the near end, staring into the blue light of his laptop.

Silk quietly closed the door.

The weekend would have been so much simpler if the Japanese biker hadn't come along, if Remy had relied on the guests to pose for her catalogue instead of bringing her own models.

Bugger, he was scared. Quaking, almost. And there were still six metres between them.

He didn't recall closing the gap, but suddenly he was at Takeshi's side.

'Takeshi.'

The word came surprisingly easily to his lips, slipping off his tongue with a lazy grace. His throat felt so thick. It didn't seem right that that it sounded so musical. The other man didn't look up, but continued to type. Silk watched the movement of his fingers racing across the keyboard, and gradually let his gaze wander up Takeshi's arms to his shoulders, and the stretch of fabric across his wiry physique. Below the silvery fabric of the T-shirt was the equally silvery creature he'd glimpsed as he'd watched Takeshi and Remy make love. Somehow, the dragon had slithered into his dreams. 'Takeshi,' he said again, his voice faltering this time. 'We need to talk.'

'You need to talk, you mean. So, talk. I'm busy.'

Silk licked his lips, and strained to see the other man's reflection in the computer screen, afraid that, no matter how hard he tried, he'd never be able to put into words what he was feeling. He could try to make this about Remy, but that was a lie, and what he wanted was a resolution, not an argument. His gaze fastened on Takeshi's dark reflection, the shaggy silver-blue hair that masked his eyes, his high cheekbones and perfect Cupid's-bow lips, which were currently closed over the end of a pencil.

He wanted to feel their soft caress again, wanted to trace their contours with his thumb.

'For someone who wants to talk, you sure don't have much to say. Is an apology really that hard?'

'No.' Breathe, Silk, breathe, he told himself. Where had his cool gone, his confidence? He'd never been this mute around women. 'That's not what I'm here for.'

'Oh!' Takeshi jerked his chair back and folded his arms. 'So, why are you here?'

Silk back-stepped, only to see Takeshi's hard expression melt into an evil grin.

'Come to bare your soul?' He snapped to his feet, forcing Silk to take yet another step back unless he wanted them to be toe to toe. 'Or is it something more that you're after?' Takeshi's hands closed around his biceps, then shoved him back against the wooden galley.

Silk hit the partition with a thump. He couldn't seem to react. The velvety blackness of Takeshi's eyes was all he could see, and he was falling, falling into their depths. Takeshi clasped his hands instead. He locked them palm to palm against the panelling, either side of Silk's head. 'I'd made up my mind not to have you after what you did with Remy,' Takeshi hissed into his ear. 'But since you've come begging . . .' His lips traced the curve of Silk's ear, then his eyetooth pressed into the lobe.

Silk gasped. 'I'm not begging.' There was a fuzzy feeling of warmth centred on his groin. His lips parted, searching for a kiss.

'Yet.'

The second whisper tickled the length of his throat. Takeshi's leg pushed between his thighs. Part of him wanted to flee; part of him wanted to stay with the struggle. He pushed against Takeshi's grip, adding to the bump and grind of their hips, but failed to free himself. He needed to be in control of this.

Takeshi's nipping kisses reached the open collar of his shirt. 'You won't have seen it,' the biker whispered, 'but there's a famous *yaoi anime* featuring two characters a little like us.' His tongue flicked beneath the line of the shirt. 'Would you like to know what happens? One becomes the other's pet. How would you like to be my pet, Silk?'

Silk laughed. He couldn't stop himself. His muscles were tensed too hard, and each of Takeshi's kisses stung him with a fevered lust. He needed to be free. He needed to respond and sink his talons into Takeshi's firm arse. Submissive little sex slave was never going to be his role, and he'd enjoy proving that point.

'Think that's funny, do you?' Takeshi's head came up, and he breathed the words straight into Silk's mouth. At the same instant that their lips touched, Takeshi released one of Silk's wrists and pushed his hand inside Silk's trouser front.

Silk swallowed hard. The sensation rippled straight down his throat to his groin. The previous time they'd kissed, it had been teasing and tender. This time it was hard and hot. A probing, aggressive kiss, that spoke in simple terms of penetration and harsh masculine edges, which made everything so very abrupt and uncomplicated. Combined with Takeshi's liquid touch, it made him feel crazy. His cock was hard in the guy's hand, but he still didn't know if he could go through with this. His body was saying it was OK, more than OK, but his mind still rebelled.

Silk pushed himself away from the security of the wall. Maybe, if he didn't feel so weak...

It took precisely two moves to reverse their positions – a simple step and turn and he had Takeshi pinned with his face to the wood and his hands held in the small of his back.

'Think I can't top you from here?' Takeshi laughed. 'Come on, then.' He wiggled his bum, so that it rubbed against Silk's hard-on. 'All you've got to do is work out how to get my jeans down and you can do me like you did Dolores.'

Somehow, Silk felt irrationally angry but horny at the same time. His skin was prickling with a static charge he couldn't get enough of. He wanted to lash out and run away from it all. He wanted to sink inside Takeshi's skin and ride out the wave of screaming bliss. 'I'm going to fuck you until you bloody scream,' he snarled.

'You couldn't even make me whimper.'

Was it possible to hate someone and desire them at the same time? He guessed it was, since that was how he was feeling. 'Oh, yeah?' He slapped Takeshi's arse, then dug his talons into the cheeks for good measure.

'Ouch!' Takeshi complained, although his smile never

wavered. 'That wasn't very nice. Think you've got what it takes to follow through?'

'Shut up and I'll show you what I've got.' He gave Takeshi another hard smack.

'You're boring me, man. Show me some action, blondie, and I might forgive you for fucking Remy.'

Silk jerked him away from the wall and flung him towards the oak table.

'The computer! Watch the computer!' Takeshi flapped frantically in the direction of the laptop. He slammed into the space beside it, sending two chairs flying, and began to laugh.

Silk tried to keep a grip on him, but he was slippery as an eel. Takeshi swung his legs up and hooked them around Silk's waist, then grabbed his upper body and pulled him on to the tabletop in a bruisingly close embrace.

He'd spent too much time this weekend letting his emotions rule him and not enough time acting. They should have fought it out on Friday night, got it out of their systems. The winner would have had Remy, and he'd never have become this riled about his sexuality.

They rolled along the tabletop, sending two of the candles flying. Wax stung as it splashed his cheek. Silk sought Takeshi's lips, even though they sent shivers through his soul.

'You're too perfect, too pretty.' Takeshi's breath was like hot smoke. He exposed Silk's chest. 'You make me want to hurt you, and do wicked, wicked things. Why did you have to have Remy?' He scored five lines down Silk's chest.

'You shouldn't have wound me up so tight. I was horny, and I thought it would blot you out.'

'Next time, try a little pain instead of pleasure.'

Silk flinched as Takeshi dashed a line of red wax from the remaining candle across his chest.

'That just makes me hungrier.' It was true: his cock

was begging to be free. He wanted to feel Takeshi's fingers working its length again. Instead, Takeshi's mouth closed around a nipple, then moved down, following the same trajectory as they had during the photo shoot in the Orangery. Those kisses had elevated him to a shivery kind of heaven and this time was no different.

Takeshi reached his waistband, undid the button with his teeth, and nuzzled open the zip. Silk's cock rose to greet him, from beneath the elastic of his pants. Each warm whispered breath caused it to buck in eager delight.

One lick was enough to have him arched off the table.

Takeshi's mouth was heaven – hot, wet and clever. He knew just how to work the length and tip in unison. Silk felt his breath grow shorter, until he was panting in time with Takeshi's bobbing head. He was good, so, so very good.

Too soon, Takeshi released him. Silk opened his eyes to find him on all fours astride his body, peering bemusedly at the slender weeping column between them.

'Seems you're all warmed up.' He bowed his head, licked the tip. 'Let's not waste it.'

Silk tensed. It was instinctive. Couldn't they do it without the dialogue? He didn't want to think about what he was doing. He could do that afterwards. Sweet Jesus, was he really gonna do this? What had happened to his reservations, his determination?

'How about I make things easy for you?' Takeshi said.

Silk wet his lips. 'Easy, how?'

Takeshi stood, his feet planted either side of Silk's hips on the table surface. He shimmied out of his jeans, to reveal smooth skin and no underwear. 'Forgot to put it on.' He winked, then pulled off his T-shirt, and sent it sailing into the gloom.

Silk stared up at his body. His eyes locked on the guy's

cock. It was ruddy, yet pale, delicate, yet hard, and, if not long, then long enough.

'Why don't you help me out a little?'

Takeshi knelt.

For a moment, Silk thought he would bring the pale stem to his lips, but instead Takeshi took him by the hand. 'Dress me and I'll dress you.'

Takeshi rolled the sheath down with his mouth, a trick that clearly required practice.

Silk rolled more uncertainly. He'd never actually touched anyone's but his own. It made this all too real. He pulled in his stomach, as inside his muscles began to knot. It felt so similar, yet so different. He smoothed his hand over the head, eased the latex down the length towards the dark thatch of hair.

'You needn't be so rough,' Takeshi joked. He batted away Silk's tentative caress and squeezed the air from the condom tip. 'There. Now, please, hurry up and fuck me.'

Silk's eyes opened wide. 'Wha –'

Takeshi planted a rough kiss across his lips, then rose into a crouch.

'Oh!' Silk's cock pushed into the tight heat as Takeshi slowly rose and fell.

The heat, the squeezing grip. He knew the sensations, but this was different. He was with a man. Stretched across a table, in a place where anyone might walk in. He was just about ready to admit this kink in his sexuality to himself. He wasn't ready to announce it to anyone else. Not yet.

'Easy,' sighed Takeshi. 'Easy.'

Silk shook his head. He wasn't going to last long.

Was this what it meant to be topped from below? No, he'd got his directions mixed up.

His hand slid all over Takeshi's body, exploring the masculine contours and the areas of muscle where he was used to soft curves. The fire streaking through his cock was almost too much. His vision felt blurred, everything was just a myriad of glowing lights and tactile sensation. Takeshi broke their embrace.

'*Ai!*' The candle wax fell as scalding raindrops and Silk was falling into the deepest, most beautiful place. His cock jerked in a rhythmic dance he couldn't control.

The next thing he knew, Takeshi was off the table and his cock was softening in the cold kitchen air. His head felt fuzzy, as though he'd drunk too much of Shaun's blasted absinthe.

Takeshi leant over him, sucking his thumb. 'Now it's my turn.' He pulled Silk towards the edge of the table, and eased apart his already bent legs. 'Ever experimented before?' He circled his thumb around Silk's tight anal whorl.

'Fingers.' Silk felt himself flush at the confession, which was crazy, since he'd just fucked the guy. 'And a small vibe.'

'Kinky boy.' Takeshi laughed. 'Not someone's bunny, I hope.'

Silk snapped his teeth.

'Ready for the real thing?'

'No.'

'Too bad.'

Silk grasped his hand. 'Don't we need some lube?'

Takeshi cocked his head to one side. 'I managed with saliva.'

'You've practised.' Silk squeezed his fingers tight.

'OK, relax. I suppose they need you to sit down at the wedding.' He sprinted the length of the room, and disappeared behind the divide into the kitchen area. A moment later, he reappeared with a can of stir-fry spray and a bowl.

'What's that?' Silk asked.

'This is for you.' Takeshi threw the lid of the can over his shoulder, then sprayed oil over Silk's rear, and his own cock. 'Ooh, cold! And this –' he spooned ice cream on to Silk's stomach '– is for me.' He immediately licked it off, leaving a wet sticky trail.

Silk squirmed. His stomach had always been sensitive. It was one of the reasons the encounter in the fountain had got to him so much.

'Ready?' Takeshi prompted. ' 'Cause this is it.' He licked away more vanilla sauce, then pushed.

Silk held his breath, anticipating pain. He must have been more relaxed than he thought, because Takeshi easily slipped inside, forcing a sharp exhalation from his lips. It felt so strange. Far stranger than doing it the other way around, but then the whole scenario was screwed up. It didn't even match the images he had in his head of their union. He'd always imagined pushing into Takeshi from behind, or perhaps on some hidden level, of being taken the same way. The possibility of doing it face to face had never occurred to him. It made it far more personal. Especially when Takeshi clasped him tight, draped his legs over his shoulders and began to rock.

The movement was slight to begin with, and gradually worked deeper. Silk sighed in time with the motion. His nerve endings were on fire, and he wanted to rub away the sensation of being so stretched. At the same time, he anticipated with pleasure the moments when Takeshi filled him to the hilt and nudged into his prostate in a crazily delicious way. Those moments were like black magic. To begin with, they were few, just dark burns that fired his senses, and revived his erection. But slowly they slid together, bursting through his abdomen like dying stars, until the rushing in his ears matched the rushing rhythmic jerks of his cock as it left sticky dots against his own stomach.

He was going to come again – and hard.

'Give it up to me.' Takeshi clasped Silk's cock and began to work its length.

Silk lost his focus. He was trembling. Takeshi seemed to glitter in the candlelight. And he was aware of their scent. He'd never really noticed it before. It was heady and sweet, with a musky undercurrent of testosterone and sweat. Then he was jerking to the rhythm of Takeshi's orgasm, and weeping opaline tears over his own stomach.

'*Omae wa ore no mono desu,*' Takeshi gasped. Their gazes locked. '*Kore kara zutto ... itsumademo.*'

15

Silk left the kitchen with a grin on his face. He couldn't help it. He had no idea what Takeshi had said to him, but he knew what he'd felt, and he had absolute faith in that. There was nothing wrong with feeling attracted to the other man. Why had he been denying himself? His body was buzzing just from the thought of feeling Takeshi's touch again.

The stairs seemed steep. His muscles felt a little tender, not painful precisely, just stretched and, well, used. He hadn't wanted it to end. That second orgasm with Takeshi inside him had felt like an explosion in his skull, or maybe his groin. It had been the most fantastic thing he'd ever felt. Normally, sex left him wanting more. Now, he just felt exhausted and relieved. Luckily the bedroom was deserted. Shaun was obviously off being primped. Silk stretched out on his bed, and watched the sunlight play out across the ceiling. He smiled, his eyelids slowly closing.

When he woke, it was dark, and there were voices in the corridor.

Silk glanced at the blurred face of Shaun's digital alarm clock. It was twenty past eight. Just over three hours left until the wedding.

'Mother! For the last time, I'm not throwing my bouquet. I'm getting it pressed.' He sat abruptly at the sound of Chelsea's voice. Dolores was obviously back and still as self-centred as ever.

'There's no need to shout, dear. We could just do a little pass outside, just enough so that people see me catch it.'

Silk drew his hands back through his hair, then noise-lessly padded to the door. He opened it a fraction and peered out, careful not to be seen.

'No, no, no, no, no! Tell her, Shaun.'

'She's not tossing it,' Shaun said, on cue. He draped a protective arm around Chelsea's shoulder. 'And she doesn't owe you any favours. Besides, catching it doesn't guarantee you'll get married, even if you could find a bloke crazy enough.'

'Your best man appreciates me.'

Silk shook his head.

Shaun laughed. 'Not enough to marry you. Not even enough for an encore.'

Thanks, buddy. Silk rubbed his jaw, where there was the faintest hint of stubble. He needed to shave.

'Well, for your information, I've found somebody who is interested.' Dolores fluffed her hair.

'Who?'

'Your dad's neighbour.'

'Cranthorpe!'

'He thought I was the hottest thing he'd ever seen when he saw me with Silk yesterday. I met him again in the pub.'

'Jesus, mother!' Chelsea turned her back in disgust. 'Remind me why you're still on the guest list. Did you ever once think of making an apology? No, you were too busy chatting up blokes in the pub to worry about how much you'd upset me. You're a Grade A bitch.' She grasped Shaun's hand, tugged him into the lounge and slammed the door.

Silk waited for Dolores to head down the stairs before he slipped along the corridor to the bathroom. He shaved, then stepped under the shower and let the water stream down his body. The euphoria he'd felt after leaving the kitchen was finally beginning to wear off. Instead, he felt a tightening of nerves that caused his stomach to flutter. What had Takeshi whispered to him while in the throws of orgasm? Had it been as romantic as it sounded, or some crude remark? And what came next? Would Takeshi and Remy go off together, leaving him here alone to dream of the best sex he'd ever had? He shook his head, causing his long hair to stick to his wet skin. There were too many variables. Besides, he had to switch off his libido and concentrate on his role as best man, make sure he had the ring and knew his speech, that sort of thing.

Shaun was buttoning his shirt when Silk returned from the bathroom wrapped in a hand towel. It seemed everyone else had already beaten him to the bath sheets.

'Hey, can you fasten these?' Shaun walked towards him, fumbling with a white cravat. 'Remy gave me a diagram, but I still don't get it.'

Silk absently knotted the neck cloth so that it hung in a fetching array of frothy lace and silk. 'À la Byron.' He grabbed his towel before it fell. 'It used to take Beau Brummell hours and an armful of starched cravats to get it right, so . . .'

'What chance have I got?' Shaun surveyed the knot in the mirror. 'Not bad, been practising, have you?'

Silk poured some aftershave into his hands and splashed it on to his skin. 'One tries.'

'You're back to your happy self, then?'

'Your advice worked a treat.'

Shaun rolled his eyes. 'Whore.'

'That's why you love me.' He clasped Shaun by the shoulders. 'How are you holding up? Not too nervous?'

'I'll be fine so long as I don't forget my lines.'

Silk shook himself free of the towel, and pulled some underwear out of a drawer. 'I think you just repeat after the vicar.'

Two storeys down, Remy sagged against the table in the windowless workroom. 'Enough already. That's the best I can do. I'm a designer, not a plastic surgeon.' The hours had melted away since she'd left Takeshi's bed. She was still dressed in her jumper and over-knee socks, with bed hair and no makeup, despite having been up about twelve hours. Dolores had just stormed in, with another crisis. She'd been back and forth all afternoon, obsessing about her outfit and appearance. Apparently, she'd found herself an admirer, and was determined to reel the poor fool in.

'But my boobs keep sagging.'

Remy bit back a remark about age and gravity. She was tired. She wanted a shower and five minutes' sit-down before she got herself ready. She'd already cinched and loosened Dolores's outfit half a dozen times and lengthened the side slit of the skirt by four inches, from knee to thigh length, between dressing Chelsea and the bridesmaids and adjusting Shaun's new outfit. Enough was enough.

'Try gaffer tape,' Alix suggested. Remy turned her head, relieved to find herself with backup. The photographer was dressed in a slinky, green velvet dress and strappy shoes. 'It's what they used in films before the invention of the Wonderbra.'

'Toupee tape,' suggested Remy. 'That's what we used at fashion college. And, no, I don't have any.'

Alix produced a roll of black tape. 'Leave it to me.' She gave Remy a deeply evil grin. 'It'll hurt like hell to get off. Go on, shoo. Get dressed.' She headed towards Dolores waving the tape.

Remy went next door and showered, swaddled herself in towels, then grabbed a brew from the kitchen and headed up to the lounge. Marianne was curled up on the sofa reading *Lair of the White Worm*.

'Borrowed it from Lulu,' she said in response to Remy's inquisitive glance. Despite her apparent love of corsets, she'd gone all Marlene Dietrich, with bow tie, shirt and tails. 'Aren't you ready yet? Everybody else's been running around like headless zombies for ages. Chelsea's still fretting.' She flicked her gaze towards the ceiling, and then back to Remy slumped in the armchair. 'It's half-ten, you know.'

Realising she wasn't going to get any peace, anyway, Remy took the hint and headed up to the cap house, to find Shadow occupying the chair, and staring at her meaningfully. 'OK, I get the message. I'll get dressed.'

She'd perfected her hair and makeup, and just slipped into her dress – a blood-red satin affair based on an Edwardian evening dress she'd once seen in a museum – when Takeshi called up the stairs.

'Ready?' he asked, appearing in the archway. 'The cars are here. We need to go before the carriage arrives for Chelsea and the bridesmaids.'

'Almost.' Remy turned towards him, while she struggled with the back of her earring.

He looked amazing.

He'd dressed in a watermarked silk suit, and the soft mauve fabric clung to his body like a second skin, emphasising his masculinity, while lending him a hint of androgyny. The whole effect was so exquisite, it almost hurt to look at him. Remy flicked her tongue across her bottom lip. 'Wow!'

'Here, let me.' He fastened her earring while she ran a finger around the inside of his cuff. He'd matched the suit with a dusky grey silk shirt, and left the collar and cuffs undone. It was so beautiful she wanted to rub up against it like a cat. She'd expected this sort of thing of Silk after she'd seen him dressed up that first night, but not from Takeshi. The outfit was a complete surprise. 'Where did you get it?'

'Relic of my past.'

'*Bosozoku* wear this sort of stuff?' At least he hadn't acquired it locally. Competition of this calibre wouldn't be good for business.

'No. It's a *Visual Kei* thing.'

'Eloise mentioned that.'

'Yeah, it's a type of J-pop. Get your shoes on.'

Remy laced her suede ankle boots and followed him to the top landing. 'Have you given Silk any more thought?' Picturing the pair naked together had sustained her throughout Dolores's many fittings.

Takeshi inclined his head a fraction. He was wearing makeup, she realised, just a faint touch of mascara and a shiny smear of lip gloss; but, still, that was unexpected, too. 'A little.' He lowered his eyelashes.

She knew immediately that something had happened. She was going to be furious if they'd been bonking like bunnies while she'd been attending to Dolores. Takeshi headed down the stairs, denying her the chance to question him. There was no opportunity to talk on the way to the church, either, wedged into an open-top Daimler with Alix, Marianne and Dolores.

The fiddler, as promised, was sending an eerie, melancholy tune through the graveyard when they arrived. The lane was lined with cars, while packs of overdressed, and in some cases clown-faced, guests lingered among the tombs. Despite the recent rains, the night was dry, and the air passably balmy.

They filed past the congregation and took their seats in the ivy-covered chapel. Alix and Marianne peeled off towards the choir stalls, where a tripod had been set up earlier. Dolores sat on the edge of the front row, where she could scan the pews behind her without getting neck strain. Remy and Takeshi sidled into an empty pew halfway back.

'Did something happen earlier?' She nuzzled against the watermarked silk covering his shoulder, but the show of affection didn't work.

'Should there have?'

She felt his body stiffen, and followed his line of vision to find Silk, resplendent in the outfit she'd made him, looking at them with a wan smile playing about his lips.

'You've shagged him, haven't you?'

A cock crowed, heralding the first strains of *Danse Macabre*. Suddenly, everyone was on their feet. Remy followed suit. Chelsea swept down the aisle like a demon princess, both majestic and resplendent in her Dark Designs dress, followed by the trinity of Gothic angels she knew as the Gorgons. They reached the altar, and stopped beside Silk and a totally gobsmacked Shaun.

'Have you?' she hissed, as they reclaimed their seats.

'What do you think?'

She didn't know what to think. That was the problem. Would he really have excluded her after his words that morning? He'd claimed he loved her.

An hour later, they filed back out into the moonlight, heads full of Lulu's crazy verse. Her performance had been even more dramatic than the rehearsal. Remy leant against a crooked cross and watched Alix bunch people into groups for photographs. She'd lost Takeshi in the crush on the way out of the chapel.

'You've done a very good job, dear,' Shaun's gran congratulated her as they were forced together for a picture. 'Everyone's been asking about the outfits. You've made Shaun look decent for a change. Hasn't got his father's style. He was always like Silk. He could pull off anything. What am I saying?' She laughed. 'He still can.'

Remy nodded politely. Richard D'Amon's dress sense was best described as eccentric. He was currently wearing a vintage Vivienne Westwood tartan.

'Are you the designer?' A group of women flocked around. 'Will you do mine? I'm getting hitched in July. You're not too expensive, are you?'

'Here.' Remy passed around some business cards. 'Give me a call, or drop into Chelsea's shop.'

The rest of her cards soon went. A surprisingly high proportion of them went to men, although, with Silk as her model, maybe that wasn't such a surprise. What had Alix said? 'Anyone looking at the images should be thinking, I want to be this person or be with them.' Well, so far that strategy seemed to be working.

The fiddler was dancing a macabre jig, surrounded by a circle of clapping onlookers by the church door. Remy stuck her head inside. 'Seen Takeshi?' she asked one of the ushers.

'Nope. Seen Silk? They're almost ready to head over to the reception.'

Remy shook her head. Coincidence, that they'd both disappeared at the same time? Not likely. Not when Takeshi was already being cagey. Why the hell was he suddenly shutting her out? The idea of their sneaking off for a secret assignation and a snog was a rather big turn-on. It'd have been nice if they'd have brought her in, but perhaps he was punishing her for being so pushy. She'd go and find him, and apologise somehow.

Silk had stuck around for all the important photos, but, once Alix moved on to snapping random friends and acquaintances, he headed away from the action along the narrow path down the side of the chapel. It was half past one now. By the time they'd got through the reception and partying, it'd be dawn. He already felt drained and yet strangely wired. At least here, away from the glare of the camera flash, he could find a moment's respite.

Silk carefully rubbed his eyes. He reached the back of the chapel. Here, where the shadows were at their thickest, and sprawling ivy obscured most of the chapel walls, there was a tiny secret garden, formed of holly bushes and a gnarled yew tree. It contained a single sepulchre, planted all around with tiny forget-me-nots. It was also his favourite time-out spot at this end of the estate. And he needed some time out. He didn't know what he'd expected to happen after the explosion of lust they'd poured into each other this afternoon, but he knew that seeing Takeshi wandering about, smiling, with Remy on his arm, was eating away at his insides. The fleeting smile in the church had not been enough. He needed more reassurance than that. He needed to be certain that, come daylight, they weren't both going to up and leave him house-sitting alone.

Silk squeezed through the tiny gateway, taking care not to catch any of Remy's exquisitely made clothing, to find Takeshi perched atop the grave, with his head resting upon his knees. 'What are you doing here?' He pulled the gate to, and walked forwards slowly.

'Escaping from Alix. Hoping you'd follow.' Takeshi raised his head. 'I'm not much for soul-sapping photographs. You?'

'After some breathing space. We need to talk.'

'Again.' Takeshi shimmied to the edge of the box.

Silk lowered his eyes, and tentatively placed a hand on Takeshi's thigh. 'I need to know if this is going anywhere.'

'Where did you have in mind?'

Silk slid his hand up the watermarked cloth towards Takeshi's crotch.

'Wasn't once enough?' Takeshi asked.

'Once is never enough.' He pulled Takeshi down towards him until their lips met. There were endless possibilities he needed to explore with this man. Accepting that he wasn't as straight as he'd thought was bursting open doors in his psyche. He wanted to make long slow love out here in the open, have hot uncomplicated quickies in armchairs and shop doorways, and in the shadows at the edge of a dance floor. He wanted to feel the intense pleasure of being filled again, and feel his loins slap against Takeshi's cheeks. He wanted to look into his eyes as he came. If he'd felt this way about any of his past lovers, he didn't recall it. Shallow vignettes to feed his craving for physical release were what most of them had been about. But what he was feeling now was something different.

Takeshi's hands were in his hair, rubbing and pulling so that the strands had locked around his fingers. Like the splashes of candle wax earlier, each tug spliced physical pain and emotional delight. They stung his senses, but only made him lust for Takeshi all the harder.

Eventually though, they both needed air. They paused with their foreheads pressed together, both breathing urgently.

'I did it for her, you know.' Takeshi's words were slightly laboured, and his dark eyes downcast. 'I can't make this just about us.'

'So, what? I have to share you with Remy?'

Takeshi shook his head. 'It's not that simple. She wants to watch us together.'

'Yes, I know about her fantasy. She told me. But, she's no simple voyeur. She puts herself right into the heart of the action. I swear, when we were in the bath together, if she could have grown a cock and buggered me herself, she would have. She's like a chameleon. If she could create a convincing enough costume and hit the gay bars, she probably would.'

Takeshi dropped on to the ground and paced as far as the gate. 'Looks like she made an impression.'

Silk inclined his head. Her whole body had been consumed by the fantasy. 'If it hadn't been for her, we wouldn't be standing here now. She was so into what she was describing. I probably owe her for making me confront myself.'

Takeshi returned to Silk's side. 'Are you saying you want to give her what she wants?'

Silk pressed an intrusive kiss to Takeshi's lips. His hands closed over the other man's bum and squeezed.

'You did suggest a threesome at the start of the weekend.'

'But that's not what she wants.' Takeshi splayed his finger across Silk's chest, and held him at a distance.

'Isn't it?' Silk clasped Takeshi's hand and forced their bodies closer. 'No way is she going to be content just to watch.' He pushed his hand between them and rubbed his palm across Takeshi's fly. 'Come on, it'll be fun. And I promise I won't steal her.'

Takeshi batted away the caress. 'I'm still not convinced. She's been adamant about not wanting to take part.'

Silk shook his head. 'Trust me on this. I know women.'

The path that wound around the side of the church seemed like the most obvious direction to start her search. Remy headed deeper and deeper into the shadows, and further from the music of the crowd. People were beginning to pile into cars; one or two had already pulled away. She could just see Chelsea, standing by the carriage, flanked by Shaun and Eloise. The glass beads on her dress winked like stars in the black fire of her skirts; here, the narrow path soon dissolved into a stretch of downtrodden grass skirting a hedgerow. She was just about to turn back, feeling faintly stupid, when Silk stepped through a virtually invisible gateway just beside her.

'Remy! Am I needed?' He fled away from her, making her wonder if he'd been receiving threats from Takeshi rather than kisses.

'Silk.'

He hurried off. Remy went through the gateway, and walked straight into Takeshi. 'What are you doing?' she demanded.

He shrugged. 'Taking a piss.'

'Was Silk holding it for you?'

'Of course not. We were just having a little chat.' He smeared a kiss across her lips and chin. 'Bet that idea turns you on, though.'

'I'd rather see you fuck.'

'Really.' There was twinkle in his eyes. 'I never would have guessed that.'

'What are you plotting?'

His infuriating grin broadened. 'Telling you would only spoil the surprise.'

16

The reception was passing in a blur of courses. King scallops followed by mushroom-and-asparagus filo parcels and now sea bass. Takeshi picked at his food. It was all very well joking with Remy about what he was supposedly plotting with Silk, but, actually, he had major reservations about the whole scenario.

He hadn't planned what had happened in the kitchen. The situation had just swept him along. Silk wanted him. Remy wanted to watch him make love to Silk. It seemed simple enough. All he had to do was go along with it, and he gained two lovers. The problem was, he didn't really want to share Remy, and he was reluctant to commit to something so potentially disastrous – even if Silk *was* hot as hell, and his philosophy *had* always been 'live wild, live free'.

OK, so it went out of the window where his relationships were concerned. If he'd taken a risk and told Megumi how he'd felt, he might not have lost out so badly, and she might still have been the reckless angel he once knew. If he tried things out with Silk and Remy, it might fall apart, but at least he'd have gained some pleasure. If he didn't act, he'd likely lose her anyway. She didn't seem interested in a 'normal' relationship.

'Something wrong with your fish?' Remy asked.

He blinked uncertainly, then realised that he'd been holding his fork inches from his mouth for the last few minutes. 'No.' He swallowed, but the whole table was watching him. To avoid making eye contact, he looked across at the top table, but that was a mistake, too. Silk was facing his way.

'I want you,' the best man mouthed. He glanced around him quickly to make sure no one was watching his frantic lip movements. Then, 'Meet me outside when they go.'

By 'they', Takeshi assumed he meant Shaun and Chelsea. That probably gave him an hour or so to come to a decision.

He turned back to Remy, and was relieved to find her talking to Alix about the catalogue photos. At least Silk hadn't just raised her expectations, even if he had just raised the stakes.

The night was growing old. Dawn was threatening to creep across the horizon.

Remy left Takeshi at their table and followed the bride and groom outside. Following the meal, Sev had run a sweepstake on the length of the speeches, which Chelsea had won, having accurately predicted seven minutes forty for Silk, and fifty-five seconds for Shaun. It had been a fix, of course. After that, they'd pushed back the tables to make a dance floor, and most of the guests had slunk off to look moody in dimly lit corners, although some had roused themselves enough to freak out on the dance floor.

It was cold on the lawn, after the press of bodies in the heated marquee. A small group of loyal friends watched the back of Chelsea's car weave its way down the driveway, the tin cans and skeletal limbs rattling over the gravel like a loose exhaust. Mrs and Mr D'Amon were flying to Bucharest at six o'clock, then heading north across the Walachian Plain and up through the Carpathian Mountains to Transylvania.

'Dracula wasn't from Transylvania,' someone had snidely remarked just as the bride and groom had got in the car.

'But Frank N Furter was,' Shaun quipped, stunning the smartarse into silence and sending a ripple of laughter through the onlookers. 'And I believe you'll find Vlad Dracula was born in Sighisoara, Transylvania.'

Remy wished them luck. She also hoped they'd let her come and visit. Shaun's parents had made a gift of the castle, and she'd become rather fond of her cap-house room. After all the frantic wedding preparations, she could do with a few days' holiday. She turned back towards Silk to ask him if he fancied some company house-sitting, but he'd already gone.

'Dammit!' She'd been hoping to pump him for information about what was going on with Takeshi, since he'd been acting weird ever since they'd left the chapel. Takeshi seemed to have lost his sense of humour and he'd been actively trying to avoid eye contact with Silk, even during the speeches.

Back inside the marquee, everyone had crowded on to the dance floor for 'Temple of Love'. The Gorgons were at the centre, performing a Gothic version of vogueing, surrounded by a ring of overdressed men whose only movement was to flick their long hair back dramatically out of time with the beat. There was no sign of Silk. Or Takeshi. He was no longer at the table where she'd left him.

Remy lifted her drink and swallowed. The champagne bubbled on her tongue, but she barely noticed the frothy fizz. They were together. She just knew it. Somehow, they'd managed to slink off the moment she'd turned her back.

Remy drained the glass and slammed it down. Her gaze flickered rapidly around the marquee. Dolores was perched on Major Cranthorpe's knee, clutching one of the bridesmaids' bouquets, which she'd somehow persuaded Chelsea to throw. Shaun's dad was still reminiscing with Steve Evans, the Gorgons' father, about their days in Toys in the Attic, and Alix was staggering towards her with Marianne a foot behind. But there was no sign of the two men.

'Remy.' Alix collapsed against her. 'Beautiful, sexy, Remy. I'm sorry. So very sorry.'

'What for?' One whiff of Alix's breath was all Remy needed to realise her friend was sloshed. She gently pushed against Alix's shoulders, trying to free herself from the drunken cuddle. She didn't have time for a repeat of Christmas. Not when her boys were MIA.

'For deserting you. I found someone else. It's Marianne,' Alix hissed conspiratorially.

Suddenly, seeing her in Alix's dressing gown that morning made sense. It also explained why Alix hadn't hounded her about the nude photo shoot. 'No problem. Good for you both.' She offered Marianne a smile over Alix's shoulder.

'I'm gonna focus on my new muse,' Alix confided, as if following Remy's thoughts. 'Already got some good ones, thanks to Takeshi.'

Eek! She'd forgotten about the photos he'd taken of them having sex. She'd have to find that memory card. She might owe Alix a few nudes but she definitely wouldn't want hardcore.

A small crowd of women had assembled to the right of the bar. Remy squinted at them. They appeared to be looking at something – some sort of tussle. Surely, nobody was fighting at a wedding reception. Suddenly there was an almighty screech. It turned virtually every head in the marquee.

Oh, God! She'd found them.

When Remy went outside to wave off Shaun and Chelsea, Takeshi stayed behind in the marquee. He wasn't going to play Silk's game. He wanted to be in control. The problem was, he didn't feel in control of anything.

The bar didn't have any sake. Good job, really, because he didn't actually like it. He just fancied something strong that might numb the cocktail of thoughts in his head. 'Give me something with a kick,' he demanded of the barman.

The tequila burned on the way down, and hit his stomach like scorpion venom. He paid for another, and walked away from the bar into the shadow of the speaker stacks. The thumping base was making the ground vibrate. It made him long for home and the roaring thunder of his custom-built bike. Everything was simple when he was on the back of that beast. The world faded into a background stream of colour and white noise.

'I can't believe you stood me up.' Silk's voice breathed straight into his ear.

Takeshi turned sharply to find Silk holding his glass aloft. 'Cheers.' He entwined their arms before taking a sip from his drink. Tentatively, Takeshi followed suit. The guy was lethal. He might have zero experience with men, but he knew how to seduce. He knew how to inspire that tantalising mix of apprehension and longing. Takeshi tensed, wondering what came next. When he hadn't gone outside, he hadn't thought Silk would come and find him so quickly. He thought it would give him deliberation time.

'Is pleasure such a hard gift to give?' Silk's voice was warm and husky. He looked gorgeous dressed in the outfit Remy had made him with, his cravat hanging loose. 'Give us what we want and you get to keep us both.'

Takeshi turned away from the invitation. He couldn't think straight looking into Silk's eyes. Would he really get to keep them both?

A crowd of onlookers had assembled a short distance away. Silk's groupies, he realised. Any one of them would jump at the chance he had.

'You're thinking too hard. Finish what you set in motion when you made me kiss you.' Silk draped an arm around his shoulders. When Takeshi turned his head, Silk turned the casual embrace into a passionate clinch. 'Now I've made the decision for you,' he whispered into Takeshi's mouth.

Even over the music, Takeshi could hear the squeals of outrage and delight. He wondered if Remy was watching.

Silk tasted good. Chocolate and brandy stung his senses, and mingled with the aftertaste of the tequila. Silk reached down and ran a thumbnail up his thigh and along the length of his trapped cock. The movement was firm, determined, arousing. Takeshi automatically rolled his hips in response.

OK, he was going to do this. He was going to live fast and dangerous again, but first they needed to thin the audience a little. This show was meant for only one lady.

'Let's take this into the castle,' he said. 'She'll find us.'

Remy's fingers tightened around Alix's shoulders. Her friend squeezed her tighter too, probably to avoid falling over. Her two men were kissing! Hell, they were more than kissing. Silk's hair was draped around them like a snowy cloak and Takeshi was putting his hands inside Silk's clothes. They were performing. And the audience was growing rapidly.

'Let go, Alix. Marianne!'

Remy launched Alix backwards into Marianne's arms. She didn't want to watch over the heads of the crowd. She wanted to be in the front row.

Remy pushed her way across the dance floor, but the men had gone when she reached the speaker stacks. She searched frantically, her heartbeat so rapid it seemed to be keeping rhythm with the thumping bass. A group of spellbound women were staring towards the exit in a sort of dazed stupor, as if they hadn't quite taken in what they'd witnessed.

Remy headed outside before any of them recovered

their wits. She didn't want to be part of a baying pack of she-wolves hungry for ringside seats of Silk in action. This was her show. She'd been the one who wanted this. She'd been behind it all – well, sort of.

There was no sign of them on the lawn. Remy raced around the outside of the marquee, then along the line of parked cars as fast as her three-inch heels would allow. Where had they gone? What was Takeshi playing at?

She slumped against the bonnet of a red Fiesta and peered into the shadows around the castle's base. Slowly, her gaze crept skywards. There were lights on in all the windows, just as there'd been on the night she'd arrived.

Of course! It'd be quiet inside, and warm, and private.

She flung open every door on the dingy bottom corridor, then started climbing. There seemed to be more steps than she remembered, and her calves protested at each one. She couldn't believe they'd just slipped away, after all the things Takeshi had said. He knew how much she wanted to see them together.

She reached the second floor. Silk's room was ahead. It was the obvious choice, being the nearest. She hesitated, wondering if she was supposed to wait for them to find her before she got the 'surprise' Takeshi had hinted at, then burst in regardless.

The room was deserted.

Disappointed, Remy limped along the corridor to the lounge, which was also empty.

Remy pressed her head to the stone mantle and stared blankly at the dead ash in the grate. A niggling seed of doubt began to germinate. Maybe they were deliberately excluding her. What if she couldn't find them, or she found them and they told her to leave? What if they didn't want a little voyeur spying on them? Not that she wanted just to stand and watch. Her fantasies were much more complex than that. She'd always been inside the minds of the fantasy men she created, living, breathing and feeling each thrust, each caress. How could she translate that into reality?

Remy kicked the coal bucket. The resulting bang was far louder than she'd anticipated, but it was the echoed thump from directly above that grabbed her attention.

Her gaze shot towards the ceiling. They were in the master bedroom. Of course! Silk was house-sitting. He was hardly going to sleep in a single bed for three weeks when there was a king-size upstairs.

Remy scooted up the spiral staircase two steps at a time, and barged straight into the bedroom.

The room was dim, the only light coming from two Tiffany lamps. Silk was sitting on the edge of the bed, his shirt open to the waist, revealing a teasing sliver of naked chest.

Her next words never made it out of her mouth. Takeshi was on his knees between Silk's thighs, still fully clothed, but with his hands clasped possessively around Silk's hips while he sucked his long cock.

His hair shimmered as he rocked. It was perhaps the most erotic thing she'd ever seen. More thigh-squeezingly good than when she'd watched them share that first dangerous kiss.

It lasted mere seconds before both pairs of eyes turned towards her.

'What took you so long?' Takeshi asked.

'I couldn't find you.' Remy edged crablike to the nearby wicker chair. Her knees felt ready to buckle. 'You knew I'd follow?'

'Once we had your attention.'

Hers and a fair few others. She swallowed hard. What came next?

Silk threaded his fingers through Takeshi's hair. 'Less talk, more action, eh?'

Takeshi laughed, then engulfed Silk's cock to the root in a single mouthful.

Remy sank her teeth into her lower lip. This was for

real. She'd never really believed it would happen, not even when she'd coaxed Takeshi that morning. Her heart gave a frightening little flutter. She loved him. How could she not? He was prepared to do anything for her, even when it was against his own better judgement. Could she reject that?

Silk was watching her expression, though his hair masked much of his own. When she locked eyes with him, he beckoned her with a tilt of his head.

'No,' she mouthed, despite the magnetic draw towards them.

'Scaredy-cat. Come and hold my hand.' He reached out towards her, while he used the other hand to quicken Takeshi's pace, his fingers curling and stretching across the back of his lover's head. He tilted his chin upward, as his back started to flex in time with the roll of his hips. Mesmerised by the motion and the smooth skin of his throat, Remy rocked her own hips to their rhythm.

Back and forth, they moved together. Back and forth, until, like the swish of a whip, Silk arched his back, shuddered, and spent between Takeshi's lips. Remy shimmied off the wicker chair in response and edged towards them on her knees.

Takeshi rose and pushed Silk down on to the bed. Their mouths met clumsily, hungrily, while their bodies locked together like Siamese twins. The energy between them crackled and sparked, as if she could reach out and get a static shock from their bodies.

Entranced by their writhing motion, conscious of the heat between her own thighs, Remy bit into the fleshy base of her thumb.

'Remy.' Takeshi's voice cut through her awareness. 'Come closer.' He patted the mattress.

This time she didn't hesitate.

Remy crossed the gap, and sat beside them. She could smell the thick musky scent of their bodies, the faint spice of aftershave, and traces of alcohol, incense and rice-paper confetti. A hot wash rippled through her from her toes. Her clothing felt too tight. She wanted to kick off her boots and unhook the corset she'd worn beneath her clothes. She wanted to press her skin to theirs and feel their heat.

Silk's shirt was thrown at the closet. Takeshi's trousers came down with his pants, so that the muscular globes of his cheeks shone like honey glazing. Instinctively, she stroked her palm over the bare skin, letting her thumb tease the shadowy channel between the cheeks, then sweep across the back of his thigh.

His head came up in response.

She wanted to sink herself into him, and feel the combined pounding of their hearts. She wanted to see Silk possess him, fuck him, until he begged for mercy and relief.

Four hands grabbed at her clothing. 'No,' she protested, but both the deep-brown gaze and the luminous-green one drew her closer.

Fingers crept beneath the lace of her panties, peeled away her dress and lifted her breasts from the corset. Takeshi's cock pressed hard against her thigh. Two mouths closed over her nipples. Long, clever fingers coaxed her clit. 'No! Oh, no,' she whimpered. She wasn't supposed to be the focus. They were supposed to concentrate exclusively on each other. She was the spectator in this. Except that it felt good. Deliciously good. Her mouth opened, only for Takeshi's tongue to push inside, as he rolled on top of her.

'But I want –'

His cock sought the warmth of her body.

'Shh! I know what you want.'

He opened her with two fingers, and guided himself into her molten heat. She felt her body welcome him, but a sense of frustration still crawled beneath her skin.

His hands came up to cup her face. 'Trust me, Remy. Trust me.'

She didn't want to. This was changing the ending she'd written. But her body was less inclined to protest. It didn't want him to stop. He was killing her with the nuzzling, concentrated kisses to her neck. They paralysed her, blanked all thoughts from her mind, and turned her into a ball of sighing and gyrating senses. She even forgot about Silk watching them. At least, until Takeshi went still.

Remy opened her eyes to find Silk above them both. There was a look of intense concentration on his face.

'Do it. All the way.' Takeshi swallowed slowly. Sweat beaded across his upper lip. Remy nibbled it away. It tasted salty.

Silk fell like a shadow. Takeshi's hips ground into hers, and she watched his eyes roll upwards. Silk was inside him. She could feel him through Takeshi and in the altered motion of their bodies. It was finally happening: her fantasy was reality.

The bedsprings whinnied as the three of them rocked, Silk dictating the rhythm.

Takeshi kept trying to talk, but the words wouldn't come out. She didn't think he'd last long. But who cared? Life didn't get any better than this. She could see both men, each beautiful in his own special way: Silk blond and fey, but with that unmistakable hint of predatory masculinity; Takeshi a study of androgynous, Oriental beauty. They were making love as she'd dreamt they would, fucking on a rumpled bed, unconcerned by thoughts of being found. The shutters were wide, the door still open, and two hundred guests were partying outside.

She'd never imagined being this close to the action, but, in her heart, it was where she'd always wanted to be. It was where she wanted to stay.

Takeshi's cheeks were blazing, growing redder by the second. The blush suited him. Silk had the glazed expression of a man on the fast train to paradise, but, in the end, she beat them both, coming with a shriek she couldn't prevent and that would have arched her up off the bed if she hadn't had two bodies above her.

'I love you. I love you both,' she sobbed, tears rolling down her cheeks.

'You'd better,' Takeshi managed to grunt. Silk bucked inside his arse, pushing him over the edge. Remy watched their faces as they came. When she finally went to sleep, she knew she'd see them again in her dreams. And again in the morning.

'Wanna help me house-sit?' Silk asked her as he leant over Takeshi's shoulder to plant a kiss upon her brow. He rolled off them on to the bed, and sank into the eiderdown. 'There's no TV and minimal heating, but the room service is excellent.' He gave a playful roll of his hips.

Remy stretched and gave a languorous sigh. 'I'm in.' She nudged Takeshi with her elbow.

'What I want to know', he said, grinning broadly, 'is whether there are enough condoms in the place. And is there a sex shop in the village so we can get Remy a strap-on?'

'No.' Silk smirked. 'But there's a cucumber in the fridge.'

Visit the Black Lace website at
www.blacklace-books.co.uk

FIND OUT THE LATEST INFORMATION AND TAKE ADVANTAGE OF OUR FANTASTIC FREE BOOK OFFER! ALSO VISIT THE SITE FOR . . .

- All Black Lace titles currently available and how to order online
- Great new offers
- Writers' guidelines
- Author interviews
- An erotica newsletter
- Features
- Cool links

BLACK LACE – THE LEADING IMPRINT OF WOMEN'S SEXY FICTION

TAKING YOUR EROTIC READING PLEASURE TO NEW HORIZONS

LOOK OUT FOR THE ALL-NEW BLACK LACE BOOKS – AVAILABLE NOW!

All books priced £7.99 in the UK. Please note publication dates apply to the UK only. For other territories, please contact your retailer.

ASKING FOR TROUBLE
Kristina Lloyd
ISBN 0 352 33362 6

When Beth Bradshaw – the manager of a fashionable bar in the seaside town of Brighton – starts flirting with the handsome Ilya, she becomes a player in a game based purely on sexual brinkmanship. The boundaries between fantasy and reality start to blur as their relationship takes on an increasingly reckless element.

When Ilya's murky past catches up with him, he's determined to involve Beth. Unwilling to extricate herself from their addictive games, she finds herself being drawn deeper into the seedy underbelly of Brighton where things, including Ilya, are far more dangerous than she bargained for.

Coming in December

THE SOCIETY OF SIN
Sian Lacey Taylder
ISBN 0 352 34080 0

Or, perhaps, 'Lust and Laura Ashley'. *The Society of Sin* is an erotic, gothic thriller set in rural Dorset in the late 19th Century, a period when educated women were beginning to question their sexuality.

The Society of Sin was conceived on a hot and sticky summer's evening inside a mansion house on a large country estate when, after an opium-fuelled night of passion, Lady P and her close friend Samantha Powerstock succumbed to desires they had both repressed for years. Now, a year later, they have invited a select few to join their exclusive association. But only genuine hedonists need apply; prospective members are interrogated over a sumptuous dinner then given an 'assignment' which they must fulfil. Failure to do so results in instant expulsion and the prospect of being 'named and shamed' in the exclusive circles they currently frequent. However, successful completion of the task opens for them a Pandora's box of pain and pleasure:

Summer sees the arrival of Miss Charlotte Crowsettle, who immediately falls under Lady P's spell.

CONTINUUM
Portia Da Costa
ISBN 0 352 33120 8

When Joanna Darrell agrees to take a break from an office job that has begun to bore her, she takes her first step into a new continuum of strange experiences. She is introduced to people whose way of life revolves around the giving and receiving of enjoyable punishment, and she becomes intrigued enough to experiment. Drawn in by a chain of coincidences, like Alice in a decadent wonderland, she enters a parallel world of perversity and unusual pleasure.

Coming in January 2007

BURNING BRIGHT
Janine Ashbless
ISBN 978 0 352 34085 6

Two lovers, brought together by a forbidden passion, are on the run from their pasts. Veraine was once a commander in the Imperial army: Myrna was the divine priestess he seduced and stole from her desert temple. But travelling through a jungle kingdom, they fall prey to slavers and are separated. Veraine is left for dead. Myrna is taken as a slave to the city of the Tiger Lords: inhuman tyrants with a taste for human flesh. There she must learn the tricks of survival in a cruel and exotic court where erotic desire is not the only animal passion.

Myrna still has faith that Veraine will find her. But Veraine, badly injured, has forgotten everything: his past, his lover, and even his own identity. As he undertakes a journey through a fevered landscape of lush promise and supernatural danger, he knows only one thing – that he must somehow find the unknown woman who holds the key to his soul.

STELLA DOES HOLLYWOOD
Stella Black
ISBN 978 0 352 33588 3

Stella Black has a 1969 Pontiac Firebird, a leopard-skin bra and a lot of attitude. Partying her way around Hollywood she is discovered by Leon Lubrisky, the billionaire mogul of Pleasure Dome Inc. He persuades her to work for him and she soon becomes one of the most famous adult stars in America. Invited on chat shows, dating pop stars and hanging out with the Beverly Hills A-list. But dark forces are gathering and a political party is outraged and determined to destroy Stella any which way they can. Soon she finds herself in dangerous – and highly sexually charged – situations, where no one can rescue her.

Black Lace Booklist

Information is correct at time of printing. To avoid disappointment, check availability before ordering. Go to www.blacklace-books.co.uk. All books are priced £6.99 unless another price is given.

BLACK LACE BOOKS WITH A CONTEMPORARY SETTING

☐ ON THE EDGE Laura Hamilton	ISBN 0 352 33534 3	£5.99
☐ THE TRANSFORMATION Natasha Rostova	ISBN 0 352 33311 1	
☐ SIN.NET Helena Ravenscroft	ISBN 0 352 33598 X	
☐ TWO WEEKS IN TANGIER Annabel Lee	ISBN 0 352 33599 8	
☐ SYMPHONY X Jasmine Stone	ISBN 0 352 33629 3	
☐ A SECRET PLACE Ella Broussard	ISBN 0 352 33307 3	
☐ GOING TOO FAR Laura Hamilton	ISBN 0 352 33657 9	
☐ RELEASE ME Suki Cunningham	ISBN 0 352 33671 4	
☐ SLAVE TO SUCCESS Kimberley Raines	ISBN 0 352 33687 0	
☐ SHADOWPLAY Portia Da Costa	ISBN 0 352 33313 8	
☐ ARIA APPASSIONATA Julie Hastings	ISBN 0 352 33056 2	
☐ A MULTITUDE OF SINS Kit Mason	ISBN 0 352 33737 0	
☐ COMING ROUND THE MOUNTAIN Tabitha Flyte	ISBN 0 352 33873 3	
☐ FEMININE WILES Karina Moore	ISBN 0 352 33235 2	
☐ MIXED SIGNALS Anna Clare	ISBN 0 352 33889 X	
☐ BLACK LIPSTICK KISSES Monica Belle	ISBN 0 352 33885 7	
☐ GOING DEEP Kimberly Dean	ISBN 0 352 33876 8	
☐ PACKING HEAT Karina Moore	ISBN 0 352 33356 1	
☐ MIXED DOUBLES Zoe le Verdier	ISBN 0 352 33312 X	
☐ UP TO NO GOOD Karen S. Smith	ISBN 0 352 33589 0	
☐ CLUB CRÈME Primula Bond	ISBN 0 352 33907 1	
☐ BONDED Fleur Reynolds	ISBN 0 352 33192 5	
☐ SWITCHING HANDS Alaine Hood	ISBN 0 352 33896 2	
☐ EDEN'S FLESH Robyn Russell	ISBN 0 352 33923 3	
☐ PEEP SHOW Mathilde Madden	ISBN 0 352 33924 1	£7.99
☐ RISKY BUSINESS Lisette Allen	ISBN 0 352 33280 8	£7.99
☐ CAMPAIGN HEAT Gabrielle Marcola	ISBN 0 352 33941 1	£7.99
☐ MS BEHAVIOUR Mini Lee	ISBN 0 352 33962 4	£7.99

☐ THE SENSES BEJEWELLED Cleo Cordell	ISBN 0 352 32904 1	
☐ UNDRESSING THE DEVIL Angel Strand	ISBN 0 352 33938 1	£7.99
☐ FRENCH MANNERS Olivia Christie	ISBN 0 352 33214 X	£7.99
☐ DANCE OF OBSESSION Olivia Christie	ISBN 0 352 33101 1	£7.99
☐ LORD WRAXALL'S FANCY Anna Lieff Saxby	ISBN 0 352 33080 5	£7.99
☐ NICOLE'S REVENGE Lisette Allen	ISBN 0 352 32984 X	£7.99
☐ BARBARIAN PRIZE Deanna Ashford	ISBN 0 352 34017 7	£7.99
☐ THE BARBARIAN GEISHA Charlotte Royal	ISBN 0 352 33267 0	£7.99
☐ ELENA'S DESTINY Lisette Allen	ISBN 0 352 33218 2	£7.99
☐ THE MASTER OF SHILDEN Lucinda Carrington	ISBN 0 352 33140 2	£7.99
☐ DARKER THAN LOVE Kristina Lloyd	ISBN 0 352 33279 4	£7.99

BLACK LACE ANTHOLOGIES

☐ WICKED WORDS Various	ISBN 0 352 33363 4	
☐ MORE WICKED WORDS Various	ISBN 0 352 33487 8	
☐ WICKED WORDS 3 Various	ISBN 0 352 33522 X	
☐ WICKED WORDS 4 Various	ISBN 0 352 33603 X	
☐ WICKED WORDS 5 Various	ISBN 0 352 33642 0	
☐ WICKED WORDS 6 Various	ISBN 0 352 33690 0	
☐ WICKED WORDS 7 Various	ISBN 0 352 33743 5	
☐ WICKED WORDS 8 Various	ISBN 0 352 33787 7	
☐ WICKED WORDS 9 Various	ISBN 0 352 33860 1	
☐ WICKED WORDS 10 Various	ISBN 0 352 33893 8	
☐ THE BEST OF BLACK LACE 2 Various	ISBN 0 352 33718 4	
☐ WICKED WORDS: SEX IN THE OFFICE Various	ISBN 0 352 33944 6	£7.99
☐ WICKED WORDS: SEX AT THE SPORTS CLUB Various	ISBN 0 352 33991 8	£7.99
☐ WICKED WORDS: SEX ON HOLIDAY Various	ISBN 0 352 33961 6	£7.99
☐ WICKED WORDS: SEX IN UNIFORM Various	ISBN 0 352 34002 9	£7.99
☐ WICKED WORDS: SEX IN THE KITCHEN Various	ISBN 0 352 34018 5	£7.99
☐ WICKED WORDS: SEX ON THE MOVE Various	ISBN 0 352 34034 7	£7.99
☐ WICKED WORDS: SEX AND MUSIC Various	ISBN 0 352 34061 4	£7.99

Please send me the books I have ticked above.

Name ....

Address ....

....

....

....

Post Code ....

Send to: Virgin Books Cash Sales, Thames Wharf Studios, Rainville Road, London W6 9HA.

US customers: for prices and details of how to order books for delivery by mail, call 888-330-8477.

Please enclose a cheque or postal order, made payable to Virgin Books Ltd, to the value of the books you have ordered plus postage and packing costs as follows:

UK and BFPO – £1.00 for the first book, 50p for each subsequent book.

Overseas (including Republic of Ireland) – £2.00 for the first book, £1.00 for each subsequent book.

If you would prefer to pay by VISA, ACCESS/MASTERCARD, DINERS CLUB, AMEX or SWITCH, please write your card number and expiry date here:

....

Signature ....

Please allow up to 28 days for delivery.